Last Summer at the Beach House

Diamond Beach Book 1

MAGGIE MILLER

D1236006

LAST SUMMER AT THE BEACH HOUSE: Diamond Beach,
book 1
Copyright © 2023 Maggie Miller

All she wanted was one last summer at the beach house...

When the unthinkable happens and Claire Thompson's husband dies suddenly, she's left wondering how to go on. Being a wife and mother is all she's ever known. Grieving and lost, she decides to take her family for one last trip to their beach house before she's forced to put it up for sale. The house is filled with happy memories, and it seems like a great way to remember Bryan.

But as she soon finds out, Bryan was harboring some complicated secrets. The kind that will change the lives of Claire and her daughter. And those secrets come to light while Claire is at the beach house, shattering her memories and making her realize she never really knew her husband.

How does she move forward with these new revelations? How will her daughter cope? What will become of them now that they know Bryan wasn't the man they thought he was?

Claire can only pray things work out for them during their last summer at the beach house.

Chapter One

Pastor Freeman shook Claire Thompson's hand, then held it between both of his. "I'll be praying for you. Call me or Susan if you need anything."

His wife, Susan, standing beside him, nodded. "Even if you just want to talk."

Claire nodded. "Thank you. I appreciate that."

She stood in the foyer as the pastor and his wife left, closing the door behind them. They'd been the last guests at her husband's memorial, which seemed fitting, since Pastor Freeman had done the ceremony.

Claire's mother, Margo, and her half-sister, Julia, who went by Jules, remained in the living room. Jules's two sons hadn't come, but they didn't live close, and Claire hadn't expected them to.

What she did expect was for Bryan to come

down the stairs, but that was never going to happen again, was it? A fresh wave of grief swept through her. She closed her eyes and leaned against the door until it passed.

A few deep breaths, a few thoughts about happier memories, and the unbearableness of the moment passed.

The memorial service had been well attended, but that was no surprise. Bryan had been well-liked by so many people, even if most of them only knew him peripherally. He'd been a tremendously ambitious man and a wonderful provider, attributes that she'd often reminded herself didn't come without a cost. One of those costs was all the time he'd spent away from her and Kat. That was the unfortunate but necessary downside when someone worked as much as Bryan did.

She understood him traveling for his business, she really did. She never nagged him about it, either. Bryan had been a financial advisor and investor with three offices spread across the panhandle and central Florida. He dealt with enormous sums of money for the very wealthy, and those kinds of clients expected to see the person handling their investments face to face. When they set up a meeting with Bryan, he had to be there. A video call might suffice in some cases, but not usually. Not when millions were at stake. A video call didn't instill confidence. He'd said it so often, she knew it to be true.

She also knew that he made as much money as he did because he worked so hard and made sure all of his clients got the personal touch. Bryan had been big on the personal touch. He claimed it was what set him apart from most other financial advisors. He sent a personally signed card with a note for every client's birthday, which wasn't so unusual, but he was always willing to meet with new clients or visit with old ones whenever they wanted him to, even if it meant flying to wherever they were.

On more than one occasion, Claire had felt deep down that his clients came before her and Kat, but she never spoke those words out loud. It wasn't a kind thought and she knew it wasn't really true. Bryan tried very hard to be there when they needed him. It was just that, sometimes, his clients needed him at the same time.

Thanks to his hard work and success, he'd kept them in a *very* comfortable lifestyle. She hadn't worked outside the home since she'd gotten pregnant with Kat. She'd gone to college to get her teaching degree, but she couldn't have taken a job even after Kat had started school. Not with Bryan gone so much. Not without some kind of extra help.

There had definitely been occasions when having him gone so often had been a hardship. She sniffed, sad again, because now he was gone forever. The finality of it felt impossible to grasp.

She supposed she should be used to his absence, but this time it was permanent and that wasn't an easy idea to accept. The one reassurance that had gotten her through him being away from home so often was knowing he was coming back.

Now she didn't have that guarantee to comfort herself with.

How was she going to manage? She'd never expected to be a widow at fifty-nine. She'd thought she and Bryan would grow old together. Older, anyway. She'd daydreamed so often about the day he'd retire and be home with her all the time. About how they were going to travel together.

They'd talked about buying an RV and seeing the country. Maybe even going up into Canada. She went back into the living room. Her mother and Jules seemed to be deep in conversation, so she continued on into the dining room, where there was far too much food that needed to be put away and plenty of mess to be cleaned up.

The RV travel was never going to happen now. The ache inside her was bottomless. Every time she thought she'd felt the worst of her grief, she sank deeper into the mire. It was a pit she wasn't sure she'd ever climb out of. Not anytime soon. Maybe never.

At least she had Kat. Thinking about her daughter provided enough of a lifeline that Claire was able to lift her head and keep on going.

"Mom?" Kat appeared from the kitchen as if knowing she was on Claire's mind. "Ray and I are going to start cleaning up in the kitchen. Unless you want me to help you out here first? Looks like as much work as what's in there."

"No, that's fine." Claire turned and offered her daughter a small smile. Her fiancé, Ray, wasn't the most manly of men, but he was always willing to pitch in. He was a podiatrist and traveled once in a while for conferences, although nothing like what Bryan had done. "You two don't have to do that, honey. Your aunt will help me."

Kat shrugged. "We're happy to do it. Ray's already rolled up his shirtsleeves to wash the big stuff. I think we'd both feel better doing something."

Claire nodded. She understood. Being busy was

better than standing still and letting the grief over-take her. "All right. Thank you."

As Kat went back into the kitchen, Jules came in. "I'm going to take Mom home. She's tired. And I need to let Toby out. But then I'll come back and help you with all of this."

Toby was Jules's dachshund. Claire nodded. "I understand. Thanks for coming, but it's silly to come back. Kat and Ray are going to help me clean up."

"If you're sure." Jules's smile was quick and sympathetic. "Whatever you need, I'm just a phone call away."

"Thanks."

Jules hugged her. Jules had always been the most affectionate one of the family. "I'm so sorry," she whispered.

Claire hugged her back, then finally let her sister go. She walked to the door with them. Claire's mother had remarried after Claire's father, Mitchell, had passed away when she was only ten. Lloyd Bloom had been a wonderful stepfather. Kind, caring, and as affectionate with Claire as he was with Jules. Sadly, he'd succumbed to cancer nearly twelve years ago.

It felt like it was just the women left now. Even more so with the passing of Bryan. Of course, Jules had two sons, but they were getting on with their lives and not around so much anymore.

Claire began collecting the paper plates, napkins, and plastic cups that were all over the house. She had a stack of them in her hands when she stopped in front of the antique buffet in the dining room to look at the photographs displayed there.

There was one in particular that made her smile, filling her with fond, happy memories. The photo of her, Bryan, and Kat in front of their vacation home on Diamond Beach in the panhandle of Florida.

They lived inland, about three hours away, and going to the beach was something special. Every summer, they spent the month of July there. Bryan still left them to work, but for Claire and Kat, it had been the most wonderful time of the year.

And when he was there with them, they enjoyed every moment of his presence. Barbequing, building sandcastles on the beach, lounging around reading, swimming in the pool, and on rainy days, working on puzzles on the big dining table.

The rest of the year, they rented the beach house out. It had paid for itself that way. But July was always theirs.

A sad thought came to Claire. Sad for many

reasons, but there was one she hadn't thought of until just now. "Kat?"

Her daughter came out of the kitchen, a dish towel in her hands. "What is it, Mom?"

Claire gestured with the cups and plates at the photo. "I was just thinking about the beach house."

Kat nodded. "We always have such a great time there, don't we?"

"We do. Or rather, we did. Unfortunately, I'm probably going to have to sell it now. I don't think I'll have a choice. I can't afford the mortgage on this house without your father's income." There would be some life insurance, but the mortgage wasn't the only bill to be paid, either.

"Oh, no." Kat's face fell. "I love that place. I didn't realize you'd have to sell it. But I understand, too."

"I was thinking before I even start that process, maybe we..." Claire almost didn't want to speak the next few words, because she didn't want her daughter to say no. "We should go. To the beach house. One last time. I'm sure your father would have wanted that. And since the damage from the last hurricane was only just finished being repaired, it hasn't been rented."

Kat looked at her without saying anything for a moment, then she nodded. "That's a great idea.

Especially if you're going to have to sell it. Maybe we could even spread Dad's ashes there. If that's okay with you?"

Claire nodded. Bryan's ashes would be ready to be picked up in a few days. She liked the idea of taking him along. "I think he'd like that. He was always so happy there."

Kat put her arm around her mom. "We all were."

Claire let out the breath she'd been holding. "I'm going to ask Grandma and Aunt Jules, too. Do you think Ray will want to come?"

"I don't know, but I'll ask him. He'll probably only be able to come for the weekend. It's nice of you to include him, though."

"Sure. He's about to be family. I know it's only April, but we should look at this like our last summer at the beach house."

"One last trip." Kat gave her mom a quick smile as she headed back into the kitchen. Back to Ray.

Claire did her best to like her soon-to-be son-in-law, but in her heart of hearts, she thought Kat could do better. Granted, Ray made good money as a podiatrist, but to Claire, he was just a dull sort of guy who seemed to go along with whatever Kat wanted, no questions asked. No real interests of his own.

Which wasn't to say he wasn't a good man. He

was. He and Kat never fought. They never even argued. He was pleasant to be around. But Claire knew her daughter. Kat would get bored with that at some point. She needed someone who challenged her. And that person was not Ray. But maybe Kat liked the comfort of Ray's stability? Or the peace in not having to work too hard at making him happy? Or how Ray seemed to put Kat's needs ahead of his own?

It wasn't Claire's place to interfere, so she'd kept her mouth shut. If Kat was happy—truly happy—then that was all that mattered.

She gathered up a few more cups and plates, thinking about that. About being happy. She'd been happy with Bryan, hadn't she?

She supposed she had been. Most of the time. She would have liked him to be home more, naturally. Involved in Kat's life more, too. He was involved to some degree, as much as he could be with all the traveling he did. Kat had certainly adored him. But then, he was big on bringing presents home when he returned, so why wouldn't she love that?

The presents had been a great way to teach Kat not to mind when Daddy went away and to look forward to him returning.

Meanwhile, Claire did all the parental heavy

lifting and sometimes felt like she was underappreciated by her husband and, occasionally, by her daughter. It was as if they had no idea how many balls she juggled to make things work. They probably didn't.

The list was endless. Cleaning the house, doing laundry, fixing all the little odds and ends that went wrong and, if she couldn't fix them, getting someone in who could, paying bills, doing the grocery shopping and the cooking, getting Kat to school, to the doctor, to the dentist, to debate practice, to gymnastics, to birthday parties, and all of the many other things that it took to raise a child.

She'd never said much to Bryan about needing help, though. What was the point? Nothing would change. He couldn't give up his clients. They paid the bills. That was just how life was. Parenting was sometimes a thankless task. Being a mother even more so. Especially with a husband who traveled as much as Bryan did.

And once Kat had graduated from college and gone to work at the actuary firm, Claire's load had lessened quite a bit. Kat, who'd chosen to stay at home, made dinner for them most nights, them being Claire and Ray, since he was almost always here.

Which, again, was fine. He was no bother whatsoever. He took the trash out, helped with dishes, did some yard work, whatever needed to be done. So there were fewer things for Claire to do. He made her life a little easier, truth be told.

Best of all, Claire and Kat had a great relationship, that was for sure. Nothing to complain about there.

Claire took the gathered plates, cups, and napkins into the kitchen and threw them away. One last visit to the beach house sounded right. A final goodbye. A chance for closure. A place to grieve but also a place to surround herself in good memories.

And, perhaps, even time to think about what the future held.

Chapter Two

It was hard to pack with such a heavy heart, but Kat managed, mostly by packing what she always took to the beach house. Shorts, T-shirts, tank tops, swimsuits, sundresses, flipflops. Early spring in Florida still meant mostly mild temperatures with some cooler ones in the evening.

Thinking about all the fun memories she had with her father at that house helped her get in the mood to pack, too. Being there would make her miss him that much more, but his presence was in that house. She felt like that would be a comfort.

He'd bought the house years ago as a surprise. It was a memory Kat recalled with crystalline clarity. He'd gotten a very good deal on it, he'd said, which was part of why he'd had to act so quickly without really saying anything.

Kat had thought it was a wonderful surprise. Until, that was, she'd seen the look of worry on her mother's face. That had dampened her excitement a little. Her father had promised them both that the purchase was no big deal and that everything was going to be all right. He had a plan for making the house pay for itself. Renting it out had definitely done that.

But now that Kat was an adult herself, she understood her mother's reaction. If Ray sprang a thing like buying a second house on Kat without talking to her about it, she probably would have dumped him on the spot. You just didn't do a thing like that to the person who was supposed to be your partner.

Of course, when her father had done it, things had been a little different. He'd been the sole bread-winner. And the times had been different, too. Men did things like that then. For all that Kat loved her mother, she acknowledged that she was not the most fearless of women. In fact, Kat would go so far as to say her mother could be a pushover.

Certainly Kat's dad had known that. He'd used it to his advantage. Something she could see now that she'd grown up. She still loved him all the same. Her parents were who they were. She wasn't trying to change them, nor could she.

Especially not her father. He was a closed book. He would forever be the man he was in her memories.

She folded her swimsuit coverup and stuck it in her suitcase. She just desperately wished her father was here to go with them. She would wish that for the rest of her life. Death was so final. She stared at the clothing in front of her without really seeing it.

Ray came in. "Getting packed already?"

His question brought her back to reality. "I know we aren't leaving for a couple of days, but I figured I might as well. Helps to stay busy. I might even work a little bit." Fortunately, she could easily do her job remotely. She was currently doing a data analysis project for an insurance firm.

"But you're on compassionate leave."

"I know, but I need to be occupied right now."

"I understand that. Anything I can do to help?"

"Nothing I can think of. Unless my mom needs something."

"Okay. Maybe I'll go check with her."

"Thanks." Ray was always willing to help out.

"I'll go home shortly and get myself packed, too.

I'll have to come back on Sunday so I can be ready for work on Monday."

"Are you sure you want to make the drive for such a short trip? We aren't leaving until my mom can pick up the ashes, so you might only get a day or two there."

"It's fine. It's not that far."

Kat nodded. "Okay. What about the week after?"

"Well, I won't be able to cancel all of my appointments, wouldn't be fair to the patients, but I'll be able to clear next Friday, I think. Then, of course, I'll have the weekend."

"That's what I figured. I know you have to work." Diamond Beach was not quite a three-hour drive from Landry, the town they lived in.

"Yep." He leaned in, kissed her cheek, then went back out.

She sat down on the bed, her head a muddled mess of thoughts and feelings. Mostly about her dad. But losing him had caused all sorts of other things to come to the surface. Thoughts about Ray.

She loved him. That was not in question. But was she *in* love with him? That she couldn't answer. And she didn't know why. A week ago, she would have easily said yes. Now? Now she no longer felt sure about that.

It was probably just grief. This kind of deep loss did all sorts of weird things to a person. It hollowed you out and made you feel like you might collapse in on yourself. She sighed, hands on her thighs, wondering how long it would take before she felt like her old self again, at least where her relationship with Ray was concerned.

Maybe it would happen at the beach house. Maybe scattering her dad's ashes and getting some closure was exactly what she needed to come to terms with her father being gone. To really accept that he wasn't coming home this time.

With a sigh, she got to her feet again and went through her closet to see what else she might want to take. She added a pair of capri jeans and some comfy leggings, because it could get cooler in the evenings, along with a pair of closed-toe gray flats and two lightweight cardigans in white and gray.

She threw in an oversized sweatshirt, too. No matter what the temperature was outside, her mother loved to keep the beach house icy on the inside. A pair of fuzzy socks got thrown in as well, just for good measure.

"Kat?" her mother called up the steps.

She went out to the landing and looked down. "Right here."

"Ray's taking the trash out, then he's going back to his place. And I'm going to lie down for a bit. Just so you know."

Kat nodded. "Okay." She went back to her room. The same room she'd grown up in. The same room she'd been sleeping in since she'd been a baby. The crib had been swapped out for a twin bed, which had then been swapped out for a queen. She stared at the room, knowing it was that same space she'd essentially lived in all of her life despite the updated, modern look it had been given after she graduated college and moved back.

She was twenty-eight and engaged. She probably shouldn't still be living at home, but it was loads cheaper than getting her own place. She was saving money like crazy, even though she bought her share of groceries and insisted on paying half the power bill and taking care of the internet, too.

But there were three much bigger reasons why she'd come back home after college.

One was her mom. With her dad gone so much, Kat worried about her mother. About her being able to do things on her own. About her taking care of herself. It wasn't like her mom had given her anything to be concerned about, not yet, but Kat knew her mom liked the company, so why not?

The second was moving out would mean seeing even less of her Dad. Or would have meant that. Not seeing him no longer factored in.

But the third reason did, and that was Ray.

If Kat decided to move out, Ray would expect her to either move in with him or for them to get a place together. He'd said as much. And Kat didn't want to do that. Not yet.

She knew it would happen eventually. They were engaged, after all, and married people tended to live in the same house, but she'd pushed for a long engagement for the same reason she knew she wasn't ready to live with him. She couldn't really put the why down on paper, but it was what felt right.

Ray, of course, in typical Ray fashion, had just nodded and smiled and gone along. That was what he did. He never rocked the boat, never made waves, never argued.

So she got her way. Deep down inside, she *liked* getting her own way. Who didn't? She frowned at that. Was that why she'd agreed to marry him? Because she knew she'd always get what she wanted? Without debate?

That didn't say too much about her. Or maybe it said volumes. Maybe she wasn't ready to marry Ray or anyone. She sniffed. She no longer had a father to walk her down the aisle. How was she ever going to get married now anyway?

Maybe she shouldn't get married at all. It hadn't worked out that great for Aunt Jules. She was twice divorced now. The alimony she received gave her a pretty nice life, but that was no reason to get married. Aunt Jules earned plenty of her own money, too. She had a vibrant career as a singer and songwriter. She was practically famous in some circles. But her success definitely hadn't transferred to her relationships.

Kat didn't want to get married if she was only going to end up divorced. She supposed no one did.

She wiped at the fresh tears spilling from her eyes and shook her head. This was just the grief again, jumbling her up inside and making her question the status quo. Now was not the time to be making any hasty decisions.

She needed to put her feet in the sand and her toes in the water at Diamond Beach. That would sort everything out. Even if being there made her miss her father all over again, it would bring so many good memories back.

They could eat at the Flying Fish, too. Her father had always loved that place. The proprietors would be so surprised to hear about his sudden heart attack.

She sniffed. She couldn't believe he was really gone. She'd only just talked to him on the phone a few days ago.

Life was so unfair. What she needed now was time in the happiest place she knew. Time with her mom, her grandmother, her aunt, and Ray. Time to reflect on all the good and wonderful things her father had done for her.

Time to figure out what she really wanted to do with the rest of her life.

Chapter Three

Claire clutched the urn containing Bryan's ashes in one arm as she unlocked the elevator door of the Double Diamond, their fabulous beach house, and pushed the call button. The elevator car stayed on the first floor, so it had to be called to the ground level, where they were.

Like all the beachfront homes in Diamond Beach, Double Diamond was built up on pilings, allowing them to park underneath the house. The gulf-front half of the ground level was devoted to shaded recreation with fans, a hammock, a big conversation area of outdoor sofas and chairs grouped around a large square coffee table, and a dining area with an outdoor kitchen. It was a great place to hang out and enjoy the breezes coming off the water. They'd shared many meals down here.

She glanced toward the water. She was already

weepy being here without Bryan, then the elevator door slid open, she saw the glass-tiled mosaic mermaid on the floor, and nearly broke down. Bryan had commissioned that as a tribute to her, telling her that she was as beautiful as any mermaid could hope to be. She inhaled and let out a soft, shuddering sigh.

Ray, who was hauling suitcases, glanced at her before loading them into the elevator. He'd driven his own car, since he'd have to go back early. "Are you all right, Claire?"

She swallowed, forced a little smile, and nodded. "Just caught up in memories."

"Of course you are. How could you not be in a place like this?"

"Yes."

Behind her came Kat, also carrying a suitcase and a computer bag, and Jules, who was helping their mother with one hand while the other kept a tight grip on Toby's leash. Her guitar, which always traveled with her, was slung across her back.

Their mother, Margo, wasn't infirm, but neither Claire nor her sister could deny she seemed to be aging faster these days. She'd never really recovered from the death of Lloyd. Toby, on the other hand, was excited to be included. In anything.

Claire held the door to let Jules, Margo, and Toby in.

Kat shook her head. "That's full enough. I'll wait. Or take the stairs."

She wouldn't take the stairs, Claire knew. She let the doors shut. The elevator whirred upward. "You could wait here with me."

"Sure, I can do that."

Claire clutched the urn a little tighter. "It's good to be here. Bittersweet, but good. Just the smell of the salt air brings back so many memories."

Kat nodded. "It does, but that's it exactly. Bittersweet."

"I suppose once we get the bags in, we should get groceries."

Kat nodded. "Maybe Aunt Jules and I can do that while you and Grandma get the house opened up. Might need a little airing out."

"I suppose that's true." What Claire really wanted was to get a tumbler of wine, go down to the water, and just sit and watch the waves until her grief retreated enough for her to breathe. She felt like her insides had been scooped out.

The elevator returned and the doors opened. Ray smiled at them. "Figured I'd come back and see what else I can bring up."

"There are cooler bags still," Claire said. They'd brought as much food from the house as they thought they'd actually eat. Most of the casseroles and dishes that had been dropped off reminded Claire of cat food. There was no way she was eating anything that involved tuna and noodles. She was grieving, not losing her mind.

In some ways, they were two sides of the same coin. She understood now why her mother was the way she was. Shut down. It was almost like a form of self-preservation.

Ray touched his fingers to his forehead in a teasing salute as he stepped out of the elevator. "I'll get to work on those."

"Thanks." Claire got in, Kat behind her.

Kat immediately reached out and pushed the button to close the doors. As they slid together, Claire looked at her daughter. "Don't you want to wait for Ray?"

Kat shrugged. "It'll take him a minute to organize what he's bringing up."

Sometimes, Claire got a little frustrated with Kat. She seemed...almost callous at times toward Ray. And while it was true that he wasn't the most assertive of men, it bothered Claire that Kat was

easier to rent out, especially to multiple families who wanted to vacation together, but still have their own space.

Ray had left Claire's suitcase in front of the master bedroom door. With the urn still cradled in her arm, she opened the door into the room, then grabbed the bag's handle with her free hand and rolled it into the room she'd once shared with Bryan.

A new wave of grief hit her. For the first time in all the years of coming here, Bryan would be absent. He wouldn't be joining them later, either. He would never be joining them again.

She wheeled her bag further in and stared at the big king bed with all its luxurious white linens and beautifully embroidered duvet. It was a vast expanse of a bed. Too large for one person to sleep in all alone. And yet, she would be.

Behind her, in the rest of the house, she heard the noises of everyone settling in. Her mother was already on the sofa, wanting Jules to put her stories on, because this TV wasn't like hers at home and she didn't know how to work it. Ray was bringing the cooler bags into the kitchen. Toby's nails clicked across the big ceramic tiles that covered all the floors.

Claire stood there, just breathing. Willing herself

not to break down again. She could do this. If they could, she could. She would just have to concentrate on the good memories.

There were no personal photos in the beach house. Because they rented it, they'd chosen not to have a lot of personal things around, which had always made sense to her, but now she wished she'd brought something from home. Their wedding picture, maybe.

"Mom?"

Claire turned, realizing she was still standing the middle of the big bedroom, staring off into her memories. "Are you off to the store already?"

"Almost," Kat said. "And I'm taking Ray, not Aunt Jules. She's going to get Grandma unpacked. I just wanted to see if there was anything specific you needed."

Claire took a deep breath and hugged the urn closer. "Wine. Red and white. And some good chocolates."

Kat nodded. "I could stop by Guilford's."

The local chocolate shop was well-known in the Florida panhandle and had several locations. Claire nodded. "Yes. I want a pound of their rum truffles. At least."

"You got it." Kat hesitated, then came into the

bedroom and put her arm around her mom in an almost hug. Claire couldn't do much while holding the urn, so she just leaned into her daughter's embrace. "We're going to get through this. I promise."

Claire nodded. "I know. It's just all so hard right now."

"It is. And it's going to be for a while." She let go of Claire and stepped back. "Maybe after dinner we'll go for a walk on the beach. What do you think?"

"I'd like that. I might go sit down there by myself for a while. In case you can't find me when you get back. I'll keep my phone on me, though."

"Okay, no problem. You do whatever you need to do. See you later."

"Later." Claire stood there a second longer, then looked around the room once more. She finally decided on a place for Bryan's ashes. On his night-stand. That seemed appropriate.

Then she hoisted her suitcase onto the bed, unzipped it, and began putting her things away. She carried her sundresses to the closet to hang them. She caught a faint whiff of Bryan's cologne as she slid the mirrored door open.

It was enough to give her a moment of weakness.

A moment where she felt as if she might sink to the ground and dissolve into tears again. Instead, she hugged the sundresses to her and sat in the nearby chair.

How was she going to do this? How would she survive? It was too hard. And yet, people did. They grieved every day, all around her, for reasons she knew nothing about, and they came through to the other side. Everyone experienced this at some point in their life. Some, like her mother, had been through it more than once. Although her mother wasn't a great example of someone who'd recovered.

Maybe Claire should join a support group. Diamond Beach might be a tourist town but there was no reason to think they wouldn't have something like that. There were still plenty of locals here. And it was the panhandle of Florida, not a Third World country.

After a number of uncounted minutes, she got to her feet and managed to get the sundresses on hangers. She left the closet door open to air out. Then she went out through the bedroom sliders onto the covered porch and stood at the screen that kept the bugs out.

There, in front of her, the Gulf sprawled like a living thing. Vast and blue and trimmed in the white

Chapter Four

*J*ules stood at the dining room windows and watched her big sister cross the sand toward the water. Her soul ached for Claire. The usual sparkle in her eyes had been replaced by the dullness of grief. It was like the light inside of her had been snuffed out. It was heartbreaking. Jules exhaled. Divorce was hard. But not as hard as this.

Grief was the kind of hard that took a piece of you with it.

Claire stopped and sat a few yards from the water's edge. She bent her knees, wrapped her arms around them, and just stared out at the waves. She looked like she'd gone as far as she could go. As if she'd run out of energy and will at the same time.

"Jules?"

Jules looked toward the sofa where her mother was sitting. "Yes, Mom?"

"Can you bring me a blanket? It's freezing in here. I don't know why your sister has to keep it so cold."

There was a soft, knitted throw along the back of the sofa. Jules picked it up and unfolded it as she walked around to the front, then draped it over her mother's knees. "Do you need anything else? I'm going out to check on Claire."

Her mother's gaze was on the television as she shook her head. "Your sister will be fine. She just needs time. Men die. It's what they do."

Jules should have been taken aback by such a comment, but she'd heard it before. Her mother had lost two husbands and it had left such a dent in her, she'd never fully recovered. Jules gave her leeway because of that. Maybe too much sometimes, but Margo was her mother. That counted for something. "I'll be back in a little bit. I have my phone in case you need me or if Toby needs to go out." He was currently asleep on the cushion next to her mom, so Jules doubted that would happen, but it was hard to tell with Toby.

Tomorrow, she'd take him for a long walk on the

beach and wear him out properly. Or maybe tonight, but she had a feeling the car ride had done him in. He was only two years old, and traveling got him wound up until he eventually crashed.

Her mother didn't say anything, so Jules went back through the dining area, out the sliding doors, and down the steps, following the path Claire had taken a few minutes ago past the pool.

She stood at the edge of the concrete pool deck and looked toward the beach. There were a handful of other people out walking. Some with dogs. Some in pairs. Some alone. The air was the perfect mix of salt, and fresh, the breeze coming off the water, shushing through the dune grass, and brushing past her like it had somewhere to be. It was rejuvenating. But not quite enough to erase her mother's morbid words from her mind.

Men die.

Well, Jules thought as she started down the steps. Everyone died, didn't they? You couldn't live your life in that shadow, or you'd never really live at all.

She took off her shoes when her feet touched sand and walked toward the water until she reached Claire. She sat beside her sister.

"Hi," Jules said softly.

It took Claire a few moments to respond. "Hi."

"How are you doing?"

Claire never took her eyes off the water. "I don't really know."

"Sounds about right. We don't have to talk. I just thought you might want some company."

Claire nodded. "I don't want to talk. But company is good." And after a couple of seconds, "Thank you."

"You're welcome."

They sat in silence, just listening to the waves and the gulls and the drifts of other people's conversations that the breeze carried to them.

This part of the beach wasn't often crowded, because while there was public beach access, there wasn't much parking, so many of the people who spent time here were staying in one of the houses that lined these shores.

How Bryan had ever afforded a home here, she had no idea. Diamond Beach was a gem. No pun intended.

Diamond Beach had been so named for the way the sun sparkled off the pristine white sand that made up these shores. It was gorgeous and as Jules dug her toes into that gleaming sand, she felt a moment of gratitude that Claire had invited her along. She loved coming to the beach house.

She only wished it had been under different circumstances.

Jules and her sister hadn't been as close growing up as she would have liked, but she understood now that she'd set the bar unrealistically high. You couldn't expect an eleven-year-old to be overly joyed that her widowed mother had remarried and, not long after, brought a new baby home.

Claire sighed so quietly Jules almost mistook it for the breeze passing by. "I don't know how I'm going to do this. I have moments where I think I'll be okay and moments where I don't think I'll ever be okay again."

Jules had no solution for that. She reached over and took her sister's hand. "At least you won't have to do it alone."

Claire sniffed and went silent again.

Jules wished she had some words of wisdom, or something pithy to say that would magically erase Claire's pain and grief, but those things didn't exist. Grief had to be experienced in its own time. No one escaped that. And while Jules knew what it felt like to lose her father, she had no experience when it came to losing the man she'd loved. She'd been happy enough to get rid of both her exes. "You could talk to Mom. She's been through it twice."

Claire blinked and kept looking at the water. "Do you think she actually loved either one of our fathers?"

The question took Jules by surprise. It wasn't something she'd been prepared for. Not something she'd ever even considered, actually. "Sure. I mean, I don't know. I'd have hoped so. Do you think she didn't?"

Claire shrugged. "She got over my father's death pretty fast. Fast enough to marry your father less than a year later. And I loved your dad, don't get me wrong. He was a good man. He was the best stepfather I could have hoped for. But I resented her for how quickly she moved on."

"She did, you're right," Jules said. "But it was a different time. A single woman then with a young daughter faced a much bigger challenge than she would now."

"So you think she married your father just for the security? Just so she wouldn't be alone?"

Something else Jules hadn't really considered. Until now. "Maybe. Is that so bad? They seemed happy together. They seemed like they loved each other."

Chapter Five

*K*at sent Ray off to a different aisle to get pasta and sauce while she picked out some meat for the next couple of days. She didn't have much appetite, and she suspected her mother didn't either, but they had to eat. There was Aunt Jules, Grandma, and Ray to think of, too. And only Ray was willing to eat most of the casseroles people had brought for the funeral.

She grabbed packages of chicken thighs and drumsticks to grill outside, a couple packages of steaks, another one of ground beef for burgers, and a bag of frozen shrimp.

Ray returned as she was finishing up her selections. His arms were loaded with jars of sauce, red and alfredo, and boxes of pasta. Spaghetti, linguine, and bowties. "Got it all." He put his items into the cart. "What's next?"

Kat checked her list. "Aunt Jules needs dog food for Toby. Wolfpack Special Selections in chicken and brown rice. And a box of small Milk-Bones."

Ray nodded. "On it."

"Wait." Kat scanned the list to see what else he could pick up. "Paper towels, too. A big pack. I'll be in dairy by then."

"Okay. See you there." He headed off to get the dog food and paper towels.

She grabbed another package of ground beef and one of ground sausage. Might be nice to have meatballs with the spaghetti. Then she went on to the dairy aisle. Eggs, half and half for the coffee, whipped cream for the key lime pie she'd picked up in the bakery, and about a dozen individual yogurt cups. Plus butter and cream cheese. And Grandma's cottage cheese, which she had for lunch almost every day with canned peaches.

Ray returned, somehow carrying the bag of dog food, the box of Milk-Bones, an enormous package of paper towels, and another one of toilet paper. "Did we need T.P.? I thought I saw it on the list."

She scanned the items. "We did. Thanks for grabbing that."

"You're welcome." He did his best to fit them all in the cart. "What else?"

"That's it. We just need to stop by Guilford's on the way home." The cart was overflowing but it was always like that when they came to the beach. They had to do a big shop to restock the house.

"You got it." He smiled.

She wasn't in the mood to smile back, but she did anyway. He tried so hard. She really needed to get over whatever reluctance she was feeling about marrying him. He genuinely was a good guy. She was sure what she was feeling was just grief.

In the checkout line, he pulled out three of the craziest tabloid newspapers and added them to the top of the cart.

She frowned. "What are those for?"

"For Grandma Bloom. She loves those papers."

Kat nodded. "It's true. She does. Thanks." She felt like a heel for even thinking Ray wasn't good enough. What was wrong with her? Again, she had to blame it on the grief. There was no other explanation. It had turned her into a different person. One who wasn't thinking straight.

She'd welcomed the chore of getting groceries for that reason. It was an easy activity with a list to follow. The right kind of tedious distraction.

They got through the checkout and Ray pushed the loaded cart back to Kat's car. They filled the trunk with bags. The paper towels ended up on the backseat.

Ray slid into the passenger seat as Kat got behind the wheel. "That should hold us for a day or two."

She did her best to smile. He made the same joke every time they went shopping. "Now to Guilford's and then home. If you want to stay in the car when we get there, it's okay. I'll just be a minute."

"And miss my chance for a free sample? I don't think so."

She glanced at him. At his body. He wasn't fat, but he wasn't fit, either. He'd be just fine skipping a helping of candy. She put her eyes back on the road, once again wondering why she'd gotten like this. So critical. So judgmental. Was she mad because she'd lost her dad?

She was. But she didn't really care what kind of shape Ray was in as long as he was healthy. Wasn't like she'd worked out since high school gymnastics, although genetics had been good to her. Still, if she ate better and got some exercise, it couldn't hurt. Genetics weren't going to last forever.

Her mother was a little plump, but time did that to you, didn't it? Women tended to spread in the hips and men expanded, getting potbellies.

She parked at Guilford's. This branch of the

was upright. She leaned against the counter. Tears followed.

Ray added his bags to the pile on the counter then put his arm around her. "I'm sorry for upsetting you. I'll get the rest of the groceries in and get them all put away. Go rest. Or whatever you want to do."

She covered her face with her hands and just nodded. It was all she could do. She waited for him to leave, going down in the elevator to get the rest of the groceries, then she went into the bedroom and collapsed on the bed.

She was asleep before Ray returned.

Chapter Six

Claire appreciated Jules coming to sit with her. It helped. She wasn't sure how, but she did feel better. When Jules's phone had rung with a call from their mother saying Toby was at the door, Claire hadn't minded being left alone again.

She knew she wasn't going to heal in a day. This was the kind of grief a person never really got over, losing a spouse. She'd learned that much from watching her own mother. But Claire was already coming to terms with the emptiness that had developed inside her. It no longer seemed like a gaping hole that would swallow her so much as a big, dark swamp she would have to slog through for an undefined period of time.

It wasn't a pleasant place to be mentally. But, physically, being in a place like Diamond Beach was the house. As she walked through the dunes toward the pool, she saw a landscaper in a wide-brimmed straw hat trimming the palms on the property next door.

That made her look at the trees around her place. They could use a trimming, too. The grounds had to be in great shape for whatever pictures the real estate agent took. She went over and spoke to the man, waving and raising her voice so he could hear her over the gas-powered saw he was using. "Excuse me?"

He turned off the saw, pushed his headphones down around his neck, and took off his sunglasses, revealing deep brown eyes and a face older than she would have guessed. Not with the shape he was in. She'd have thought him to be in his thirties or forties. Instead, she was looking at man probably a few years her senior. There was a smattering of gray at his temples, too. "Yes, ma'am?"

"I was wondering if I could get your information? Or maybe you could just give me a price? I'm Claire Thompson. I live next door and I need someone to trim my palms, too."

He smiled, his teeth brilliantly white against his deeply tanned skin. He pointed at the Double Diamond. "Is that your house?"

"Yes."

He gave Claire a nod. "Nice to meet you, Claire. I'm Danny Rojas. I live here."

"Oh." Coming here only once or twice a year meant she'd never really gotten to know any of the neighbors. "I didn't realize. I'm sorry for bothering you." She'd mistaken him for a landscaper, but she didn't know if he understood that.

He kept smiling. "No bother. Always nice to meet one of my neighbors. Seems like most people around here are just renting for the week. Your place has been vacant for a while. I guess to get those repairs done."

She nodded. "That's right. Otherwise we'd have renters in, too."

"I understand. It pays the bills." He glanced at her palm trees. "I'd be happy to trim those up for you."

"Oh, I couldn't ask you to do that."

"You didn't ask. I offered."

"Still, that seems like an awful lot of work. You could at least let me pay you."

He laughed. "That's kind of you, but that wouldn't be very neighborly. How about I trim your trees and you have me and my dad over for dinner some night. That's getting off pretty cheap."

"Dinner? I'm, uh..." She'd been about to say married. Except that wasn't true anymore. "I'm a terrible cook." She closed her eyes for a second. "No, sorry, that's a lie. I'm actually a great cook, but I'm in a weird place and I didn't know what to say and I'm sorry, but can we just forget this whole thing?"

He frowned. "Are you okay? I didn't mean to impose."

She shook her head, taking a deep breath. "It's not you, I promise. It's just that...my husband just passed away and I'm not myself." She hadn't been expecting him to invite himself to dinner, either. Not a good-looking guy like him.

Did he think she was an easy mark? Because there was no way he could be attracted to her.

"I'm so sorry to hear about your husband. My wife passed four years ago. Cancer." He stared at the ground for a few seconds. "I don't think you ever really get over it."

"No," she whispered. "I don't think you do." His confession had pulled her emotions to the surface again, causing tears to threaten. She cleared her throat. "I'm sorry about your wife. Cancer is a terrible thing."

He nodded solemnly. "Your husband, too?"

"No. Heart attack."

"Even worse."

That surprised her. "You think that's worse than cancer?"

"Yes. At least I had a chance to say goodbye."

She sniffed, blinking hard to keep the tears at bay. "True. I wish I'd had..." But she couldn't finish. The muscles in her jaw tightened as she fought to regain control, but she wasn't winning that battle.

"It's okay," Danny said quietly. "I understand completely."

She sucked in air, trying to breathe through the pain. "I should go. Sorry." And with that, she ran off toward the house. She took the front stairs, not willing to wait on the elevator.

She'd made a fool of herself. Why had she thought coming here was a good idea? She was clearly not ready to be around people.

It was her own fault. She'd approached him. Lesson learned. She went inside on the first floor and just stood there for a moment, staring up the steps that led to the second floor. She could hear the television and some other sounds. Maybe someone in the kitchen?

Going up the steps led to a landing barred by the baby gate that was usually kept closed. Directly in front of the landing was the door to her bedroom.

Turning right put you immediately into the kitchen, so it made sense that she could hear someone in there. Ray, maybe. Jules was probably out with Toby and their mother was obviously still watching TV. Could be Kat, but she was usually louder.

Ray was very quiet. Almost like he didn't want to bother anyone with his presence. And if they'd both been in the kitchen, there would have been conversation. Mostly Kat telling Ray what to do next.

Claire didn't want to go upstairs. She didn't want to talk to anyone. Didn't want to help with dinner. She just wanted to go to her room and lie down in the dark and wake up again when this nightmare was over.

Except that wasn't going to happen.

She ignored the steps. Instead, she went through the first floor's little foyer, past the elevator doors and around the corner into what they called the reading nook. It was really just a wide hallway with a comfy couch that faced the bedroom doors on that floor. In between those doors and the entrance at the end that led into the kitchen-living room area were a couple of bookcases.

The shelves were mostly full and, over the years, the books had changed without any effort on their part. Sometimes guests took a book home with them. Sometimes guests would leave books behind. She'd always loved that. You could get to know a person based on what they read.

She took a seat on the couch and looked at the spines to see if she could recognize anything new from the last time she'd been here.

There were still plenty of books by David Baldacci, John Grisham, James Patterson, and Lee Child. Bryan loved those kinds of stories. Lots of action. Then there were her picks. The cozy mysteries. The hearth-and-home stories. The occasional romance.

She didn't read too many of those. She found them unrealistic, which she imagined was to be expected in such perfect, happily-ever-after tales, but hers and Bryan's relationship hadn't followed that sort of pattern.

Neither had most of the relationships she knew about. Like those of her friends. The other mothers she'd met through Kat's school events and extracurricular activities.

Very few had fallen in love at first sight. There were the exceptions, of course. Specifically, a few couples at church who seemed made for each other.

The thought made her look toward the end of

the house, as if she could see through the walls to where her neighbor was working on his palms.

Suddenly, she wondered about his story. He'd lost his wife to cancer. The look in his eyes had been one of genuine pain and grief. He'd loved her, clearly. Had theirs been a storybook romance?

Probably not. Because those only happened in books. Grief had made her bitter enough to believe that.

She put her feet up on the couch, rested her head on one of the throw pillows and lay there, watching the golden light that spilled in from outside grow dim. The sun would be down soon and it would be dark outside.

She could go to bed without anyone fussing then.

A new thought came to her. Did anyone else in the house even care where she was?

Probably not. And, honestly, she couldn't blame them.

Chapter Seven

*T*oby's barking woke Kat. She blinked a few times, trying to get her bearings. It took a moment, then it all came back to her. They were at the beach house. She'd laid down to take a nap. And, from the sounds of it, someone was making dinner.

She got up and went to the bathroom to splash water on her face. She'd obviously needed the nap, but she wasn't sure she felt better. Sleep anytime it wasn't night often left her feeling groggy and disoriented, which was exactly where she was at right now.

She dried her face and went out to the kitchen. Ray was chopping vegetables and making a salad. Grandma Bloom was still on the couch, watching television. Some news talk program. There was no sign of her mother or aunt.

Ray smiled at her. "Hello, Sunshine."

She smiled back. "Hi. Sorry about before." She couldn't even remember why she'd been angry with him, just that she had been. She sighed. She was a mess.

"Nothing to be sorry for. Grief gives you a pass."

That was sweet of him. Which was all Ray ever was. She felt contrite. "What can I do to help?"

"Well..." He looked at the empty stove top. "You can tell me what to make for dinner. Right now, all I've got is salad."

She nodded. "No problem. We can do spaghetti with meat sauce. It's simple and easy. And it goes great with salad."

"Sounds perfect."

She got out a big pot and filled it with hot water and salt, covered it, then set it on the biggest burner to come to a boil. Next, she grabbed one of the packages of ground beef from the fridge and started it frying in a pan.

She stood at the island, breaking up the beef to get it all cooked. She added a little salt. "Did Aunt Jules take Toby out?"

Ray nodded. "Yes. And your mom just came in. She went straight to her room. Said she was going to take a shower."

"I guess everyone will be ready for dinner soon then. What time is it?" She looked over her shoulder at the microwave to check the digital clock.

"A little after six," Ray answered.

The day was nearly over. Did she feel any better than she had this morning? Maybe the tiniest little bit. Tomorrow was a new day, though. There was hope and thinking about that helped. All she had to do was make it through each day and after enough of them, she'd be happy again. Or at least, not so sad.

The mechanical hum of the elevator being called came from the shaft. Aunt Jules must be on her way back with Toby. His short legs were okay for walking and running, but he wasn't so good on stairs.

The elevator whirred back to the second floor and the doors opened. Toby exited first, but didn't make it far, thanks to the leash attached to his collar.

"Hang on," Aunt Jules said to the dog. "I need to clean your feet. Hi, Kat. Hi, Ray. Dinner smells good." She scooped him up and took him straight into the pantry-laundry room.

"Thanks." Kat heard the water running in the big laundry sink.

Ray took the salad out to the dining table, then went to work setting it with plates and utensils. As he pulled things from the cabinet, he glanced over at her. "Want to go for a walk on the beach after?"

She nodded. "Sure."

"Great."

Her mom came out of the bedroom, dressed in pajama pants, a matching T-shirt, and slippers. The ones Kat had given her for her birthday. "Hey, Mom."

Her mother's response was a quick smile, but her eyes still held a lot of pain. "How long before dinner?"

The water had just started to boil. Kat opened the box of spaghetti and dumped it in. "About ten minutes."

Her mom opened a bottle of red wine. "Anything I can do?"

Kat was about to say no when Ray answered. "You could get the salad dressings out. Whatever kind you think people will want."

Claire seemed pleased to be given a job. "All right." She poured herself a glass of wine, took a big sip, then went to the fridge.

As her mom got the bottles of dressing out and carried them to the table, Kat caught Ray's gaze. "Thanks," she said softly.

He nodded. He got the strainer from a cabinet

and set it in the sink so it would be ready when the pasta was done.

Didn't take long to bring the meal together and, in a few more minutes, they were all sitting down at the table. No one sat at the head. That was her father's seat and if his chair had been under a spotlight, his absence couldn't have been more obvious.

Kat held her fork but didn't eat. She just stared at the empty chair, her heart slowly disintegrating once again.

Ray lightly cleared his throat. "Anyone up for a puzzle later? If I remember, there are some in the game closet. Kat and I are going to walk on the beach, but I'd love to do one when we get back."

Aunt Jules nodded. "Sure. I'll do one with you. And Claire and I will clean up, since you and Kat made the dinner."

Ray shook his head. "You don't have to do that."

"Yes," Kat's mom said. "We do. Mother? Are you going to help?"

Grandma Bloom looked over. Her attention had been on the television, which had been turned down but not off. "Help what?"

Kat twirled noodles around her fork.

Claire gestured at the table. "Help us clean up."

"We only just sat down to eat. Or did I fall asleep?"

Jules snorted. "No, Mom. We mean after the meal."

Grandma Bloom arched her slim brows. "You two can clean up. I'm going to take a bath and watch *Forensic Files*."

Kat laughed, despite her mood. "I don't know how you can watch those shows. They're so gruesome."

"They're not that bad," her grandmother said. "Better than those insipid Hallmark movies where people are always falling in love because someone gave them a cupcake."

Jules shook her head and chuckled.

Ray lifted his fork to point toward the kitchen. "Speaking of cupcakes, we have key lime pie for dessert and rum—"

Kat kicked him under the table. Those truffles were meant for her mother, not for sharing. Even if they *had* gotten two pounds.

Claire's gentle smile said she knew exactly what had just happened. "It's okay. I'll share. There are rum truffles from Guilford's. Kat and Ray got them for me, but there's no way I'll eat them all. I'll put the box on the table for dessert."

Kat noticed her mom had said box, not boxes, as if there were just the one. That had to mean she was keeping the other one in her room. Good for her for being a little selfish. Her mother always put others first. Time she did something for herself.

After dinner, Aunt Jules practically pushed her and Ray out the door to walk on the beach. They headed for the water, the light from the half-moon and the houses lining the shore enough to see by.

Kat kept her hands in her pockets so she didn't have to hold Ray's. She just wasn't in the mood. And doing so anyway would have felt disingenuous. She really didn't know what was going on with her and how she was feeling.

"You're awfully quiet," Ray said. "Which I understand. I just want you to know we don't have to talk."

She was about to say thanks, when a realization struck her. "Actually, I think we do."

He shrugged. "Sure. What do you want to talk about?"

She stopped walking. "Us."

That brought him to a standstill, too. "What about us?"

Was she actually doing this? It felt like she was teetering on the edge of a cliff, too far gone to save herself from falling. She needed to say what was on her mind and in her heart. Not telling him would only make a bigger mess of things, because either way, she was headed in a new direction.

She took a breath as she looked down at the diamond on her finger. She pulled the ring off and handed it to him. "I don't want to be engaged anymore."

He blinked, mouth open in shock. He took the ring from her, moving slowly, like a robot running out of juice. "You're breaking up with me?"

"No. It's not that. I just need time to think."

"About what?"

"About us. About my life and where it's headed. What I'm doing with it. About what I want. What I need." She shook her head. "I'm sorry, but there's something going on with me. Something more than just losing my dad. I don't know what it is, and I need time to figure it out."

"I'm confused."

"So am I. That's part of the problem."

"But we're not breaking up?"

She shook her head. "We're just...taking a step back. It doesn't mean you're not welcome here. You are. I'm just not in a place mentally where I can be anyone's fiancée right now. I don't even know if I want..." She'd almost said, "to be married," but she held back, not wanting to hurt him any more than she already had.

"If you want what?"

She offered him a little smile. "Losing my father has broken something inside of me. I need time to heal. I'm sorry I can't explain it more than that."

Ray exhaled, a long, deep sigh that wavered at the end. "Okay. Whatever you want. Whatever time you need. I don't understand, but I don't have to. Just know that I love you, whatever the outcome. And I'm here for you. If you need me."

And just like that, Kat's spirit felt a little bit lighter. Still shattered into tiny pieces that all felt as if they belonged to someone else, but also impossibly lighter.

Giving back the ring had been hard, but obviously, it had also been right.

"I know. But what if he's not the right guy for me?"

Claire sighed. She understood her daughter was going through some things. They both were. Grief had a way of infiltrating even the happiest of emotions and making you feel guilty for the split second you'd felt anything but despair.

"What?" Kat asked.

Claire slid her hand toward her daughter, unable to reach her, but wanting her to know the sentiment was there. "If you're thinking all of this because you've suddenly come to the realization that Ray isn't your soulmate, then it's time you learned that soulmates aren't a real thing. Maybe they are for a tiny percent of the population, but for the rest of us?" She shook her head. "We find someone who is kind and caring, who treats us well, who can help us carve out a decent life, and we love them for who they are. It's the best any of us can hope for."

Kat looked horrified. "Are you saying you didn't love Dad?"

"Of course I loved him. But we weren't some fairytale romance. There were no fireworks or butterflies or any of that. We liked each other very much and that turned into loving each other. He took care of me, and I took care of him, and that kind of mutual respect made things work."

Claire pulled her hand back. "No one actually tells you how hard marriage is. Nothing truly prepares you for the amount of work necessary to keep that kind of commitment going. It's one of the great illusions of life, that marriage just happens like this magical, effortless thing when the right two people get together. It doesn't. Not without determination and sacrifice and a lot of forgiveness. Prayer doesn't hurt, either."

Kat's expression had gone from horrified to bleak. "You're really not selling me on the institution."

"I'm not trying to. I'm trying to be honest with you. I guess this is a talk we should have had a while ago. But I say all of that to say that I believe with all my heart that Ray is a good choice. He might not be the most exciting of men, but excitement is overrated. Stability is far better."

Kat let out a soft groan. "I don't know if it is or not. But just to be clear, I'm not looking for excitement. I'm not looking for anything. Except maybe to figure out who I am and what I want. And how to make my life matter."

"Dad's passing brought this all on?"

Kat nodded. "I feel ... I feel like I lost my center."

Claire got that. Her center still felt like a swamp, dark and murky and impossible to wade through. "Do you want to go home?"

Kat reared back. "No. This is definitely where I need to be. Why? Do you?"

Claire shook her head. "No. I feel like this is the right place for us, too. I think your dad would have wanted us to come here." She glanced over at the urn. "I can sense him here. Not in a woo-woo kind of way, but there are so many good memories here."

"There are," Kat said. "When he was here with us, he was the most present."

Claire tipped her head to look at her daughter again. "What do you mean?"

"I mean, when he was here with us, he was really *here*. He engaged with us. Sometimes, at home, he'd be there, but he'd be a million miles away at the same time. On his phone, working, or just thinking about work, I guess."

A small knot formed in Claire's throat. She hadn't been aware that Kat had picked up on that, but why wouldn't she have? Kat was a smart woman with a working set of senses. She could hear and see what Claire could, just the same. She tried to smile. "Your father only worked as hard as he did because he wanted us to have the best possible life."

Kat stared at the duvet. "I know. Except..." She picked her head up. "Don't you think we could have had a pretty great life just by having him around more?"

A muscle in Claire's cheek twitched as she fought back tears. "Yes," she said quietly. "I'm sorry that wasn't the case." She sniffled, a little liquid spilling down her cheek. "I don't want to say anything bad about your father—"

"It's okay. I'm not going to judge you."

Claire wiped at her face. "I wish he'd been home a *lot* more." She stopped trying to hold the tears back. "It was hard being in charge of the house and raising you and trying to make sure nothing got overlooked. I felt like a single parent. Even when he was home, he wasn't that much help. Not engaged, like you said."

Kat got up and came around to her mother's side of the bed and sat closer to her. She leaned in and hugged Claire. "You were a great mom. I don't tell you that enough. But you were. You still are. I hope you don't ever doubt that. I'm sorry that dad wasn't your soulmate and that there was no fairytale romance or fireworks. You deserved better."

Claire held onto her daughter. She inhaled the scent of her hair and absorbed the warmth of her skin. The hug wasn't a common thing. They weren't the most affectionate family, and she didn't know why. Maybe they could change that. "Thank you."

When Kat leaned back, her own cheeks damp. "You know, it's not too late."

Claire narrowed her eyes in confusion. "For what?"

"For you to...take another crack at love."

Claire shook her head. "No. I have no interest in—"

Kat held her hands up. "I don't mean right this instant. I know you're not at that place yet. I just think you shouldn't count yourself out."

"I don't know. I've been alone so long that I—I mean, not alone but—" She shrank back, aware her words painted her marriage in a very unfavorable way.

"I know what you mean. You've been doing things your own way for a long time, because dad was pretty much a non-factor in all of the decision-making, and it's hard to think about having to bring another person into your life after that. Right?"

Claire nodded, slightly embarrassed by her admission.

"It's okay. I think that might even be a little of what's going on with me. The idea of losing some of my independence is hard to accept."

Claire wanted to tell Kat that wasn't true, that she wouldn't lose her independence or anything by being married to Ray or anyone else, but that would have been a lie. Claire was done with that kind of nonsense. This was the realest conversation she'd ever had with anyone. The fact that she was having it with Kat felt like a significant moment.

Kat arched her brows. "Aren't you going to tell me that won't happen?"

"No. Because I'm not going to lie to you or sugar-coat anything. Ever again." Claire cupped her daughter's cheek. "We should always be honest with each other, you know that? It feels good. It feels..." She tried to think of the right words. "Very adult."

Kat smiled. "We are both adults. But, yeah, I know what you mean. We've never really talked like this. I like it."

"I do, too." She patted Kat's cheek before settling back on the pillows. "Marriage doesn't have to mean losing your independence, but I think those kinds of relationships are rare and I'm the last person to tell you how to get one. I was very dependent on your father." *Almost trapped by him.* The stray thought shocked Claire. Had she actually felt that way? No, that couldn't be right.

Kat took Claire's hand. "Thank you for giving up so much of your life for me. I see it now with a kind of clarity I never knew I was lacking, but you sacrificed for me."

Claire swallowed and said nothing.

"Mom, whatever you want to do with the rest of your life, I just want you to know that it's okay with me. No judgment. About anything. You've earned the right to make your own choices from here on out."

"Thank you, sweetheart. If there's anything you ever want to talk about, I'll offer you the same deal. No judgment. About anything."

Kat kissed Claire on the cheek. "I love you. We're going to get through this. Try to get some sleep."

"You, too," Claire said. She had no doubt they'd get through this. She just didn't know what kind of shape they'd be in when they made it to the other side.

$\mathcal{K}$at stayed up watching *Forensic Files* with her grandmother until well after Ray had gone into bed. Her mom and Aunt Jules had turned in, too. Kat wasn't a big fan of the show, but she enjoyed spending time with her grandmother. And she didn't want to lay in bed with Ray beside her and have to make small talk or, worse, big talk about what had happened between them on the beach.

Because Ray would definitely want to talk about it. He'd give it up after she said she didn't feel like talking, but that would disappoint him. Even if he didn't actually put that into words. And she didn't have the energy for any of that.

She didn't have the energy for much. It had been a stream of long, emotionally exhausting days and despite the nap she'd had, she was ready for bed when her grandmother finally turned off the television.

"Night, Grandma."

"Sleep well, Kat." Grandma Bloom got up slowly and went off to the room she was sharing with Aunt Jules.

Kat turned off the rest of the lights and tiptoed into her bedroom. Ray was snoring softly. He'd be headed back home at some point tomorrow, because it was Sunday, and he had to work on Monday. Whether he'd return the following weekend remained to be seen. Not because of his work schedule, but because of her.

Maybe by then she'd have everything figured out and they'd be back on track. Or not. She really had no idea.

She grabbed her nightgown and took it into the bathroom with her to brush her teeth and change. She closed the door before turning on the light so she wouldn't disturb Ray.

His things were all neatly lined up on the left-hand side of the sink. Hers were still in their plaid cosmetics case. She unzipped it, took out her toothbrush and toothpaste, then brushed her teeth.

She replayed the conversation she'd had with her mother, thinking through what her mom had said about marriage and soulmates. Had Kat ever had fireworks with Ray?

She rinsed her mouth out. No, she hadn't felt fireworks, but he did make her reasonably happy. Most of the time. But since her father's death, she no longer felt sure she knew what real happiness was.

And therein lay the issue. It was completely possible that she was settling for Ray. The truth was, he might have been just slightly out of her league. Not by much. She wasn't so vain that she couldn't honestly assess herself.

She was pretty enough, but she wasn't the most beautiful girl in the world. She was okay with how she looked. She prided herself on being natural. Her hair was the same dark blond she'd been born with. She didn't pluck her eyebrows, or wear a lot of makeup, or try to be someone she wasn't.

She'd done very well in school, but she hadn't been valedictorian. Stylistically, she tended to dress in safe, classic pieces, because fashion was a bit of a mystery to her. And as an actuary, she needed to look a certain way when meeting with clients. Safe. Trustworthy. Responsible. No one wanted a woman in a hot pink zebra-striped suit and stiletto heels handling their important data, especially when it came to finances.

At least Kat didn't think they did.

She moisturized, then changed into her nightgown, which was a simple, shell-pink cotton knit that looked like an extra-long T-shirt and proved exactly her point about her views on fashion.

She turned the light out and went to bed, slipping quietly under the covers and turning her back to Ray. She lay there, staring into the dark and thinking about her life and hoping that sleep would come fast. She didn't want to lay here all night, filled with sad thoughts about her life and her father.

Apparently, sleep happened before she knew it, because a noise woke her up sometime later. Bleary-eyed, she looked at her phone where it was charging on the nightstand. Nearly one a.m., so she'd been asleep not quite two hours. She put her phone down and listened, attempting to figure out what she'd heard. Maybe it had been a dream.

But then, she picked up on a few more faint sounds. She was mostly awake now, trying to determine what she was hearing. They seemed to be coming from downstairs. That brought her fully around, because all she could think of was that Toby was down there and couldn't get back up. Even worse, he might have fallen down the steps. If he was hurt...

She tossed the covers back, slipped her feet into some flipflops and headed for the stairs. There was the baby gate at the top, but it was very possible that hadn't been latched. It was too dark to see, so she felt around for the latch. The gate was open. Her heart caught in her throat.

If Toby was injured, she'd never forgive herself. Or whoever had left the gate open.

Fresh, outside air drifted up the steps. Was the outside door open, too? Then she saw movement, just a dark shape, but it wasn't Toby. In fact, it was human. There was someone in the house.

She froze, hoping whoever it was didn't look up and see her. She didn't know what to do. Her phone was still on the nightstand and the beach house didn't have a landline.

A second shape appeared. And a third. As her eyes adjusted further, she realized they were female. And rolling suitcases behind them. Except for one who was shorter and a little stooped.

The shorter one sighed as she disappeared from view, muttering something about being tired and too old for this and she just wanted to go to bed. All three disappeared from view and a light came on.

Kat jerked back into the shadows. Oh, crap. Had the house been rented, and her mom hadn't realized it? She couldn't think of any other reason there would be people with suitcases on the first floor.

She grimaced as she turned toward the door behind her and opened it as quietly as she could. She crept into her mother's room, carefully closing the door behind her. "Mom," she whispered as loudly as she dared.

Nothing.

"*Mom*."

"Hmm?" Her mother came awake. The pale moonlight filtered through the plantation shutters, giving a small amount of light. "Kat?"

"Yes. Wake up."

Her mother stirred, turning toward her. "What is it?"

"There are people downstairs. I think the first floor must have been rented and you didn't realize it."

"What?" Her mom rubbed at her eyes. "No, that's not possible. We told the agency we were closing down rentals until the repairs were done and since that was just two weeks ago, they never got started up again. Mostly because of everything with your father."

"Well, that might be true, but there are still people downstairs."

"I'm getting my robe." She hesitated as soon as her feet touched the floor. "Or should we call the police? They could be burglars!"

"They have suitcases." Kat thought about that. "Although I guess that could be for carting stuff out?" She shook her head. "I don't think they're burglars. They all looked female. And one of them was sort of hunched over. Like an old lady. She mentioned wanting to go to bed."

Her mom made a face. "That doesn't sound like burglars." She got up, put on a robe, and gave Kat a nod. "Let's go see what's going on."

"Grab your phone," Kat said. "And keep it handy. Just in case we have to call 911."

"Right. Good idea." Her mom hesitated, finger-combing her bedhead into place. "What if they have weapons?"

Kat doubted that. "I seriously think they're renters." But she understood her mother's reluctance to confront them. It was late, they were sleepy, and it was just a prickly thing to have to deal with at such an odd hour. "Do you want me to get Ray?"

Her mom yawned. "No, it's okay. I'm sure you're right. Let's go make sure they're in the right house."

"How else would they have gotten in if they

didn't have the code for the keypad?" To Kat, that confirmed they were renters.

"Good question." Claire headed for the door. "We'll soon find out."

They went out to the steps. Kat pulled the baby gate open and they descended. At the bottom of the steps, Claire called out, "Hello? Is there someone here?"

The small side lamp in the reading nook was on, as well as the lights in the three bedrooms, the doors all open.

One by one, three women appeared in the doorways. The first was a middle-aged redhead with big hair, tight clothes, and a lot of makeup. She was barefoot.

The second was a younger version of the first woman, but her hair had streaks of blond and was tied up in a high ponytail. Both women were in leopard print. The first in pants with a low-cut black top, the second in what could only be described as a romper accessorized with a hot pink belt and hot pink platform flipflops.

The third woman, the older, slightly stooped one Kat had seen, scowled at them. She had an elaborately curled cloud of pale pink hair that not-so-faintly resembled cotton candy and cat-eye glasses bedazzled with rhinestones. She was dressed in a loud floral tunic and leggings with orthopedic sandals. "What's going on? Who are you people?"

Claire straightened, drawing herself up to her full height of five-foot-four. "I'm the owner of this house. Who are you?"

The middle-aged woman stepped out from the doorway and put her hands on her hips. "That's not possible, because I'm Roxie Thompson and *I'm* the owner of this house."

Chapter Ten

Claire shook her head. What were the odds the woman would have the same last name as her? This had to be some kind of a scam. "Impossible. I own this home."

Roxie kept her hands on her hips. "Listen here. I don't know what you're trying to pull but this is my place. We've been coming here for years. Now, it's late, we're tired, and I'm in no mood for games."

Claire frowned. "We've been coming here for years, too. You must be in the wrong place."

Roxie dangled a pink puff of fake fur that had keys attached to it. "If I'm in the wrong place, how do I have the key to the front door? I know the keycode, too."

Claire was utterly confused. But also ready to be done with this. "I'm calling the police. They can sort this out."

Roxie wasn't fazed. "Go ahead. The sooner they get here, the sooner I can have you removed."

Kat put her hands up. "Everyone just hold on a sec. Why don't you just tell us who you rented through and maybe that will help clear some things up."

Roxie rolled her eyes. "Aren't you listening? I'm not renting the house from anyone. I own it. My late husband, may he rest in peace, bought this house years ago."

A sick feeling wormed its way into Claire's stomach. "Your late husband?"

Roxie nodded and sniffed, putting her hand to her chest and thankfully covering some of the overabundance of cleavage on display. "Yes. He just passed and we've come here to remember him and the wonderful times we had here. He bought this place for us."

Claire reached out and grabbed Kat's arm to steady herself. "*Your* husband. Bought *this* place."

Roxie gave her a look like she was a few sandwiches short of a picnic. "That's what I just said. Bryan Thompson."

Claire gasped, but no sound came out. She couldn't get enough air and all the strength seemed to leave her body. She squeezed Kat's arm, trying not to let her knees buckle. She couldn't have heard the woman right.

Kat stared at the woman. "Your husband's name is Bryan Thompson?"

The younger one leaned against the door frame. "Why? Do you know him? Because if you do, you'd better not say anything bad about my father, you understand? He was a good man and we're in mourning."

Claire managed to pull in a breath, but weakness still filled her body. There was no way this was real. "I don't feel well."

Kat blinked. "This can't be right. There's got to be some explanation for this."

"There is," Roxie said. "Everything I just told you."

Claire let go of her daughter and collapsed into a nearby chair. She lifted her head to keep eye contact with Roxie. A faint screeching filled her head, probably the sound of her sanity being ripped away. "My husband's name is Bryan Thompson. I'm Claire Thompson. He bought this house for us years ago and we've been coming here every year since. Every July."

Roxie paled slightly. "Every June."

The older woman snorted. "I told you he was up to something, Roxanne."

"Mimi," the younger woman said. "He wasn't, don't say that."

"Sorry, Trina, but the proof is in the pudding. I'm going to bed." With that, the older woman shuffled back into the bedroom and shut the door.

Roxie stared at Claire. "You mean to tell me you were married to Bryan? That can't be. *I* was married to Bryan."

Trina, now twisting a loose strand of hair around her finger, let out a sad sigh. "Seems like he was married to both of you, doesn't it?"

Kat put her hand on her head and looked at Trina. "Bryan was your father?"

Trina nodded.

"How old are you?"

Trina grinned. "Twenty-eight. About a month from turning the big two-nine. Hard to believe, huh?"

"About a month?" Kat glanced at Claire before looking back at Trina. "When exactly is your birthday?"

"September twenty-sixth."

Kat sat on the arm of Claire's chair, looking as dazed as Claire felt. "How can that be?"

"What?" Roxie asked. "How can what be?"

Kat rubbed at her throat. "My birthday is September twenty-seventh. And I'll be turning twenty-nine, too."

Trina got a strange look in her eyes. "What's your name again?"

"Kat," Kat answered. "Short for—"

"Katrina?" Trina snorted. "I guess it was easier for him to remember that way."

Kat let out a soft, strangled sound. "Your name is Katrina, too?"

"Yep."

For the space of several heartbeats, no one said anything. Claire was glad for the silence and the chance to think without interruption.

But the more she thought, the more puzzle pieces fit together in her head, and the picture became very clear. Bryan hadn't just been a workaholic, he'd been a bigamist. All these years she'd thought he'd been unable to spend as much time at home as she'd wanted him to because of his work.

She'd never imagined in a million years that it was because he'd had another family. Not just another wife, but another child?

All those excuses he'd made about being busy. About having to meet with clients. About why he couldn't make Kat's recital or be there when Claire had a small operation or the church Christmas party or *any* of the multitude of things he'd missed. All for *these* people. All for his *other* family.

A shiver went through her, a mix of revulsion and the recognition of how deeply he'd betrayed her.

She fixed her gaze on Roxie. There was nothing about the woman she liked. She looked cheap and easy and it gutted Claire that this was the sort of woman Bryan had chosen to spend so much of his time with. That he'd thought enough of this woman to marry her, too.

How could he have done this to her? It was like being punched in the gut and smacked in the face at the same time.

All the years that Claire had worried about presenting herself in a manner befitting the wife of a businessman such as Bryan, and he'd taken up with some woman who looked like she waitressed at a honkytonk.

His blatant infidelity cut through her like a blade, slicing away the sadness of his death until it only remained by the thinnest of threads. She'd given him the best years of her life. Her youth. Her beauty. Her time and energy.

Was it possible for love to become hate in the blink of an eye? It certainly felt like it. How could he do this to her? To Kat?

Claire had been nothing but loyal. She'd never even thought about cheating, because even that would have felt like infidelity to her.

Obviously, Bryan had had none of those qualms.

The anger started down deep, but then it unfurled and bloomed like a drop of black ink in a glass of water. It seethed through her, pushing out the last of the grief and despair she'd been wallowing in.

She shook with rage and a bone-deep sense of betrayal that almost made it hard to see. She did not deserve this. She'd been a good wife. Her nails dug into her thighs where her hands rested, bunching her robe.

"Mom? Are you all right?"

She shook her head. "No, I'm not all right." She might never be. She took a breath, once again unsure how to go forward but for reasons that had nothing to do with being a widow. She spoke to Roxie. "How did you find out about his passing?"

"Dr. Welling. He called me and told me that Bryan had had a heart attack and, according to his wishes, was being cremated and that he'd call me when the ashes were ready to pick up."

"Then Dr. Welling knew about you?" Claire ground her teeth together. "He has a lot of nerve hiding Bryan's secret for him."

Roxie shrugged. "Doctor-patient confidentiality, I guess."

Kat stood and put her hand on her mother's shoulder. "Why don't we go to bed and figure this out in the morning?"

Roxie nodded. "I think that's for the best."

"None of this is for the best," Claire muttered. But she got to her feet, moving without really being aware of what she was doing, but her body seemed to understand where she needed to go. She cut her eyes at Roxie. "Just so you know, I've already picked up his ashes. And it's a good thing he's dead," she said quietly. "Or I'd kill him myself."

Chapter Eleven

Roxie sat on the side of the bed and stared out the window into the dark. Somewhere out there was sand and water that stretched to the horizon. Didn't matter that she couldn't see any of it. She knew what the view looked like from all the other times she'd been here. But she wasn't focused on the view anyway. Bryan had another wife. And another kid.

The kid was all right so far, but the wife was a doozy.

Maybe him having a second family shouldn't have been such a shock to her system. They'd always had a pretty passionate relationship, one based more in the physical than anything else. Their love had been a wild, reckless thing, heightened by the time they spent away from each other. She'd thought it was part of what kept the magic alive between them.

What made the spark burn so bright. And Bryan had always felt like her soulmate. She'd told him as much and he'd said the same about her.

But if that was true, why had he married Claire?

Roxie had an idea, but it hurt to think about. She pushed herself to do it anyway, to face the painful truth that had been presented to her that night.

Claire was respectable. Claire was the kind of woman he could take to business dinners, the kind he could introduce to clients.

It was easy to tell just by looking at her that Claire kept a neat, tidy house, always had dinner on the table when Bryan walked through the door, and probably sent Christmas cards to every one of his clients without fail.

Claire might be uptight, but she was also the model wife. Roxie was not. She was more the good-time girl. She wasn't, not really. She'd been a nurse most of her life. Being who she was, being a fun person and wearing bold colors and living life loudly helped alleviate a lot of the stress and sadness of her job.

Despite all of that, Bryan *had* married her. Claire, too, obviously. But he'd loved Roxie enough to want to make it official. That meant something. Although maybe not as much as if she'd been his only wife.

She narrowed her eyes at the question that arose in her mind. Which one of them had Bryan married first?

And how had both of his daughters been born on nearly the same day? A few more minutes and Trina would have been born on the twenty-seventh.

She exhaled a long breath, trying to figure out what it all meant. She remembered how he'd insisted on the name Katrina, telling her that it meant "pure" and that their child was exactly that— a pure expression of their love.

She'd been swept away by how much thought he'd put into the name, never once thinking it was because giving two children the same name would make his life easier.

What a low-down, dirty... She sniffed and started to cry. The truth was, she still loved him very much. Missing him was an ache she couldn't get rid of. A void she knew she would never fill.

That ache had lessened a little since finding out about Claire and Kat, but Roxie couldn't bring herself to hate him. She could be mad at him. That was easy. She'd been mad at him a lot over the years.

All the times he'd never made it home, for example. The long stretches where she survived on the occasional text. But she'd come to understand that was just what it meant to be married to a busy, successful man like Bryan.

She'd thought of him as a blessing in her life and been willing to accept his absences.

Now, of course, she realized that he *wasn't* always working. He was with Claire and Kat. How often, she wondered? What had his real schedule been like?

She fell back on the bed. The last time she'd slept in this bed, Bryan had been beside her. There were so many memories in this house.

If what Claire had said about them coming here for regular visits was true, then she and her daughter had their own set of memories. There were more memories in this place than there should have been.

Roxie sighed but that did nothing to lessen the weight on her. Or how totally messed up this whole situation was.

She got up and went to the bathroom to wash off her makeup and change into a nightgown. A few minutes later, she walked out in a slip of red silk, one of Bryan's favorite nighties, and got into bed. She sat for a second just staring at the wall. She'd spent enough time alone that life without Bryan wouldn't be that much different.

She spread her hand over the empty side of the

bed. There were certain aspects of life that would be very different, and, in those areas, she ached for him. Like the way he'd held her and whispered sweet things in her ear and made her laugh and gave her the kind of companionship she'd never experienced with another man. He made her feel so wanted and desired.

That was part of why she'd married him. That connection they'd shared. And then, of course, Trina had come along, cementing their bond by making them a family.

They'd had a good, if rather unconventional, life. She regretted none of it.

But Claire didn't seem to be having those same kinds of feelings. She seemed to be having a lot of regret. Was that going to be a problem?

Roxie slipped further under the covers. She had a sinking feeling it wasn't just going to be a problem. It might turn into some kind of a fight.

She hoped not. But if that was the case, she wasn't about to back down and slink away. She'd been married to him just the same as Claire. Maybe for longer. Who knew? She deserved her fair share of things. Bryan would have wanted that, she was certain. He would have taken care of them. He would have at least taken care of Trina. He doted on that girl.

She frowned at the ceiling. Did he have a will? He must have. She knew he had life insurance. Or at least he'd told her he did. Had the will already been read? There were so many unanswered questions.

She groaned softly, thinking about how she was going to have to explain all of this to her mother in the morning.

Willie had never really liked Bryan. She'd always said he acted like a man hiding a secret and that he smiled too much to be honest. How right she'd been. And what a crazy-big secret he'd been hiding. Insanely big.

Part of her was definitely mad at Bryan. Hurt that he'd been so boldly unfaithful. But also, it hurt a lot that she hadn't been enough. She got it, though. She knew exactly who she was. Loud. Boisterous. Fun. Flirty. Colorful. Too much for some people's tastes.

He'd needed someone the opposite of that to instill confidence in his clients, she supposed.

Was it really so awful to live your life in full color? She didn't think so. And she wasn't about to change. Not now. Not ever. She liked herself. She'd certainly had no problems attracting men.

But when Bryan had come along, that had been

it for her. She'd found the one she was meant to be with. And that was that.

She'd suspected him of cheating a few times, but she'd let it go. They were only suspicions, after all. He always, eventually, came home to her. Always convinced her that she was his one and only.

He'd been around for Trina as much as he could be. He always brought her a present when he came home, made sure their bills were paid, that Roxie's car had a full tank of gas, and that there was money left over for them to live on. As fathers went, sure, he was a little absent, but he was always there for holidays and birthdays.

So that meant...he hadn't been there for his other family. Or had he? She thought back to how many Christmases he'd been called away early. Or shown up late because of a work emergency. He'd been there for every one of Roxie's birthdays. And always there for Trina's birthday celebration. But he'd always left that evening.

Roxie hoped that meant he'd spent the next day with Kat. No kid should go without their father on a day like that.

Those kinds of thoughts raised her irritation level. She didn't have a lot of sympathy for Claire, mostly because she knew Claire had no sympathy for her, but Kat was different. She might be grown now, but what about her childhood years?

The idea that Kat might have suffered bothered Roxie. "Oh, Bry, what a mess you've made. Why did you have to marry both of us?" She sniffed. "And why did you have to have a heart attack?"

She hugged his pillow to her and sobbed into it.

She'd almost drifted off when a low voice brought her around.

"Ma? You sleeping?"

She looked at the figure in the doorway. "No, honey. What is it?"

Trina let out a small sigh. "I can't sleep. Too much on my mind."

"Come on, get into bed with me."

"Thanks." Trina climbed in and a few moments ticked by until she got settled. "Are you mad at Dad?"

"Sure, a little bit. Are you?"

"Sort of. But I'm kind of excited to have a sister. Although I don't think she's so excited about me."

"Maybe not yet." Roxie tugged on a stray lock of Trina's hair, her heart broken as much for her daughter as for herself. "But she'll love you once she gets to know you."

Chapter Twelve

*T*rina stood at the bottom of the steps, out of sight around the corner where she could listen undetected. There were definitely people moving around upstairs. Someone had made the coffee she smelled. Was there a better smell? She doubted it.

But somebody was definitely awake up there. That was good enough for her. She and her mom hadn't had the chance to get groceries yet and she was dying for a mocha latte, but coffee with a lot of sugar and creamer would have to do for now.

She'd already dressed and finished her hair and makeup, so she bopped up the steps to see who was around. Hopefully Kat. Trina was eager to get to know her new sister better.

As she reached the top of the stairs, she sang out

as she went around the corner and into the kitchen. "Morning!"

Claire, Kat and a woman who looked like a younger version of Claire but with long, dark hair stood there, staring at her.

"Morning," Kat said without any warmth.

The younger version of Claire looked at Trina with great curiosity. "I'm guessing you're the other daughter?"

Trina nodded. "That's me. Katrina 2.0. Or Katrina 1.0." She laughed. "I guess that's more accurate, seeing as how I was born first." The woman had well-layered long hair with expensive highlights and lowlights. Nice brows and skin that looked taken care of. Trina pointed at her cup. "Would it be all right if I had some of that coffee?"

"Sure," the woman said.

Claire took her coffee and headed for the bedroom. Her hair was more of a blond helmet. Sort of typical for women who didn't have a stylist willing to tell them better. "I'm not doing this."

Trina paid her no mind, just opened cabinets until she discovered the mugs. She wasn't as familiar with where things were up here as she was in the downstairs kitchen. She filled half the cup with coffee, found the sugar and added several teaspoons, then pointed at the fridge. "Creamer?"

The younger Claire waved her hand at the appliance. "Help yourself."

"Thanks," Trina said. "Who are you, by the way?"

"I'm Julia. Claire's sister. But everyone calls me Jules."

Trina let out a happy gasp. "You're my aunt!"

Jules nodded, amusement in her eyes. "I suppose I am."

"Auntie Jules." Trina grinned. "I'm so glad to meet you. You look like Claire but hipper. Which is totally cool. What do you do?"

"I'm a singer and songwriter. You'd probably know some of the commercial jingles I've written."

Kat rolled her eyes. "She's really underselling herself. She sang at the White House for the birthday of one of the former First Ladies."

"Wow. That is so cool. I'd love to hear some of your music sometime." Trina pulled open the fridge. "I see half and half but no creamer."

"That is the creamer," Kat said. "What did you expect?"

"I don't know, something good like French Vanilla or maybe that new Italian Pastry Cream one. That one is the bomb."

"That stuff is filled with artificial ingredients and nasty chemicals." Kat's lip curled. "And do people actually still say things are 'the bomb'?"

Trina bobbed her head to one side. "I do. And I'm people." Kat's hair looked like it had never been touched outside of the occasional trim. Sad, because it wasn't doing much for her. But that wasn't Trina's business. She grabbed the half and half and poured it into her coffee until it was lighter than the tan she planned to get later on the rooftop. "You're not a morning person, huh?"

Kat made a face. "What's that supposed to mean?"

Trina took a big sip of the coffee as she lifted one shoulder. "You seem sort of cranky, that's all."

"I am not cranky."

Jules tipped her head back and forth. "You actually are a little."

Kat glared back. "Aunt Jules."

Trina tried not to laugh. "Listen, there's no reason for you to be mad at me for what our father did. It's not like I had anything to do with it. Neither did you. We were just born."

Jules tipped her cup at Trina while looking at Kat. "She's got a point."

"And," Trina went on. "I have always wanted a sister. So you might think this is a terrible thing that's happened, and maybe it is, but I'd rather look on the bright side. Can't we try to be friends? Seeing as how we're related and all?"

Kat's unhappy expression melted into something unreadable. Maybe that was her thinking face. "I don't know. I'm just trying to process all of this."

Trina drank some more of her coffee. "I get that. I am, too. It's bad enough that he's gone but now on top of that I have to deal with my dad also being your dad and my mom not being his only wife. You must be thinking that, too, right?"

Kat nodded.

Trina shrugged. "So, look, we've got that in common already. We're in the same sort of metallurgical boat."

"Metaphorical," Kat said.

"That's what I meant." Trina should have put more sugar in her coffee. "And we share a name. And almost a birthday. It's like we were meant to be sisters."

Kat sighed. "I don't know. I need to take this slowly. I'm still dealing with the fact that I no longer have a father. Adding in that he had a whole other family really cranks up the difficulty level."

Before Trina could respond, a man walked out of one of the other bedrooms. He was thin and seemed to have the same amount of muscle tone as a pool noodle, but he had a full head of thick, dark hair that was in desperate need of an actual style. She immediately thought about how she'd cut it. Which didn't mean he was her type. She preferred her men with muscles, tattoos, and, as Mimi would say, full of vinegar.

He smiled at her. His smile was nice. "You must be the sister."

"I am. Who are you?"

"I'm Ray. Kat's fiancé, er, uh, boyfriend?" He looked at Kat like he needed her approval.

Kat shot him a look that went by too quickly for Trina to catch it. "Ray is my boyfriend. He's headed home today, since he has to get back to work tomorrow."

Ray nodded. "I'm a podiatrist."

Trina sipped her coffee. "That's feet, right?"

"Right," Ray said. "You know what they say about podiatrists." He grinned. "We're always one step ahead."

"No one says that." Kat picked up her coffee cup. "I need to shower." She headed for the bedroom Ray had come from.

At the sound of the door closing, Jules moved a little closer to Trina. "Don't take any of that personally. She's pretty upset. Although I'm sure you are, too."

Trina held her cup with both hands. "Sure I am. I miss my dad so much it hurts, but there's not much I can do to change any of it, is there? I'd rather focus on what I can change. And that's getting to know my sister."

Jules nodded. "There's a silver lining in everything. Good for you."

"So you don't mind if I call you Aunt Jules?"

"Not at all." She tipped her head toward Claire's room. "That one's going to take a long time to come around. If it happens at all. She's hurt and lost and furious right now."

Trina glanced toward the room. "So is my mom. Not furious, exactly. More like low-key mad. But she's pretty hurt. And grieving. And full of questions."

"I think we all are."

Ray, who'd fixed his coffee and was just standing quietly, suddenly spoke up. "Should I make breakfast?"

Trina turned around to face him. "I can help. Although I'm not a great cook. We mostly do pancakes from the box mix or cereal. Have you got any pancake mix?"

"No, but nothing wrong with that," he said. "We have everything to make them from scratch, though."

"Wow, fancy," Trina said. "Maybe you can teach me."

"You two have fun." Jules refilled her coffee. "I'm going to check on my mom and then I'm going to shower, as well."

Trina looked at her. "You mean your mom is here, too? Kat's mimi?"

Jules nodded. "Yes. Kat's grandmother. Mine and Claire's mother."

"Cool," Trina said. "My mimi's with us. I call her Mimi. Obviously. You guys can call her Willie."

Ray laughed. "What kind of name is that?"

"Short for Wilhelmina," Trina said. "But if you call her that, she'll give you the stink eye. Say it twice and she'll smack you." She rubbed her hands together, pleased with how the morning was shaping up. "All right, Ray. Let's make some breakfast."

Chapter Thirteen

Claire stood in the bathroom, tweezers in hand, staring intently into her magnifying mirror in an attempt to find any errant hairs that needed to be plucked. That girl had a lot of nerve acting like she was suddenly part of the family. If Bryan were here, Claire would have strangled him.

What a mess he'd made of things. What a nightmare he'd left her with. The muscles in her jaw tightened. She was so mad she could spit.

A low buzzing outside her window distracted her. Sounded like the dull, brassy whine of power tools.

She put her tweezers down and went to see what it was all about. It seemed like it was coming from the front of the house that faced the street. The only window that looked out onto that side was the transom over the bed and those plantation shutters were closed.

She kicked off her house shoes, grabbed hold of the headboard, and climbed up. She pulled one of the shutters back.

Danny Rojas was up on an extension ladder, trimming her palms.

She frowned. She hadn't asked him to do that. And if he thought he was going to get paid for something she hadn't asked him to do, he had another think coming.

She climbed down off the bed, put on some sandals, and headed for the door. She stopped, went back to the bathroom, and took a quick look at herself. She ran a brush through her hair then slicked on a hint of tinted gloss. She hesitated. She really needed mascara, too. And maybe a swipe of blush. Without those, she looked washed out and pale. It was bad enough that she'd become essentially invisible, thanks to her age, but she didn't have to just roll over and take it.

Mascara and blush quickly applied, she went out the sliders, through the screened porch to the uncovered porch and down one flight on the circular stairs. From there it was easy to access the front of the house on the second wraparound balcony. In fact, moving toward the corner of the residence put her a few feet away from Mr. Rojas.

He cut the engine of his power saw as she got closer, resting the handle on his hip. "Morning, Claire. How are you today?"

"I'm—Mr. Rojas, I did not ask you to trim my palms."

"Please, call me Danny. And no, you didn't. But I figured I'd do it anyway, since it needed doing and it was the neighborly thing."

"I'm not paying you for this." She wasn't made of money, if that's what he thought. In fact, depending on how things went with the will and the life insurance, she might be flat broke.

He smiled. "I would hope not. Me asking for or expecting payment would be the opposite of neighborly. Unless, as I suggested yesterday, that payment was in the form of dinner, but I also understand that due to your current circumstances, you probably don't feel like company, so I really don't expect anything. Trust me. I've been there."

She frowned, the wind completely gone out of her sails. "No, I don't feel like company. But it is very nice of you to trim them for me. Thank you." She sighed. "I didn't mean to snap at you. I'm just..."

"I know." His expression was kind and full of

compassion. "And you're welcome." He gestured toward the ground. "Those flower beds could use some weeding and probably a couple more bags of river rocks in each one. You've got some bare spots."

She glanced down. They did look a bit sparse. "I see that. I'll get to the weeding. I can handle that." She wouldn't mind having something to do that would require her to be out of the house. Away from the reminders of Bryan's infidelity.

"I have to run to the home and garden center later today to pick up a few things. I can get the rock if you'd like." He glanced down again. "Six bags ought to do it."

She didn't want to be beholden to him, but she knew the bags of rock were heavy and it was more lifting than she could do. She nodded reluctantly. "I would appreciate that. I'll write you a check for whatever it costs."

"I'll let you know." He shifted the power saw into his other hand and dug in the pocket of his jeans for his phone. "If you give me your number, I'll text you when I'm back. I can send you a copy of the receipt that way, too."

She narrowed her eyes. Was this a ploy to get her phone number? Did he think she was some lonely widow who'd be easy to take advantage of? Or was she just so angry at Bryan that she was painting all men with the same traitorous brush? Probably the last. Danny was a widower. He understood. He wasn't trying to put the moves on her. Also, she hated everything about her life right now. "That would be just fine."

"Great. Ready when you are."

She gave him her number slowly so he could punch it into his contact list. "I'll wait to hear from you."

He touched his forehead in a salute, then fired up the power saw again.

She went back inside through the first floor's front door but stood by the sidelights looking out. The palms were looking better already. He was a nice man. And he was a neighbor. She needed to stop assuming the worst.

"What are you doing down here?"

Claire turned to see Roxie in a purple bathrobe, her hair wound up in a towel. Without makeup, she looked even younger than Claire had assumed. "I was just talking to the neighbor, who's trimming the palms for me."

"Well, that's nice of him to do that for *us*."

Claire pursed her lips and ignored the plural

pronoun. She was in no mood for small talk. "How old are you?"

Roxie's spine went a little straighter at that question. "Fifty-two. How old are you?"

Claire was tempted to lie about her age, but what would be the point? She certainly didn't look younger than she was, like Roxie did. "Fifty-nine."

Roxie's artfully shaped brows rose. "You look all right for your age."

"Thank you. I think." It wasn't exactly a compliment. Claire moved toward the steps. "I should go back up. Smells like something's burning in the kitchen."

Roxie laughed. "Probably Trina's doing. She's a terrible cook but she makes up for it by being a whiz with hair. She's not bad with makeup, either. She does me and Willie's hair."

Claire had no idea who that was, and she was sure her face expressed that. "Willie?"

"My mother. Wilhelmina. But call her Willie."

Claire had no intention of calling her anything. "Well, like I said, I should be getting back upstairs." She put her foot on the first step.

"We still need to talk," Roxie said.

"Later," Claire shot back. Much later. Like, when Claire figured out how to make her go away.

She ignored the kitchen and whatever was going on in there and went directly into her room, where she picked up her phone and sat on the bed to call their attorney. Hers now, she supposed, since Bryan was gone. Although Bryan had been friends with him first. They were members of the same fraternity and as adults, they golfed together once a month. When Bryan was home.

Or at least, that's what Bryan had told her. She really couldn't assume anything was true anymore.

"Attorney Charles Kinnerman's office."

"This is Claire Thompson. My husband, Bryan, just passed and Charles is handling the estate. Can I speak to him? Something urgent has just come up."

"Just a moment."

Music played briefly, then a new voice filled her ear. "This is Charles."

"Hi, Charles. It's Claire." He'd sent her a condolence card but hadn't come to the memorial. He had sent a nice flower arrangement, along with his regrets.

"Claire, hello. How are you doing? I can't imagine how hard this has been for you."

She glanced toward the kitchen through the closed bedroom door. "No, I don't think you can."

"I'm sure. Again, my sympathies on the passing

of Bryan. He was a good friend and I miss him. Although not as much as you, no doubt."

"Thank you. Listen, something's come up. I know you're handling the estate and you'd said it would be a few more days before you were ready to execute the will, but..." She paused, searching for the right words.

Then she decided she didn't care if they were right or not, so long as she explained what was going on. "It's come to my attention that Bryan had another family. Another wife and daughter, to be exact. He was *married* to the woman. Roxie. Roxanne. Anyway, I'm sure she thinks she's entitled to part of his estate. What on Earth am I supposed to do? How do I get rid of her?"

Charles cleared his throat softly. "I see. How did you find this out?"

"She's at our beach house in Diamond Beach. That's where I am with Kat. This woman showed up last night with apparently the same idea I had about taking one last trip here before I have to put this place on the market. The nerve."

He sighed. "I'm sure she didn't do it intentionally. She couldn't have known you were there. Or even known about you."

Claire frowned into the phone. "Why aren't you

surprised by this news? And why are you sticking up for her?"

"I'm not sticking up for her. Just attempting to see both sides."

"Both sides? Bryan was *married to another woman.*" A couple of seconds of uncomfortable silence went by and in those seconds, Claire realized something. "You knew."

"I was his attorney." Charles cleared his throat softly.

Claire felt sick. "How could you? I thought you were our friend." Him and Dr. Welling. Who else had known?

"I was Bryan's friend first. And his attorney first. I'm sorry. He had me draw things up very early on."

Draw things up? The twisting in her gut got worse. "How early on?"

"Right before Katrina was born."

A little steel returned to her backbone. "*Which* one?"

"Ah, yes. Both of them, really."

"What does this mean? In plain terms. Is she getting half of everything? A third of it? What?"

"It's...complicated. That's why I've asked for a little time to work things out. We were in the middle of adding a codicil to his estate planning when he had the heart attack. It had already been filed, as a matter of fact. Just waiting on the final paperwork. Once I get that, we should be able to proceed."

She hated Charles in that moment. He'd been complicit with Bryan and helped him keep his secrets. Another traitorous man. But she had no one else to turn to. She'd just have to get through this and pick up the pieces, whatever was left, when it was over.

"Fine," she said. "You keep me posted. Because I want this over as quickly as possible."

"Understood."

She doubted that very much. She hung up.

Chapter Fourteen

*K*at needed to get out of the house and away from everything. She changed into shorts and a tank top, stuck her phone in her pocket, then put on sunglasses and a hat to keep the sun off her face. She went out to the kitchen where Ray was making breakfast. With Trina.

She wasn't happy with him about that. It felt disloyal. How could he smile and laugh with her? Because he was a nice guy, that was why. But she still didn't like it. She grabbed a slice of bacon off the serving plate. "I'm going out for a walk."

He looked surprised. "Breakfast is just a few minutes away."

"I'll eat when I get back. I need some fresh air." And some time to think. By herself.

He nodded. "Sounds like a great idea. Whatever you need. Beautiful day for it."

She took a second piece of bacon and ate it on the way down to the beach. She left her flipflops on the pool deck and took the path that led through the grass-covered dunes. There were more people out this morning than there had been last night. But then, today was Sunday. A lot of the rentals went Saturday to Saturday, so maybe they were people who'd just arrived and were eager to get on the beach.

Bacon finished, she wiped her fingers on the edge of her shorts and stood for a few moments to stare out at the waves. The water was too bright to look at where the sun reflected off it. The sky was so blue it seemed unreal. Behind her, a gentle breeze swished through the dune grass with a soft, shushing sound.

It was so beautiful here. She needed to hold onto that, to remember it, and not let Trina—or anyone—get to her. Even Ray had annoyed her this morning. Kat knew she was not in a great place to be around people. She started walking again. Maybe if she walked far enough, she could change her mood.

She imagined her mother was dealing with a lot of the same feelings. Mostly about Roxie. It had to be worse for her mom. She'd been cheated on, after all. And not just once. For a long time. Nearly thirty years, at least. Kat shook her head. What a thing to find out.

If her mother went completely nuts, Kat wouldn't blame her. This was by far the craziest situation she could imagine. There was no easy way out, either. Not really. You couldn't just turn your back on a thing like this and pretend it had never happened. Nothing would ever be the same again.

And all of it was her father's fault.

That stopped her in her tracks. And filled her with sadness. The man she'd loved and idolized was deeply flawed. It was a hard thing to think about. A hard realization to accept, that her hero father was so far from the perfect man she'd always imagined him to be. That the pedestal she'd put him on was completely undeserved.

She sat down in the sand to watch the waves. There was peace in that. In the sameness of it. The waves felt like a form of meditation sometimes. She let herself drift as her mind wandered, thinking about Trina and Roxie and her father, and wondering what had made him want a second family. Why hadn't she and her mom been enough?

That's really what hurt. Thinking they hadn't

measured up in some way. A pang of self-pity went through her, and tears pinched her eyes. She was so tired of crying. She exhaled and willed herself to snap out of it.

"Hey, there. We're having a sandcastle-building contest to raise money for the firehouse and we're looking for more entrants."

She gazed up into the face a very handsome guy in navy shorts and a gray Diamond Beach Fire Department T-shirt that fit him snugly. He was bronzed from head to toe. Tanned skin, sun-bleached hair a little too long. He looked like one of the many surfers who called Diamond Beach home.

He also looked like trouble. The kind of laidback beach bum who got by on his looks and went through girlfriends like shots of tequila at a frat party. Not that she'd ever been to a frat party. Or tried tequila.

Hmm. Apparently, her father's infidelities had made her judgmental. She managed to respond with an even tone. "Oh?"

He held out a bright yellow flyer. "Here's the info."

She took it, because she didn't know what else to do. "Thanks, but I can't. I'll take it back to the house in case anyone else wants to."

They wouldn't. But she wasn't in the mood to explain that to him.

He smiled. "You can't?"

"No. I'm busy."

Sunlight glinted in his eyes, and he squinted. "You don't know when it is yet."

She laughed. "No, I suppose I don't." She looked at the paper. "It's tonight? Isn't that kind of late in the day for building sandcastles?"

"We've got permission from the town to set up tiki torches." He shrugged one nicely rounded shoulder. "We thought we'd try something different, see if we could get more people to enter that way. There are only so many spaghetti dinners people will attend. Anyway, we're firefighters so I think we can handle a few torches."

She'd been assuming he was a volunteer, but if he was a fireman, maybe he wasn't quite the slacker she'd imagined him to be.

He stuck his hand out. "I'm Alex, by the way."

"Hi, Alex. I'm Kat." She shook his hand. He had quite a grip. A little spark of something flared in her belly at the contact. "It does sound interesting." She looked at the paper again. It was a twenty-dollar donation to enter and that got you a T-shirt and a spot in the contest. First place was a seventy-five-dollar gift card for Waterman's Seafood House. "Do I have to build it by myself?"

"No, you can have a team of two." He tipped his head. "Thinking about bringing your boyfriend?"

"No. He has to go back home tonight."

"Sorry to hear that." But he was smiling, so he didn't look *that* sorry. "Tell you what—if you enter and you lose, I'll take you out to dinner as a consolation prize."

She almost rolled her eyes. "And if I win?"

His smile got bigger. "*You* can take *me* out."

She snorted. Mentioning the fact that she had a boyfriend didn't seem to faze him. Definitely a playboy. Or at least a player. "You're just using this as a way to fill your social calendar, aren't you?"

He chuckled. "I guess it probably sounds that way, but you're the first one I've made that deal with."

She shook her head, amused. "It's what time right now? Nine? Nine-fifteen? The morning is young. I'm sure you'll manage a few more dates." Not with her, though. Suddenly deciding it was time to go, she got to her feet and brushed the sand off her backside. "I have to get back to the house for breakfast, but maybe I'll stop by the contest just to see how things are going."

"Okay, Kat. Looking forward to it."

She started backwards for the house, keeping eye contact with him. "I said maybe."

He gazed after her. "Hope springs eternal."

She laughed and turned around. She folded the flyer and stuck it in her pocket. What was she doing? Flirting with another guy while Ray was just yards away. Even if they were in a weird place right now, it didn't feel right. Especially after all the thinking she'd done about her father's disloyalty. Was she cut from the same cloth? Maybe she was overreacting, but what did it say about her?

She dug into that question a little deeper. She supposed it said she was a woman who wasn't really happy with the path she'd been poised to take. That maybe Ray wasn't the right guy for her. How would she know? She hadn't done a lot of dating. They'd met in college, but he'd had a lot more schooling to go through and hadn't wanted to get married until that was behind him.

She'd been all right with that. She'd admired his dedication, actually. But she'd changed during that time. Grown as a person. Something that was bound to happen from age twenty to twenty-eight.

She knew they'd fallen into the complacency of the long engagement. They'd even stopped talking about the wedding, for the most part, constantly putting it off. Partly because weddings were a lot of work, and they were both busy people. But partly because there didn't seem to be a lot of need to change the status quo.

Or was she the one who'd been putting it off and Ray was just going along with it? She wasn't sure anymore.

She would not be going out with Alex, no matter what happened at the contest. But a little flirting never hurt, did it? Assuming that flirting was actually what they'd been doing. He could have just been talking to her. Wasn't like she was an expert in flirting.

She wasn't even a novice, really. She didn't flirt. With anyone. She wasn't sure she could recognize it being directed at her, either. But that little interaction with the surfer fireman? That felt like flirting. Even her stomach had reacted with—she stopped walking and put her hand flat against her belly.

Had that been a firework? A butterfly? Had Alex made her feel something that Ray hadn't, at least not for a long, long time?

It frightened her, mostly because she wasn't sure, but also because it made her feel like she'd done something...shady. But she couldn't help what her body did. She had no control over that.

Maybe she could talk to Aunt Jules about this. She wouldn't judge. And she'd had plenty of experience with men.

Kat broke into a jog through the dunes, grabbed her flipflops off the pool deck, and kept going up the circular stairs until she reached the second floor.

Trina was laying on one of the lounge chairs on the open part of the deck, smiling at her. "Hey. Who was that hot guy you were talking to?"

"I wasn't. I mean, he was just handing out flyers about some sandcastle-building contest tonight." Kat shook her head, trying to brush off the question. "He was no one. It was nothing. It's a benefit for the fire station."

Trina's mouth curved in a sly smile. "What time is the contest?"

"Sometime tonight. I have no idea."

Trina pointed at Kat's hip. "Is that the flyer in your pocket?"

"What?" Kat looked down. "Yeah, I guess."

"Sounds like fun. We should go." Trina shrugged. "I'm sure you'd usually go with Ray, but since he won't be here, I'll go with you."

Was Trina being coy on purpose? Was she

hinting that she'd say something to Ray if Kat didn't agree? Kat couldn't tell. But befriending Trina might keep her quiet. Kat forced a smile. "I guess it's a date then."

"Great!" Trina got up. "Let's go eat. I'm sure breakfast is ready. Ray was just finishing up."

Kat nodded, but she didn't have much of an appetite.

Chapter Fifteen

Margo sat in one of the recliners in the living room, a cup of tea on the side table, along with her current book. She hadn't turned her shows on yet, but she would soon, after the rest of them finished breakfast.

She never had much appetite in the morning. Tea was enough. Sometimes a slice of toast. Getting old was awful. The older she got, the more she lost.

It was why she watched so much television—to distract herself from the reality of her life. And to avoid people. She knew it was no way to live, but the truth she'd never say out loud was that she just didn't care.

"Mom," Julia said. "Come sit with us."

Margo shook her head. "I'm fine where I am. I can see and hear you."

"It's not the same."

"It's not much different." Margo picked up her cup and took a sip. "Go on and eat."

She shifted enough to see them all better, though. Kat and the other Katrina came in. Kat looked uncomfortable. The other one looked happy. She always looked happy. Maybe she was simple.

Margo envied her if that was true. Sometimes being blissfully unaware was the best way to get through life.

Kat knocked on Claire's door and got her to the table. Ray brought a big platter over with pancakes and bacon on it, then two big bowls. One was filled with cheesy scrambled eggs and the other with hashbrowns he'd made from the shredded potatoes you could buy at the store these days.

Everything was about convenience these days. Too convenient, if you asked her. In her day, if you wanted hashbrowns, you had to start with actual potatoes. Now you just bought a bag. Or, even lazier, you could buy them already browned and ready to heat. No one knew what real work was.

Not many, anyway.

Certainly not her late son-in-law. She'd known from the get-go that he wasn't the big businessman he pretended to be. Sure, he made good enough money, but all that hullabaloo about taking care of his clients was just noise. A total load of bunk. What he was really taking care of was his own needs.

Lousy two-timer. And now poor Claire was reeling, looking like a lost, frightened bird who'd flown into a window and didn't know which way was up. She needed to get ahold of herself and take charge of this situation before that other woman caused real trouble.

Margo put her book in her lap but fixed her eyes on her eldest daughter. Her heart broke for the girl's pain. She knew what it felt like to bury the man you loved, but to have that man tear your heart in two because he'd strayed in such a significant way? That wasn't something Margo had ever experienced.

She could imagine it pretty well, though. She knew what she was feeling on behalf of Claire, so Claire was going through twice as much. Maybe more.

She didn't deserve it, either. Maybe she was a little naïve, but Claire had worked herself to the bone to raise Kat. That child had had the best of everything that Claire could give her. More than that, she'd had the best of Claire. Her time. Her talents. Her energy.

Kat had wanted for nothing. Except a father. That no-good so-and-so.

Heat built in Margo's belly as she thought about Bryan's many shortcomings. He was better off dead. Because she'd have made him a batch of cookies laced with rat poison otherwise. Why not? She had nothing to lose.

Kat turned to look at her. "You sure you don't want to join us, Grandma? These pancakes are really good."

"No, thank you, sweetheart. But I appreciate the offer."

Trina helped herself to another pancake and a few more slices of bacon. That one was an eater. Margo hadn't seen the mother yet, Bryan's floozy. She imagined the woman must be a real looker if she'd snagged Bryan.

Claire wasn't pretty but she *was* beautiful. To Margo, there was a difference. Julia was pretty. She could be beautiful, too. But she didn't have the poise and sophistication that Claire had. Julia was a performer. She had charisma and charm. Claire, however, she could have been a First Lady. She had the right kind of bearing. The right kind of quiet determination.

Instead, Bryan had married her and disappeared into his work, showing up often enough to get her pregnant and make her think she had a real husband.

The louse. Margo tried to focus on her book before she broke a crown from gritting her teeth.

"Mrs. Bloom?"

Margo looked up to see Trina talking to her. What on Earth could she want? "Yes?"

"Maybe you and my grandma would like to go out later? I'll drive you into town if you want to do a little shopping."

Shopping didn't sound bad. The only thing Margo liked as much as watching her shows was spending money, something she could do without much worry, thanks to her two late husbands. But she had no intention of keeping company with the mother of *that* woman. Margo shook her head. "I don't think so."

"Well, you let me know if you change your mind."

When pigs flew.

When the meal was over, breakfast got cleared away by Ray, Kat, and Trina. Julia took Toby out and Claire came over to be by her mother, sitting at the very edge of the couch to be as close as possible.

She leaned in, voice low and conspiratorial. "Mom, maybe it wouldn't be a bad idea for you to do some shopping with Willie. That's the grandmother. You know, get to know her. See if you can learn anything."

What kind of a name was Willie? Margo looked over her book at her daughter. "I already know everything I need to know about those kinds of people.

"Please, Mom. I need all the help I can get. I talked to the attorney this morning and he told me nothing. Except that he already knew about Roxie, which means she might be in the will." Claire took a breath, the lines around her mouth deepening. "For all I know, Roxie might be planning to fight me for everything Bryan had. Or she might already be getting it."

Margo relented, nodding. She hated seeing Claire like this. If shopping would help, she'd endure it. "I will abhor every minute I spend with that woman, but for you, my darling girl, I will endure."

Claire exhaled. "Thank you. I know I owe you for this."

Margo shook her head. "You owe me nothing. This is what a mother does. You'd do it for Kat, wouldn't you?"

"In a heartbeat." Claire smiled. "I love you."

"I love you, too."

Claire gave her knee a pat, then got up and went back to her room, announcing as she did, "I'm going out in a little bit to weed the flower beds if anyone needs me. Which I hope you do not."

Margo let a few minutes pass, watching the flurry of activity in the kitchen. Trina seemed to be pulling her weight, which was surprising for someone who dressed like a streetwalker. Then she cleared her throat slightly. "Trina?"

She looked up brightly. "Yes, Mrs. Bloom?"

"I've decided I could use a few things. I'd like to go shopping. When can your grandmother be ready?"

Trina grinned. "Cool beans! I'll pop down and ask her." She wiped her hands on a towel and disappeared down the steps.

Kat gave Margo a strange look. "Seriously?"

Margo waggled her finger. "Don't question the mysterious ways of your elders."

She came over, hands on her hips. "Mysterious ways? What are you up to?"

"To know your enemy, you must become your enemy."

Kat squinted. "Are you quoting Sun Tzu to me?"

Margo smiled. "*The Art of War* teaches you everything you need to know about how to succeed at life."

"Sure, if you're actually going to war."

"How do you think I defeated Mrs. Albertelli in bridge?"

"I have no idea. Are you sure you want to go shopping with them? You'll be outnumbered."

"I'll be fine." Margo got up. Her knee was bothering her ever so slightly. That might mean it was going to rain later. She'd better wear closed-toes. "Now I'm off to change. I can only imagine what that woman is going to wear, but I will be in something sensible."

"Good for you, Grandma." Kat leaned in and kissed her cheek.

Margo smiled as she went off to the bedroom. She loved her granddaughter dearly. She loved her entire existing family. They were all she had left.

She wasn't about to see them run over by a pack of she-wolves in leopard print and false eyelashes. She opened the closet and decided on a pair of powder-blue slacks with a matching floral twinset. Maybe today she'd glean some information that would be the catalyst that finally galvanized Claire and Kat into action.

They were *good* women, the best, but they were

so passive at times. Letting life happen to them instead of pushing back against the obstacles, content to just go around instead. Going with the flow was fine until the flow dragged you down and you lost yourself.

That was no way to live. No way to be happy.

She might not be completely happy now, but she had been. She at least understood what it felt like. She put her clothes on the bed. She remembered what it meant to be genuinely happy. She'd had the great fortune to find real love with two wonderful men.

She was content with the sort of melancholy existence she had. She had her memories. Her books and her shows helped pass the days and she enjoyed spending time with her family. That was all that mattered.

Whatever time it was that she had left.

Chapter Sixteen

illie looked away from the crossword puzzle she was working and screwed up her face in response to her granddaughter's outrageous suggestion. "Are you kidding me? A shopping trip with one of them?"

"No, Mimi, I'm not kidding. Come on," Trina said. She lingered in the doorway of Willie's room, then took a step inside. "It'll be fun. We need to get to know these people. They're our family now."

"Pfft. They are not our family." Willie had known right down to the very bottom of her soul that Bryan Thompson would be trouble. It was like a sixth sense she had for picking out men who could ruin a woman's life.

She'd felt it when she'd met Zippy Klausen and look how that had turned out. Well, he hadn't ruined her life, but she never should have married him. Even if his magic act had been the best thing she'd ever seen and that little Vegas chapel so romantic. They'd had so much fun together but combining their lives just hadn't worked. Sadly. At least they'd remained friends. Seriously, though. Five husbands really was too many.

"They're *my* family," Trina said. "And doesn't that make them yours, too, by extension? Please? I'll give you that lilac rinse you've been wanting."

The girl drove a hard bargain. Willie wanted to say no again, but there wasn't much she wouldn't do for her granddaughter. And not just because Trina kept Willie's hair looking so good. "Fine. I'll go. But I won't like it. And we have to get a coffee first. I am dying for a mocha latte."

"We totally will, because I totally am, too." Trina clapped her hands. "And you don't have to like it, just be nice and show her that we're good people."

"You're the best people, sweetness." Willie gave her a wink. "Now let me get dressed and put my face on."

Roxie came out from the bedroom still wearing her purple robe, hair tied up in a scarf, and looking very much like she needed a coffee IV. She yawned.

"It's bad enough I got woken up early. Why are you all up?"

"Because," Trina said. "We have things to do and places to go. Plus, it's nearly ten o'clock."

Roxie, squinting against the light, nodded. "Don't remind me. I could have slept longer but Claire came in through our door and woke me up. Doesn't matter, I guess. We need to go to the store anyway. I need my Diet Cokes. Is that what you were talking about? A trip to the Winn-Dixie?"

"No." Willie shook her head. "And you need to quit those things. It's like drinking battery acid. They eat up your insides and they're bad for bone density."

Roxie cocked her microbladed brows at her mother. "So I should stick to gin and tonics like you?"

Willie pursed her lips. "Nothing wrong with a little medicinal sip now and then. Besides, tonic water is full of quinine. Keeps you from getting malaria."

"I'll bear that in mind when the mosquitos get bad." Roxie supported her right elbow with her left hand crossed over her body and held the first two fingers of her right hand casually near her mouth.

Like she was holding a cigarette. It was a habit that had never died after she'd quit smoking some years ago.

Trina looked at her mom. "You want some coffee? I could run upstairs and get you a cup."

Roxie made a face. "As much as I hate to take anything from that woman, I could desperately use a cup. Thanks, love."

Trina headed for the door. "I'll be right back." She stopped. "Oh, they don't have any good creamer. Just half and half."

Roxie nodded. "Extra sugar, then. You know how I like it."

"I do." Trina went toward the stairs.

Willie opened her suitcase as her granddaughter left. She hadn't had a chance to unpack yet, but she'd do that when she got home from this shopping trip. She pulled out a teal velour tracksuit with a little bedazzling on the collar.

"What are you getting dressed up for?" Roxie asked.

"Trina wants me to go out shopping with Claire's mother. Margo." Willie rolled her eyes. "Just her name sounds snooty. But I'm supposed to get to know her and make nice. Trina thinks it'll help smooth the way." She set the tracksuit on the bed.

"Smooth the way for what?"

Willie cut her eyes at her daughter. "Trina is desperate to be friends with her new sister. She's always wanted a sister. You of all people should know that."

"Yeah." Roxie sat on the bed. "I do. But I don't know about getting chummy with these people. I don't see that happening."

"Well, do your best to be...understanding. Or at least nice."

Roxie snorted.

Wille cut her eyes at her daughter. "I mean it, Roxanne. I know you're still grieving. I know you're dealing with a lot. But try."

"Okay, I heard you." She got to her feet as the sound of footsteps reached them.

Trina returned with a big mug of coffee. "Here you go, Ma."

Roxie took it. "Thanks." She brought the mug to her mouth and sipped. "Not bad. All right, I'm off to take a shower. You two have fun on your little excursion."

"Thanks," Trina said. "You and I can go to the store when we get back."

"I'll work on a list." Roxie went into her bedroom.

Trina turned to Willie. "How long until you're ready, Mimi?"

"Ten or fifteen minutes? All depends if I can get my eyebrows to match on the first go." They needed to be sisters, not twins, but sometimes they ended up looking like second cousins twice removed.

"You want me to draw them in for you?"

"No, no. I like a challenge. Thank you, though."

"Okay. Meet you down at the car? I'm going upstairs to tell Margo that's where we'll be."

"Yep."

Trina headed out.

Willie changed into her tracksuit, adding a white T-shirt with a rhinestone martini glass on it. Then she did her makeup. Nothing too dramatic, just penciled in her brows, which magically worked out on the first try, added a dash of eyeliner on her top lids, some mascara, a little blush, and her favorite lipstick, Cherries In The Snow.

She spritzed on some Jean Naté, put on her bedazzled orthopedic sneakers—something she'd had to pay someone to do, because they did *not* come that way—secured her fanny pack around her waist, and headed for the elevator. She could do the stairs if she had to, but with her tricky hip, she preferred not to.

She pushed the call button, surprised to see Margo in the car already when the doors opened shortly after. Willie reminded herself to smile as she stepped in. "Hello, there."

Margo gave her a curt nod. "Hello."

They didn't say another word on the ride down.

The doors opened to reveal Trina standing by her Nissan Cube. Willie headed for the front passenger seat.

Margo only made it a few steps out of the elevator. "What kind of car is that? Looks like something that ought to have clowns getting out of it."

Trina's smile disappeared. Willie knew that look. Trina loved her quirky little car. Even if it was a box on wheels.

Willie turned to look at Margo and put a soft warning into her voice. "It's a Cube. They don't make them anymore, so it's kind of a collector's item. Not only that, but it's paid for, gets good gas mileage, and can haul a surprising amount of cargo. Including clowns. Anything else you'd like to know?"

Margo's lips firmed into a hard line. "No, that will be all." She gave Trina a quick smile. "It's a lovely color."

"It's called Caspian," Trina replied, her grin

returning. "Reminds me of the color of the Gulf water."

"That it does," Margo said. She opened the rear passenger door and got in.

Trina hopped into the driver's seat and started the engine. "All right, first stop is Java Jams, the coffee shop. My treat as a way of saying thank you to both of you for coming along."

Willie patted Trina's hand where it rested on the wheel. "Such a sweet girl." She turned to try to see Margo, but she was directly behind Willie's seat and Willie couldn't twist quite that far these days. Instead, Willie lifted her head to direct her voice back. "Do you drink coffee, Margo?"

"Yes. Not usually coffee shop coffee, though. I prefer to make my own."

"I can understand that," Willie said, reminding herself to be nice. "Then you can make it just the way you like it. But this place does a dynamite mocha latte."

"I'm not sure I've ever had one," Margo said.

Trina gave her a quick glance, brows raised. "Then you're in for a treat."

"If you say so," Margo responded.

Willie figured the best way to thaw out the iceberg sitting behind her was to keep her talking and get to know her likes and dislikes, so she did her best to make small talk all the way into town.

By the time they arrived at Main Street and Trina parked out in front of Java Jams, Willie didn't feel like she'd made much progress. Margo hadn't offered much in the way of information about herself.

They all got out and headed into the shop. It was busy but because it was past peak coffee hours, not outrageously so. Trina looked at them. "Three mocha lattes, right?"

"Works for me," Willie said.

Margo shrugged. "I suppose I'll try one. But don't expect me to drink the whole thing."

"No problem. I'll get you a small," Trina said. "Why don't you two get a table outside and I'll bring the drinks when they're ready."

"Great. Thanks, honey." Willie didn't wait for Margo, just headed back to the street side where a few little tables lined either side of the entrance. She nabbed the last one with an umbrella.

Margo joined her. She set her purse on her lap and looked at Willie but said nothing.

"What?" Willie wasn't about to be stared at without an explanation.

Margo hesitated, then came out with it. "Well, since you asked. Why do you have pink hair?"

Willie grinned. "Why don't you?"

"Because I'm a grown woman."

"That's exactly why I have pink hair. I'm a grown woman and I can do whatever I want. And I'm at an age where I don't care what people think of me. I live to entertain myself. To make *me* happy. Simple as that."

Margo apparently couldn't let it go so easily. "But it's not...dignified."

"Do I look like I care about dignified?" Willie laughed. "Besides, dignity is a thing you hold inside yourself. It's not something bestowed on you by those around you." Of course, Margo looked exactly like someone who cared the world about what other people thought. Willie didn't fault her for that. Lots of people cared about the opinions of others. "Haven't you ever wanted to do something fun just for the sake of fun?"

"I...I'm not sure. Probably. When I was younger, certainly."

Willie pursed her lips, giving Margo a hard look. "But now that you're this age, there's no room for fun?"

Margo looked out onto the street, watching a

young couple go by. "I've buried two husbands. Fun doesn't enter into the equation much anymore."

Willie shrugged. "I've buried one. The love of my life. Roxie's father. And I divorced four more. Fun is about all I have left."

Chapter Seventeen

Trina walked toward the door carrying the mocha lattes in their cardboard holder, but she hesitated as she looked outside. Mimi and Margo were talking. Like, *actually* talking. Engaged in what seemed like meaningful conversation. She didn't dare go out and interrupt whatever might be happening.

Could they be bonding? It was possible. She wasn't sure what they'd bond over, but she'd figured they were of similar age. They had to have things in common, right?

She watched as the two women seemed to exchange a moment of real emotion. Sympathy, maybe? Empathy? Understanding? She couldn't really tell.

But if she waited much longer, the drinks would

get cold. She put on a smile, hoped for the best, and made her way to the table. "Here we are. Three mocha lattes with whip." The barista had added a sprinkling of chocolate shavings, too, making the coffees look even more inviting than the ones she usually got at the place back home.

She put the cardboard carrier on the table, then set the small in front of Margo and a large in front of Mimi, before taking a seat with her own drink.

Margo blinked at hers. "This looks more like dessert than coffee."

Mimi lifted hers. "Tastes like it, too. That's the whole point." She gave Trina a wink. "Enjoy!" She took a sip, leaving a mustache of whipped cream on her top lip.

Trina laughed. "Mimi, you have a little whipped cream..." She gestured to her own lip, then got up again. "Which reminds me, I forgot napkins. I'll be right back."

She ran inside and grabbed a small handful off the counter and returned to the table. Margo didn't look happy, although she sort of always looked that way, so it was hard to tell if that was just her usual face or her current mood. Trina handed out the napkins. "Everything okay?"

"This is impossible to drink without..." Margo tipped her head at Willie. "Looking like that."

"I brought napkins. Would you like me to get you a straw?"

Margo made a face. "For hot coffee?"

Trina raised one shoulder. "I could get you a spoon and you could take the whip off the coffee altogether."

Willie gently nudged Margo with her elbow. "Just drink it and then wipe your face. Trust me: It's worth it."

Margo sighed but picked up her cup. She took a small, delicate sip, but still ended up with whipped cream on her face.

Trina pressed her lips together and made herself not laugh.

Willie clearly felt no need to restrain herself the same way. She snorted loudly. "That's the ticket. What do you think, Margo?"

Margo picked up a paper napkin and dabbed at her mouth. "It's tasty, but I'm not sure I could drink something like this every day. Not while maintaining my figure. I do my best to avoid an excess of sugar and carbs."

Trina nodded. "Yeah, it's not exactly carb-free. Or

calorie-free. And it's definitely not sugar-free. But it's a nice treat."

Willie's mocha latte was already a third gone. "I could have one of these every day and be perfectly happy. Who am I maintaining a figure for? No one, that's who." She waggled her brows at Margo. "I guess that means you either have a man in your life or you want one."

Margo scowled. "Neither."

"Then why do you care about your waistline?"

Trina sipped her mocha latte, eager to hear more. She wasn't sure the two women were getting any closer to becoming friends, but at least they weren't sitting like bumps on a log. Conversation was good. Willie probably wasn't capable of being quiet anyway.

"Because," Margo said. "I care about my appearance."

Trina joined in. "I get that. We all do, right? I mean, we're women. We want to look nice. It's in our nature. If it wasn't, I'd be out of a job." She leaned in toward Margo. "I do hair."

"So I understand." Margo slanted her eyes at Willie's pink curls.

Trina gestured with her cup. "If you don't mind a

little professional advice, a couple of highlights around your face would really brighten you up."

Margo stared at her without speaking. Trina knew she shouldn't have said anything but sometimes she couldn't help herself.

Willie had just about finished her latte. "Mmm, that was good. But now I have a taste for more chocolate."

"We could go by Guilford's," Trina said. "There's one just up the street."

"Perfect," Willie said.

"None for me," Margo said. She pushed her half-full cup away. "Are we walking, then? We should. Might help burn off some of that drink."

Trina drained the last of hers, got to her feet, threw the cups away, then offered Willie her arm. "Sure. Let's go see if the shops have anything good."

The three of them headed down Main Street. Most of the shops were designed with tourists in mind and the prices reflected as much, but they went in a few anyway.

One of the shops, Sunshine Sundries, was her grandmother's favorite.

Willie pointed. "We have to go into Sunshine. I love that place."

Margo glanced at the storefront and the windows filled with touristy T-shirts and apparel and shook her head. "Why?"

"Because they have a whole section of bedazzled things." Willie let go of Trina and marched toward the door. "I can't wait to see what's new."

"Right behind you, Mimi," Trina said. She wasn't sure Margo would come in, but she glanced back and saw her reluctantly moving closer.

Willie made a beeline for the rear corner of the store, where glittery T-shirts, hats, shorts, leggings, bathing suits, reusable cups, sunglasses, and other items made up the display. "Oooh, Trina, look at these." She held up a pair of sunglasses, the large red frames covered in dazzling red crystals.

Willie put them on. "What do you think?"

"I think they're totally you, Mimi."

She took them off and looked at the tag. "Twenty-four ninety-five. Should I splurge?" She put the glasses back on. "I don't need them, but I do look fabulous in them, don't I? The girls would get a kick out of these at bingo."

Margo joined them, looking very much like she was trying not to touch anything in the store. "No one needs those. But if you're really going to get them, at least get the black. Those could almost be workable."

Trina liked to think she had a pretty long fuse, but Margo was such a buzzkill. Trina wanted to speak her mind, even if the older woman was intimidating. She cleared her throat softly and kept her voice calm. This wasn't the place to be making a scene. "No one really needs anything outside of food and shelter but having fun's pretty important. And those sunglasses are fun. Wearing them is fun, too. So is being sparkly and girly and a little outlandish. What's wrong with that? What's wrong with wanting to be a bright spot in a world that feels so dark sometimes?"

Willie smiled approvingly. "Well said, my girl."

She looked at Willie. "I'll buy them for you, Mimi. You do have a birthday coming up. They'll be my gift to you."

"No," Margo said quietly. "You're right. I apologize for my comment. Just because we don't share the same tastes doesn't mean you shouldn't enjoy the things you enjoy."

She looked miserable.

Trina frowned. "Are you okay? You look so sad."

Margo swallowed and looked away. "Sorry. I'll be outside."

She left. Trina raised her brows at Willie, who just shrugged.

"Beats me," Willie said. "But she did tell me she'd buried two husbands. Maybe she's living under a shadow of grief she can't get out of. Some people never recover from a spouse dying, you know. And she's been through it twice. Your dad's passing has probably stirred all of that up again."

"I bet you're right." Trina glanced the way Margo had gone, her own emotions turning toward sadness as she thought about her dad. "I feel bad for her. What would that much pain feel like? Trying to keep your head above water when you're already too tired to swim?" She turned her attention to her grandmother again. "We have to help her."

"You have a good heart, Trina." Willie picked up the black sunglasses covered in black crystals. "What do you say we get her a little gift?"

Trina nodded. "Those are perfect. She'll probably never wear them, but maybe she'll put them someplace she can see them. Maybe they'll be a good reminder that there's more to life than being sad."

Willie handed the red sunglasses to Trina. "You can buy me those for my birthday, but I'll buy these."

They went to the register together and made their purchases.

Margo was on her phone when they went outside, but she quickly hung up and offered them a brief smile. "Anywhere else you'd like to go?"

Trina looped her arm through Mimi's. "We've only just begun to shop."

Chapter Eighteen

Claire wiped a bead of sweat off her forehead with the back of her arm, then moved the foam knee pad over about six inches and went to work weeding the next section of the flower bed. Her favorite podcast played through her earbuds. It was a show that delved into the history of England and all its kings and queens, how they rose to power, and the intrigues that surrounded them. Fascinating stuff for a history buff like her.

She'd always planned on being a middle school history teacher. She knew she would have been able to make the subject come alive for her students. But that wasn't the direction her life had gone.

She focused on the flower bed. Weeding was the kind of hard work she liked, the kind that yielded an instant, noticeable result. It felt honest and it was good to get her hands dirty, even if she was wearing gloves. There was something about connecting to the earth in that kind of ancestral way that eased the soul. She would sleep good tonight from the exertion. Probably after a nice long soak in the tub.

She had an old drywall bucket next to her and all the weeds went in there. She moved the rocks out of the way, then grabbed the weed as close to the ground as she could, pulling it up by the roots.

When she didn't get the whole thing, she used her three-pronged digger and got the rest out. Roots left behind would sprout new growth and she wasn't about to have her efforts spoiled by laziness.

She sat back on her heels. As much as she wanted to distract herself with the weeding, Bryan and Roxie remained at the forefront of her thoughts. Had he known her before Claire had met him? Before they'd married? She was dying to know. It felt important. And probably would be when it came to who ended up with what.

She looked up at the house.

She had a feeling Bryan had made Roxie his insurance beneficiary. Which meant if Claire didn't get this place, wasn't able to sell it, she was going to be in serious trouble. She'd have to sell the house she was living in, because there was no way she could make that mortgage without Bryan's income.

Even if she could get a job, she doubted she'd make enough. And what kind of job could she get? She'd been a mother and a housewife, she'd helped organize bake sales and fundraisers, she'd volunteered at the church's food pantry, driven her share of carpool days, and helped sew costumes for school plays, but none of those were really marketable skills.

Were they?

Maybe some of them. But she wouldn't know how to begin turning any of those skills into a job. And she doubted any of them would give her enough income to replace Bryan's contribution.

She exhaled, the weight of what might be coming already heavy on her shoulders. Could she get an apartment that she could afford? That really depended on whether she was able to get a job. And whether she got any of Bryan's life insurance.

Maybe she'd have to rely on Kat and Ray. Although she wasn't sure those two were going to end up together. Kat had said they were taking a break from being engaged, and she must have meant it, since Claire had noticed Kat was no longer wearing her engagement ring.

Could Kat handle the mortgage by herself? That was such a big thing to ask of her daughter. Claire would be willing to give up the master bedroom and move into Kat's smaller room. That would only be right. If Kat and Ray did get married, maybe they could make the house their new home?

And if they didn't get married... Well, it wasn't fair to expect her daughter to take care of her. Claire might need the insurance more than ever, but her instincts said she wasn't going to get it.

That sent a new wave of despair through her. What if his insurance really did go to Roxie? What if it *all* went to Roxie?

Claire wanted to press the heels of her palms against her eyes, but her gloves were dirty, and she was wearing sunglasses. Instead, she clenched her hands and put her fists against her thighs.

How could Bryan do this to her? She closed her eyes and willed herself not to cry. That would help nothing. She pulled off her gloves and turned off her podcast. She was too much in her own head to pay attention.

"Looks like you're making good progress."

With a sharp intake of breath, she looked up. "You startled me."

"Sorry." Danny Rojas stood nearby, a large bag of river rock balanced on his shoulder. That bag had to be forty pounds, at least. He handled it like it was no big deal.

She was glad for her sunglasses so he couldn't see how tired and bloodshot her eyes were from all the crying and restless sleep. "I see you got the rocks."

He moved around to her other side, slipping the bag from his shoulder to rest it on the ground. "I did. Like I said, I had to pick up a few things myself anyway. I'll get the bags unloaded and start spreading the rocks in the bed you already finished."

"You don't have to do that." She was currently beholden to him for the work he'd done. She didn't need to add to that. "You must have work of your own to do. I can manage it."

He nodded like he was seriously considering her words. "I'm sure you can, but those rocks are heavy. What kind of man lets a woman do that kind of heavy labor? Plus, I don't mind helping out." He grinned, almost knocking her out with his megawatt smile. "And I could use the exercise."

He didn't look like he had an ounce of extra fat on him. She reminded herself what they were talking about. Rocks. She knew he was right, too. Spreading those rocks would be a lot of work. "Well, it's very kind of you."

"Just being neighborly." He headed back to his truck.

She watched him for a moment. Danny was about the fittest man in her age group she'd ever seen. At least up close and personal. Maybe in several age groups.

He hoisted another bag of rocks onto his shoulder.

After another second or two, she reluctantly went back to her weeding.

Danny deposited the remaining bags of rocks on the other side of the driveway that split the two main beds. Then he disappeared for a couple of minutes, only to return with a box cutter and a narrow metal rake.

He slit open the first bag and parceled out the rocks around the bed, then began spreading them evenly with the rake.

It was hard not to watch him. She'd never really seen Bryan do that kind of work. He was home so rarely that yard work fell to her. His time at home was mostly spent with them doing what he called "quality" things.

Meals, watching movies, hearing about Kat's friends or time at school. Occasionally, he'd take Claire out on a date night, which was dinner out.

He paid a local service to mow the grass and edge the lawn, so Claire had never had to do that. But she'd managed everything else. Which didn't always mean she'd had to do it physically. She had a few people she hired for the big jobs, like power washing or cleaning out the gutters.

But sometimes she did take on the big jobs. A lot more frequently when she'd been younger. It meant saving money. In the early days, that had been pretty important.

It might soon be again.

Danny straightened, leaned back, and lifted the edge of his T-shirt to wipe his face.

The breath caught in her throat. The man had actual, visible abs. How was he in that kind of shape? Not even Ray had abs and he had to be half Danny's age.

He dropped the shirt and caught her looking. He smiled.

She played it off by asking questions that had nothing to do with how he looked. "How do you have time to do all this? Are you retired?"

He shook his head. "Semi-retired. Which means I only work forty hours a week, not sixty."

She laughed. "That's not semi-retired. What do you do? If you don't mind me asking."

"Ever heard of Mrs. Butter's Popcorn?"

She nodded. "Sure. Who hasn't? It's an institution in the panhandle." The shops sold all kinds of flavored popcorn but were best known for their caramel corn and kettle corn varieties. It was a given that if you came to the beach, you'd eventually end up with some Mrs. Butter's Popcorn. The brand had been around for as long as Claire could remember.

"You're looking at Mrs. Butter."

She stared at him. "You own those shops? I thought the Shipley family owned them."

He nodded. "My dad went to work for the Shipleys when he was a young guy. About ten years after Frank Shipley died, Delores, his wife, decided to sell. My dad, Miguel, bought the business from her. We've run it since 1998. My dad is eighty-two and fully retired, but he still goes by the main shop once in a while, just to make sure we're doing everything the way Delores would have wanted."

"I had no idea. But you're semi-retired?"

"I am. My son and daughter are now in charge.

And my daughter's oldest boy, Dylan, works in the business, too."

"Keeping it in the family. I like that." She wondered if he knew how blessed he was to be able to keep his family close like that.

He put his hand to his heart. "It's a good life."

"You're very fortunate."

He grabbed his rake again. "In some ways, yes. Very."

She remembered immediately that his wife had passed. "I didn't mean to imply—"

"I know." He gave her a quick smile. "I am fortunate. I just wish Maria was still here to see how well we're doing." He crossed himself and looked up. "I think she knows."

He went back to work.

She sat there for a moment longer. She envied him. He might have lost his wife, but he hadn't lost his love or affection for her. He hadn't had the craziness of a secret second family to deal with. He hadn't been betrayed.

Darkness fell over her again. Bryan had complicated her life in ways she'd never fathomed possible and now even the act of mourning him was nearly impossible to navigate. She was more angry than sad and that made her feel guilty. At least some of the time.

He'd ruined so much and left her no way to tell him about it. Nothing about this was fair. Nothing.

She got up, yanked off her gloves, and, leaving her tools behind, went back inside, her only goodbye to Danny a muttered, "I have to go."

Chapter Nineteen

*R*oxie took a long shower, indulging herself in the hot water. She was careful with her hair, though. Just a quick rinse and then she fixed it up with a clip to keep it out of the hot spray. Red was a hard color to maintain.

If her daughter wasn't a hairdresser Roxie would be coloring her hair herself, which meant it wouldn't be looking this good. Red was hard to maintain *and* hard to get right. Box dyes couldn't hold a candle to Trina's skills.

Roxie got out of the shower, dried off, then wrapped her hair in a special towel meant to absorb as much water as possible.

She hoped Trina would get back soon so she could blow it out and style it. Roxie could do it, but it never looked as good as what Trina did. Never got as big or bouncy.

She stuck her head out of the bedroom door and listened but didn't hear anything that sounded like her daughter had returned. She was about to shut the door and get dressed when she heard a soft, mournful sound. She stepped out into the reading nook to hear better.

Someone upstairs was crying.

She hesitated. She should go about her business. It wasn't her problem. But her own heart was heavy, and she understood.

Roxie pulled on her robe and padded up the steps. The sound was coming from the master bedroom directly in front of her. The door was slightly ajar and through the crack she could see Claire sitting on the bed, knees pulled to her chest, head down, arms wrapped around herself.

Roxie frowned, not because she wasn't empathetic. She was. But she already knew Claire wouldn't want comfort from her.

Feeling like she was about to get smacked down, she pushed the door open anyway. "Are you okay?"

Claire looked up, face wet with tears. Her despair turned into anger for a brief moment, then she looked away and wiped at her face. When she made eye contact again, the anger was gone, replaced by something Roxie couldn't read. "How are you not crying all the time? Did you not love him? Aren't you angry about what he did to you? About the lies he told? He ruined everything. All of my memories are tainted."

Roxie hugged her arms around her body. "I am angry. And I did love him. More than I thought I could love anyone. But I guess..." She felt the words fill her mouth, but she wasn't sure if telling the truth would help or not.

"You guess what?"

Roxie exhaled. "I guess I never expected him to be completely faithful to me. There was something about him, something that told me he had the sort of spirit that couldn't be contained. That he'd find a woman to love him wherever he was."

Claire's brow furrowed. "And you were okay with that?"

"No. Not even a little bit." Roxie shrugged and leaned against the door jamb with a sigh, her grief rising up again. "But if I wanted him in my life and in Trina's life, I knew I had to accept it. So I did."

Claire shook her head. "I never thought in a million years that he'd cheat on me. I really thought he was busy with his work all this time. I believed him. I guess that makes me a fool."

"No, it doesn't," Roxie said. She straightened

and took a few steps toward Claire. "Don't say that. You weren't a fool for loving him. You were just being a normal, trusting person. A good person. He wouldn't have been with you if you'd been anything different." She tugged the belt on her robe tighter.

"I don't know about that," Claire said. "I don't think he was that picky. No offense. I just meant that with two wives, he was clearly more in love with being married than with us."

"I wouldn't be so sure about that," Roxie said. "I think he was with you because he needed a different kind of woman than me."

Claire looked at her without saying anything for a moment. "What do you mean?"

Roxie snorted. "You know what I mean. The difference between us is as plain as looking in the mirror. We are pretty much opposites."

Claire wiped at her face. "We're both idiots who fell for the same lies."

Roxie edged closer. "We're not idiots. We didn't know. Not really. How could we? I might have suspected him of cheating, but I certainly never had proof. And I'd never have guessed he had a whole other family." She sat on the far corner of the bed and stared at the bright purple glitter polish on her toes. Claire's were the soft pink of ballet slippers. "And if one of us is an idiot, it's me."

Claire stared through her. "I'm still not sure I understand what you meant about me being a different kind of woman. You mean because of the way we look?"

"It's more than that." Roxie was amazed Claire hadn't told her to get lost. Yet. "You're everything I'm not. You're refined and classy and proper. You have to know that. You had to realize how different we were when you saw me."

Claire shifted her gaze to the white cotton comforter. "Looks aren't everything."

"No, they're not. But in this case, they're a lot."

Claire's gaze dropped further. "I'm sure you were more...fun." She sighed. "You're younger than me, too. And probably more adventurous in other *areas*."

Roxie's mouth pursed in a restrained smile. "Maybe. He was my physical equal when it came to those sorts of things."

Claire shook her head. "I don't want to hear about it. I really don't."

"Sorry." Roxie held her hands up. "I won't mention it again."

Claire lifted her head. "How long were you married to him?"

"Twenty-nine years. You?"

Claire seemed to exhale in relief. "Thirty-three. I guess that means I was first."

Roxie nodded. "You were. Does that make you feel better?"

A long, silence went by before Claire spoke again. "Not really. But it probably means his estate belongs to me."

Roxie gave a quick nod. "It might." She hated that Claire could be right, but she wanted to believe Bryan had left her and Trina something.

Claire's eyes narrowed. "Why do you say it that way?"

Roxie got off the bed. "Bryan always told me he'd make sure me and Trina were taken care of. I don't know what he meant by that, but I believe he was telling the truth. Of course, he used to tell me I was his soulmate, too."

Claire's expression went dark again, her face clouding over like a storm was coming. "We'll see soon enough." She lifted her chin toward the door. "Close it behind you."

Roxie left, pulling the door shut like Claire had asked. She hesitated at the top of the steps, staring back over her shoulder for a few heartbeats. What had she said to make Claire so angry?

Roxie went downstairs. Was Claire worried about the will? About getting her share of things? She looked like she had money. Bryan had always been a good earner. Although he had been taking care of two households.

Was Claire in trouble financially? Roxie hadn't considered the possibility until now. She felt for the woman. What could be harder than losing your husband and your financial security at the same time?

She must feel adrift. Roxie wasn't in the most economically stable spot in her life, but then she never really had been. She was used to it. To doing without or cutting corners or having to take a few extra shifts at the hospital now and then. That was something she didn't love, because not being full-time meant she had to take the worst shifts, but it helped pay the bills when Bryan's deposit ran out and Willie's alimony payments or Trina's income didn't quite meet their needs. Both of them lived with her, something Bryan had never minded.

Of course, Bryan's monthly deposits into their household account had always taken care of the big bills. The money she earned went to building up a cushion, something they'd never had too much of. Just when she got a nice little nest egg, something would happen. Her car would need a repair or the hot water heater went bad or *something*.

Now that he was gone, was she going to be in a tight place, too?

She supposed that would depend on whether he'd been true to his word and taken care of them.

And whether Claire contested anything he'd tried to do for them.

Roxie glanced toward the second floor, wondering if there was a fight coming. She had a feeling she already knew the answer.

Chapter Twenty

Still in her shorts and tank top, Kat had retreated with her tablet to the ground floor. It was good to be out of the house. She was currently on a lounge chair by the pool, under the shade of an umbrella. No one else was down here, which made her happy.

Being alone had become a rare thing with the arrival of Roxie and her family. Kat was used to having Ray at her side most of the time, too.

Something that had never really bothered her until now.

Was that really all because she was grieving? Because if it wasn't, then what *was* going on with her?

She wished she knew.

Behind her, she heard the elevator doors open

and close. So much for being alone. Should she pretend to be asleep?

"Hello, Sunshine."

Too late. She glanced up at Ray. "Hi."

"Mind some company?"

"Sure, but I'm reading."

He held up the book he'd brought with him. "I'm going to do the same. Figured I should get a little fresh air before my drive back."

He settled into the lounge chair next to her.

She focused on her tablet. She'd read the same paragraph three times now. She was determined to pay attention to it this time.

"Listen," he started.

She almost sighed. Of course, he wanted to talk. She looked over. "Yes?"

"I know you don't want to talk about us and whatever's going on with you, but I just want to say that I'm here when you do."

"Thanks. I appreciate that." She still didn't want to talk. Mostly because she had no idea what to say. She couldn't explain what she didn't understand, and she definitely didn't understand how she was feeling. Or, rather, why.

She'd never had such a jumbled mess of emotions inside her before.

"I'll miss you this week."

So much for not talking. She glanced at him. "I'll miss you, too." She meant it. She might not know exactly what was going on with her and Ray right now, but he was very helpful. And easy to be around.

He smiled. "I put your engagement ring in that little ceramic shell box on the dresser. Just in case you changed your mind about wanting to wear it."

She smiled back but she didn't think that was going to happen. "Trina and I are going to a sandcastle-building contest this evening. It's a fundraiser for the fire station."

"Putting the fun in fundraiser, eh?" He grinned at his own joke.

She snorted, despite herself. "I guess so."

"Are you actually going to compete?"

"Maybe. Probably. Although if we do, I don't expect to place. I can't imagine we'll make anything worth looking at." An image of Alex appeared in her head. She tried to make it go away.

"I hope you have a good time, no matter where you finish."

"I don't know how good of a time it will be. She's really eager to get to know me. I hope she doesn't make things weird."

"She *is* your sister."

"Half-sister."

"So are your mom and your aunt and they get along great. Nothing half about that relationship."

"True, but they grew up together. Trina is a complete stranger to me. Not to mention one of the biggest unwelcome surprises I've ever gotten."

Ray nodded. "I know, but that wasn't her fault. And she's certainly not treating *you* like an unwelcome surprise."

Kat shifted her gaze to the sparkling pool water. "No, she's not. But why isn't she?" She looked at him again. "Don't you think that's odd?"

He shook his head. "Trina strikes me as the kind of person who always sees the bright side of life. Nothing wrong with making lemonade out of lemons, right?"

Ray really was an old man trapped in a young man's body. "I guess not, but you'd think she'd be a little angry about it."

"Maybe she is. Not everyone expresses their feelings the same way."

Kat returned to her book. She wasn't interested in talking about Trina anymore. Especially not when Ray seemed to be taking her side.

She felt better about going to the sandcastle contest

since she'd told him about it. Not that anything was going to happen there except for her and Trina attempting to build a sandcastle. That was it. Alex could ask all he wanted; she was not going out with him.

Maybe she'd put her engagement ring back on for the night. Except that probably wasn't the smartest thing to do when she'd be digging in the sand. Well, she'd mentioned she had a boyfriend. That should be enough.

She attempted the paragraph for a fourth time and made it all the way through. The book was a spy novel. She and her dad had always read the same books so they could talk about them when they were done.

She wouldn't have anyone to talk to about this one.

The words on her tablet went blurry.

Ray sat up. "Hey, are you okay?"

She sniffed, ignoring the tears rolling down her face. "No, I'm not okay. I miss my dad."

He leaned over as best he could with the umbrella pole between them and put his arm around her. "I know you do. I know it hurts. I'm so sorry."

She leaned into him and let him comfort her.

"I'm never going to get to talk to him about books again."

Ray kissed the side of her head. "You two loved your books, didn't you."

She nodded and sniffed again.

"Hey," he said softly. "How about I read that book, too? Then you and I can talk about it all you want."

She looked up at him. "You'd do that? You hate spy novels."

He smiled. "I don't hate them. They're just not my favorite. But for you? Anything."

Her heart melted a little. Her doubts about him being the right one receded. "Just the fact that you offered is enough."

He let go of her to wake his tablet up. "What's the title? I'll buy it right now. When I get back next Friday, we can have a nice long discussion about it."

She smiled. "*Honor Among Thieves*, by Martin Dutch."

He tapped away, then gave her a nod. "Done."

"Thank you."

His small act of kindness had made her feel better than she imagined possible. She sat back and returned to her book. Alex might be nice to look at, but he probably didn't even read.

Ray might not be the most exciting guy on the planet, but he was kind and considerate and thoughtful. There was a lot to be said for those qualities.

Even without the fireworks.

Chapter Twenty-one

*M*argo gestured ahead to the Garden Bistro. "How about some lunch?"

She was a little hungry. They'd been shopping for nearly two hours, a remarkable amount of time, considering the fact that she'd expected to be home in about forty-five minutes.

But Willie and Trina, for all their rough edges and questionable sartorial choices, weren't as awful as she'd believed. In fact, Margo and Willie definitely understood the heartache and pain brought on by losing a husband. Widowhood had a bonding effect, even when the other person wasn't someone you'd normally spend time with.

And Trina had a certain innocence about her. She never seemed bothered by much, although it was clear she missed her father and worried about her mother. Neither of which Margo could find fault in.

Trina's brows lifted in surprise. "Lunch would be good, but isn't Garden Bistro kind of expensive?"

"It's all right," Margo said. "Lunch is my treat. You bought the lattes, after all. And the two of you invited me out. Let me get lunch."

"That's awfully kind of you," Trina said with a smile.

"Very kind," Willie agreed.

They went into the restaurant and Margo let the hostess know there would be three of them.

The young woman led them to a table by the window.

"Thank you," Margo said.

They all sat, and the hostess handed out the menus. Margo immediately checked to see if they still had the Asian chicken salad she'd enjoyed so much last year. They did.

"Wow," Trina said. "Everything looks so good." She looked over the menu at Margo. "What are you getting?"

Margo closed her menu and put it aside. "The Asian chicken salad. It's very good."

Willie set her menu down, too. "I'm getting the tuna melt. I haven't had one of those in years."

Trina snorted. "Mimi, we made tuna melts at the house last week."

"Yes, and your mother put American cheese on them. I hate American cheese." Willie glanced at Margo. "I like a good sharp cheddar myself."

Margo just nodded, unsure if she was supposed to chime in with her own cheese preference.

Trina went back to her menu as a server brought them each a glass of water.

He introduced himself. "I'm Tom and I'll be taking care of you ladies today. Can I get you anything else to drink?"

"I'd like an unsweetened iced tea," Margo answered.

Willie piped up next. "I'll take a sweet tea."

"We have regular or peach," Tom offered.

"Peach sounds good."

Trina nodded. "I'll try one of those, too."

Margo almost laughed. The pair of them never seemed to shy away from anything with extra sugar in it.

"Be right back," he said.

Trina shook her head. "I don't know if I should get the club sandwich or the soup and sandwich combo, because that looks really good, too, but the club sandwich has bacon."

Willie leaned in. "Get half a club sandwich with the soup."

"I don't think I can do that," Trina said. She studied the menu. "Hey, I can. Awesome! Club sandwich with a bowl of tomato soup it is." She put her menu to the side. "I love tomato soup. It's about the only thing I can cook. That and a grilled cheese, although about half the time I burn the bread." She shrugged. "It's all right. I still eat it."

The girl was such a curious creature. She had a childlike quality that Margo was unconvinced was real. "Have you always wanted to be a hairdresser?"

Trina shook her head. "No. I wanted to be a therapist. To help people, you know?" Her smile was wistful, and maybe a little sad. "But college was really expensive, and my dad said we'd have to get loans." She shook her head. "It was a lot of money. And being in that much debt scared me. So it never happened."

Margo frowned. Bryan hadn't had a problem with the cost of Kat's college tuition. Why had Trina's been an issue?

"It's all right," Trina said brightly. "I'm still helping people but in a different way."

"That's wonderful," Margo said. But she was lost in thought, trying to figure out why Bryan had balked at paying for Trina's college. Had he doubted her ability to succeed? Thought she wasn't smart enough? That was a terrible thing for a father to think of his child, but Margo's opinion of Bryan was low enough to believe he'd have done such a thing.

She felt sympathy for Trina. Everyone deserved a shot at their dreams. And for some reason, Bryan had shut hers down.

Willie lifted her chin. "She's the best hairdresser I've ever been to, and I've been to a lot of them."

Trina smiled. "Thanks, Mimi."

Tom returned with their drinks and took their food orders.

After he left, Trina leaned in toward Margo. "I hope you didn't take offense to what I said earlier about adding some highlights to your hair. It's just what I do, and I know I should probably keep my thoughts to myself, but when I see someone with hair I could improve upon, I just can't help myself."

Margo touched the ends of her short shag. She paid a hundred and twenty dollars every six weeks to have the gray touched up and the cut freshened. Jonas, her hairdresser, had mentioned highlights once but she'd shut him down, thinking he was just trying to pad the bill. "I suppose it would be no different than a chef giving you advice on how to cook something."

Willie laughed. "Wouldn't help my girl. She'd still burn it."

Trina nodded. "You're right, Mimi. I would."

Maybe Margo felt sympathetic toward Trina. Maybe Margo was starting to like the young woman. Or maybe Margo was losing her mind. All the same, she smiled at Trina and said, "If you think I should get some highlights, then maybe I should."

Trina gasped. "You mean it? You'd let me do it? I'd love to. We could do it tomorrow. I brought supplies with me, since I'm about due for a touchup myself, but there's a beauty supply place at the mall. I'll run out there in the morning and get everything we need." She clapped her hands. "This is going to be so much fun!"

That hadn't been what Margo had meant at all. She'd meant she'd let her own hairdresser do them, but Trina had gotten so excited, Margo didn't have the heart to tell her no. What had she gotten herself into? She glanced at Willie's cotton candy pink hair and swallowed.

Willie grinned at her. "You know what else is fun?" She reached into the bag she'd been carrying and pulled out a pair of sunglasses. The black ones with the black crystals.

Margo nodded. "I see you took my advice. Smart choice."

"No, silly." Willie pushed the sunglasses toward her. "Trina bought me the red ones for my birthday. These are for you."

Margo stared, aghast. She didn't know what to say.

"Calm down," Willie said. "You don't have to wear them. Just keep them as a reminder that not everything in life has to be so serious all the time."

Relieved, Margo tucked the sunglasses away in her purse. "That's very kind of you."

She really didn't know what to make of these two. They were not her usual sort of people, yet they were kind and down to earth and generous.

It was going to be hard not to like them.

Chapter Twenty-two

Jules pulled her hair into a ponytail and threaded it through the back of a ball cap. She put her sunglasses on next, then attached Toby's leash to his collar and led him to the elevator, although he didn't need much leading. He was always happy to go to the beach for a walk. Even better if he could wade into the water, which she tried to prevent.

They got off at the ground level and walked toward the Gulf, headed by the pool on the way.

Ray and Kat were sitting on the lounge chairs, reading. But Ray got up and started folding his towel. "Hi, Jules."

"Hi. Are you going in?"

He nodded. "I'm going to get a shower then drive back. I'll see you next Friday."

"You have a safe drive. And don't work too hard this week."

He smiled. "I'll do my best." He gave Kat a kiss on the cheek, then headed for the house with a little wave to both of them.

Jules stopped next to Kat's lounge chair. "How are you two doing? Or shouldn't I ask?"

Kat lifted one shoulder. "We're doing all right."

"Wow, that was convincing."

Kat sighed. "We're fine. Losing my dad has just twisted my head up a bit, you know? Made me think about the future and life and what I want from it. If I'm doing anything valuable with it. If there's purpose to it. That kind of thing."

Jules's brows went up. "Lots of deep thoughts, but grief can do that to you. If you ever want to talk..."

Kat nodded. "I do, actually. But it can wait." She smiled at Toby. "Someone's going to chew through their leash if they don't get to the beach pretty soon."

Jules smiled. "How about when we get back? He'll be pooped out by then. Probably literally as well as figuratively."

"Ew!" Kat laughed. "Thanks for sharing. That would be all right. Or even later tonight. Hey, that reminds me—Trina and I are going to a sandcastle-building contest tonight to benefit the fire station. You want to come?"

Jules was surprised to hear the two girls were doing something together. "So I can act as a referee?"

Kat smiled. "Maybe something like that."

"All right, no problem. Might be fun." She gave Kat a wave as she went on down to the beach, much to Toby's pleasure.

He trotted through the sand straight to the water.

She pulled back on the leash slightly. "No swimming, buddy boy. I do not want to carry a wet, sandy dog back into the house. If that happens, you will be getting a bath in the laundry sink."

He tugged harder, his little feet digging in. She gave a few inches. Sandy feet were easier to deal with than a whole wet dog.

Then two things happened at the same time. A new, bigger wave rolled toward the beach, and a large streak of golden fur charged between them, causing Jules to lose her grip on Toby's leash and her balance.

She flailed, her arms windmilling while she was desperately trying to grab his leash again, but Toby had bolted for the waves and was immediately swamped.

Her backside hit the wet sand and she sucked in

a breath as the water seeped through her shorts. The golden retriever that had knocked her down went zipping past again. He or she was also trailing a leash.

Much further down the beach, a man called out, "Shiloh! *Shiloh!*"

Jules got herself up and went after Toby, who was now completely soaked and utterly thrilled.

The golden retriever made another running pass. This time, Jules stomped on the leash as it went by, stopping the dog. She bent down to grab the end. The last thing she needed was interference trying to get hold of Toby. She went after his leash next, but he scampered off in the opposite direction, thrilled with his new freedom.

He ran right into the arms of the man who'd been yelling at the golden retriever. The man picked him up, soaking wet as he was, and carried him toward Jules. The man smiled at her, crinkling the lines at the corners of his eyes. He had a full head of dark hair and a kind, open face. "Want to swap?"

"Thanks." She took Toby's leash as the man put him down. She held out the end of the retriever's leash. "Is this troublemaker yours?"

He sighed. "I'm afraid so." He looked at the dog. "Shiloh, what is wrong with you? Zoomies on the beach are fine but you can't be knocking people over." He glanced at Jules. "Are you okay?"

She looked over her shoulder at her damp backside. "I'm fine. Wet, sandy, and slightly embarrassed. But fine." She tried to brush a little of the sand off herself.

He frowned. "I'm really sorry. She's not a bad dog. She's just a puppy, really, and full of more energy than any one animal should be allowed to have. I thought letting her burn it off out here would be safe."

"It's okay. I understand. Puppies are their own kind of crazy." He was a good-looking guy. Probably ten years her junior, but that didn't mean she couldn't appreciate his handsomeness.

"That's for sure. Thanks."

She nodded. "And thanks for grabbing Toby. He thinks he's a seal." She looked at Toby. "Who is now getting a bath."

The man laughed and stuck his hand out. "Jesse Hamilton. I live that way." He gestured back behind him with his thumb.

She shook his hand. He had a nice grip. Strong, firm, a little callused. "Julia Bloom." She pointed to the Double Diamond. "I'm staying there, at my sister's place."

He got a strange look on his face. "You're not *the* Julia Bloom, are you?"

"Maybe? I don't know how to answer that."

He laughed. "I know of a musician by the name Julia Bloom. Her *Deep Water* album is one of my favorites."

Jules smiled as Toby wound around her feet, clearly thinking about making another attempt to get back into the water. "This is weird. But cool. I'm glad you like it. That is me."

His mouth came open. "Seriously? Of course. It *is* you. I just didn't recognize you with the hat and sunglasses. Wow."

She got a little tongue-tied. She'd run into fans before, but it wasn't something that happened often, so she usually struggled with figuring out what to say. "Always nice to hear that someone's enjoyed my music. I really appreciate it."

He shook his head. "I don't want to get weird, but *Deep Water* is more than one of my favorites. It got me through my divorce."

Toby gave up and sat by Jules's feet. "I actually wrote that when I was going through a divorce."

"No wonder it spoke to me." He stared at her for a second. "Hey, would you like to get some coffee sometime? I'd love to talk to you a little more. If that's not too forward of me."

When she hesitated to answer, he added, "I'm not some weirdo, I swear. I own the Dolphin Club in town. I have a serious interest in music."

"The Dolphin Club? I like that place." It was probably the best music venue in town. And it also meant that talking about music was really all he wanted to do. She relented. "Coffee would be okay."

"If you have your phone, I can give you my number. You can text me when it's a good time. Or you can call me at the club. I'm there from four until midnight."

She stuck her arm through the leash's loop handle so she could get her phone out. "I'll take your number." It might be good to talk to someone who was in a similar industry. Maybe that would be just the thing to get her out of the creative dry spell she'd been in. Although that would *not* be a topic of conversation. Losing her creative mojo wasn't a rumor she needed to get started.

He gave her his number and she plugged the digits in, adding his name to the contact before saving it. She put the phone back in her pocket. "Maybe tomorrow?"

He nodded. "Sure. My days are pretty free. What are you working on now? A new album?"

She took a breath. "I'm always working on new music." Not a lie. There was no need to explain that the work wasn't going so well. She looked around. "This place always seems to inspire me."

"Me, too. It's a phenomenal place to live. How long are you here for?"

"I'm not quite sure." Toby tried to take off after a seagull. She laughed and took a few steps backwards in the direction he'd gone. "I should get going. I'll text you."

"Great." Jesse waved as she continued to retreat. "Nice meeting you. And talking to you."

"You, too." She turned and went after Toby. Jesse was a nice-looking man, obviously younger than her, and in the same kind of business she was in. Sort of. But if he owned the Dolphin Club, he was definitely successful.

The kind of guy she would have been interested in, if he'd been older and she'd been even slightly open to getting involved again, which she wasn't.

So did he really just want to talk about music or was there more to it? What was he hoping for? And should she consider getting coffee with him a date?

Looked like she'd find out tomorrow.

Chapter Twenty-three

*T*rina parked under the house and jumped out to get her grandmother's door. "Hang on, Mimi. I'll get the elevator down here, too."

"Thanks, sweetness. That was quite a day of shopping."

Trina opened Margo's door as well. "That was a ton of shopping. Don't worry about the packages, I'll bring them up. You two just go on and get in the elevator."

"I'm old, I'm not dead," Margo muttered.

Trina ignored the comment and ran over to the elevator to push the button. She glanced toward the water before returning to get the packages out of the car. Kat was lounging by the pool, reading.

Trina wondered if she'd care if Trina joined her. After she got her grandmother, Margo, and the packages inside, of course. She went back to the car. Mimi and Margo were gathering their purses and making their way to the elevator.

Trina opened the back of the car and got the bags out. Wasn't all that much. A small shopping bag from Guilford's with a box of chocolate-covered cherries, one of Mimi's favorites, and a bag of chocolate-covered raisins for Trina's mom, something she loved. Mimi had also bought a new straw hat to wear on the beach.

Margo had a few more bags. She'd bought a pair of sandals, pretty leather things with little cork wedges. A floaty chiffon top from one of the pricey ladies boutiques. And a couple of books at Beachside Bookstore.

Trina had gotten a magazine in there and Mimi had picked up a new book of crossword puzzles.

All in all, a very successful trip. Made even better by two things: Margo's generous treat of lunch, and her agreeing to let Trina give her some highlights.

In truth, that's what Trina was most excited about. Nervous, too, because Margo was probably the most important client she'd ever had, outside of the mayor's assistant, who came in every couple of months for a full head of highlights herself.

Trina scooped up all the bags and ran to the elevator.

"Did you lock the car?" Mimi asked.

"Not yet, but I'm coming back down. I can always do it from the porch."

"All right," Mimi said. "Just don't forget, crime is everywhere these days."

Margo looked at her as the elevator doors closed. "I agree with you, but Diamond Beach still seems very safe to me."

"Let's hope so," Mimi said. "I'd hate to see this place ruined."

"Same here," Margo agreed.

Trina kept her head forward and smiled so neither one of them could see her. They were actually getting along, which to her meant the trip had been a success. She was tickled pink about it, too.

She and Mimi got off the elevator on the first floor. She handed Margo her bags. "Thanks again for lunch. I can't wait to do your hair."

Margo's smile looked hesitant. "Yes, about that..."

"Don't be nervous," Trina said. "If you really hate it, I can always change it back."

That seemed to surprise Margo. "You can?"

"Oh, sure."

"Oh. All right then." Margo nodded. "See you later."

Trina stepped out of the doors so they could close. "Later!"

Roxie came out from the living room where the TV was on. She was in white capris with a sparkly pink shirt and white espadrille wedges. "There you are. I was starting to think you two were never coming back. We have got to go to the store. I had to have a can of soup and crackers for lunch. It was about the only thing I could find to eat in the pantry. And I'm pretty sure the crackers were stale."

"I'm sorry, Ma." Trina realized they'd kind of forgotten about her. "We can go to the store right now."

"Hang on," Mimi said. She dug into the shopping bag Trina was holding and pulled out the bag of chocolate-covered raisins. "These'll make you feel better."

She tossed the bag to Trina's mom, who caught it and took a look at it. She smiled. "Yes, they will. Thanks." She glanced at Trina again. "I'm ready to go right now. Just let me grab my purse."

Trina nodded. "I'll wait right here."

Roxie opened up the bag of candy, took a small handful, and popped them in her mouth as she went into her bedroom. She came back with her purse, the candy left behind. "All right, let's go."

She didn't say another word until they were in the car. "How did it go with those two? Any fights?"

"No, not at all. I think we made great progress. Margo even bought us lunch. And she's agreed to let me give her some highlights. Although, I have to give Mimi that lilac rinse she's been wanting now. That was the deal I made with her to get her to go."

"Claire's mother bought lunch?" Her mom looked stunned. "If I'd known she was going to do that, I would have gone, too." She laughed. "Nah, probably not. I'm not sure I could have put up with her for that long just to get a salad."

"Margo's not that bad," Trina said as she pulled out of her parking spot and headed for the road. "Mimi told me she's twice widowed. She didn't tell me that, though. She told Mimi. They talked a lot. Well, more than I expected them to. Mimi and I think she's never gotten over losing her husbands and that's why she is the way she is. She's just stuck in her sadness."

Roxie put her sunglasses on. "I've had a few moments since losing your dad that make me under-stand how that could be possible." She stared out the side window. "I still think he's going to call or text and then I realize that's never going to happen again and I just sink down into the same dark place where I was the last time."

"I'm so sorry, Ma," Trina said softly. "I miss him so much, too."

Roxie let out a small sniff as she patted Trina's leg. "I know you do, kitten. I know you do."

When Trina pulled into the Winn-Dixie parking lot, her mom got her list out. Trina parked and they went in, grabbing a cart on the way.

"We have a lot to get." Her mom looked down at the list.

Trina's phone buzzed. She pulled it out and checked the screen. "Mimi wants English muffins and raspberry jam. Do you have that on the list?"

"No." Roxie dug out a pen from her purse and scrawled the additions onto her list. "Now I do. All right, let's get this done."

"What are we having for dinner tonight?"

"Something easy. Ziti and sauce? We could get a bag of frozen meatballs."

"Or," Trina said. "We could do mac-n-cheese and a rotisserie chicken."

"True. Is that what you want?"

She nodded. She liked pasta but not with tomato sauce as much as with cheese sauce.

"Your grandmother won't be happy unless we have a vegetable. We'll get some frozen peas. Tomorrow night, I'll make meatloaf. Or maybe taco pie. Either way, it'll last us a few days."

"Works for me."

They loaded the cart, getting enough food to keep them fed for about a week, including two bottles of the good kind of creamer in Irish Cream and Italian Pastry Cream, and a couple of twelve-packs of Diet Cokes for her mom.

As they checked out and went to put everything in the car, Trina asked the question she'd been dying to get an answer to. "How long are we staying? I only cancelled this week's appointments."

Her mom put the last bag in, then closed the hatch. "I don't really know. But I don't want to leave before they do. Can you ask for a longer break?"

"I rent my chair. I can make my own schedule. But I worry about losing clients if I'm gone too long."

Her mom nodded in thought. "Maybe you could go back for a couple days next week? Just reschedule as many people as you can for two or three days, get them done and then come back?"

"Yeah, maybe. Are you worried that leaving before then will affect something? Like the outcome of the will?"

"No, that's going to be whatever it's going to be." Her mom sighed and put her fingers by her mouth like she was smoking an invisible cigarette. "I guess I'm worried she might change the locks and we'll never see the inside of the Double Diamond again."

Trina shrugged one shoulder. "Why don't you ask her?"

Her mom frowned. "I would, except I don't want to put ideas into her head."

Trina nodded but she figured that Claire, with a mother like Margo, probably had all kinds of ideas already.

Chapter Twenty-four

Claire had pulled herself together and gone back out to finish the weeding, only to discover Danny had done the weeding and spread the rest of the rocks. She felt bad that he'd worked on that all by himself. She should have been out there to help him.

The feeling of imbalance motivated her to do something she'd never pictured herself doing—she went next door to his house and rang the bell. It was a nice house. Three stories like hers, but possibly a little bigger.

He answered dressed in a nice Hawaiian shirt, dress shorts, and loafers. He was showered and clean-shaven, and it was the first time she'd seen him without some combination of hat, sunglasses, or stubble.

He cleaned up well. In fact, he was better-looking than she'd realized, and she'd already thought he was handsome.

"Sorry, you look like you're about to go somewhere."

He nodded, his smile sympathetic. "I was just headed to the store to see how things are going. Mrs. Butters, I mean. But I can be late. That's one of the perks of being the boss. How are you doing?"

"I'm fine. I'm sorry about earlier. About not finishing the weeding. My emotions still get the best of me sometimes."

"Nothing to apologize for. I get it."

She knew he did. "Well, I do need to apologize for you having to finish those flower beds on your own. I should have come back out sooner to help. Anyway, I wanted to thank you for all the hard work you did for me today. That was so kind and so helpful, and I am truly grateful."

"I'm happy I was in a position to help."

"I'd like to invite you to dinner. You and your dad."

His smile turned into a grin. "Yeah? You don't have to, you know."

"No, I want to. It's the least I can do after everything you did for me. Plus, I still owe you for the rocks, but I've just realized I left my checkbook at the house. How about tomorrow night for dinner and I'll give you the check then? Would that work? I'll do some barbeque chicken. If that's all right."

"Sounds great. What can we bring?"

"You don't need to bring anything. Just your-selves. Around six?"

"Perfect. Thank you."

"You're welcome. See you then." Her heart was racing, and she had no idea why. She'd entertained plenty of people plenty of times. Never alone, though. Never a single man.

"Looking forward to it."

She went back to her house, trying to shake off the sudden case of nerves. She couldn't uninvite him, so she'd just have to get over whatever was going on with her.

And pray she got through the dinner without making a fool of herself.

The key to that was surrounding herself with family. Her mother, Jules, and Kat would have to be there. That would help.

She went inside and looked for Kat, then remem-bered she'd gone out to read by the pool. Her mother was puttering around in her room, and Jules was...Claire wasn't sure where Jules was.

She decided to go back down to the ground floor

to talk to Kat. She took the circular stairs and found Jules on the lounge next to her.

They both turned to look at Claire, alerted by the sound of her footsteps on the metal stairs. She lifted her hand in greeting. "Hello."

"Hi, Mom."

Toby lay on the pool deck next to Jules's chair looking exhausted. And damp.

Claire stopped a few feet away. "What happened to him?"

Jules shook her head. "Long story, but basically he got away from me and plunged into the waves before I could stop him."

Kat had a goofy smile on her face. "She's leaving out the part about how she also met a man."

"What?" Claire came to sit on the end of Jules's lounge. "You met someone?"

Jules cut her eyes at Kat. "It's not like that. His dog is the one that knocked me down and—"

"You never said you got knocked down." Claire frowned. "Back up and tell the long version of the story."

"Okay," Jules said. "Here's what happened..."

Claire listened intently as her sister regaled her with the beach adventure she'd had. At the end of it, Claire smiled. "Only you would have an encounter with a handsome man named Jesse who also happens to run the best music club in town. So, are you going to have coffee with him?"

Jules glanced at her phone, which was beside her on the cushion. "I'm thinking about it. But I really don't want to get involved. I'm happy to sit and talk music with him, but that's it. It's not going to be a date."

Kat snorted. "Right. Are you going to tell him that?"

Jules nodded. "Yes, I am. I don't want to lead him on. I've had enough of being married and divorced. I'm not going through it again."

Claire knew how distraught Jules had been by both of her failed marriages, especially the last one. She'd bought Trevor's promises that he was going to treat her like a queen and do everything she needed him to so that she could focus on her music.

Then he'd cheated on her with one of the producers working on Jules's next album. Claire had never seen her sister so broken. How Jules had gotten over that, Claire wasn't sure but she knew she didn't want that to happen again. "You do whatever you need to do to make sure he understands. It's your right to be upfront."

"Thanks," Jules said. "So, did you come down to

hang out with us? You don't look dressed for chilling by the pool."

"Oh, no," Claire said. "I came to tell you that tomorrow night I need you to be here for dinner. I've invited our neighbors over to say thank you for trimming our palm trees and doing some other landscaping odds and ends. Nothing fancy, just barbeque chicken and probably potato salad and baked beans. Maybe some corn bread. I haven't figured out dessert yet."

"I got a key lime pie when I did the shopping," Kat said. "We could have that."

"That works," Claire said.

Kat sat up a little more. "Are we talking about Aunt Jules's potato salad?"

Claire smiled at her sister. "If she wants to make it."

"Sure," Jules said. "Who are these neighbors again?"

Claire gestured to the house next door. "The Rojas. It'll just be Danny and his dad, Miguel. Danny is the one who trimmed the palms. And get this— they own the Mrs. Butter's Popcorn stores."

"I love that stuff. Their caramel corn with salted peanuts is addictive." Then Kat's brows went up like she'd just realized something. "Wait. No wife?"

Claire answered, "He's a widower."

"Recently?" Kat asked.

"No," Claire said. "Four years ago, I believe. Anyway—"

"Is he cute?" Kat grinned.

"Kat! I don't care about that." She frowned at her daughter. "He's a nice man who helped us out. It's only right that we thank him."

"I agree," Jules said. "But seriously, is he cute?"

Claire rolled her eyes. "Really, Jules? Bryan has been gone barely a week."

"I understand that, but there's nothing wrong with making friends. And listen, Bryan wasn't exactly Mr. Wonderful." Jules gave her sister a serious look. "The regular rules of mourning don't apply to you, not with the kind of special circumstances you're in."

Claire didn't know about that. But she also didn't know what exactly was okay in a situation like hers.

Kat touched her mom's leg. "You know what I said earlier about being happy. You do whatever you need to do. You deserve it after what you found out about Dad. I still love him and miss him very much, but that doesn't stop me from seeing that he was a big fat cheater who hurt both of us. If you want to explore your options, then you go right ahead."

Claire put her hands up, hoping to end the conversation. "I do not need to make friends and I do not want to explore my options. I am simply trying to be neighborly and thank Mr. Rojas for his help. End of story. All right?"

"If you say so," Kat said. "I can run to the store for you tomorrow if you need me to."

"Thank you." Claire got up. "I'm going back up to sit on the porch and read."

She didn't wait for their responses, just headed for the steps.

Tomorrow night's dinner was going to be very interesting. Danny was a very handsome man, something she had no doubt Jules and Kat would notice right away.

Chapter Twenty-five

*P*utting the groceries away had given Roxie an idea. She finished up, then went to see how Trina and Willie were getting on with Willie's new look.

She went into her mother's bathroom. Willie was sitting in front of the mirror on a stool from the kitchen while Trina applied the new color, which was a shockingly vibrant lavender.

Roxie leaned on the door. "You already took the pink out?"

Trina nodded. "I did a nice mild bleach bath and just like that, we've got a blank slate again."

Willie had a gossip magazine on her lap. "She knows what she's doing."

"I know she does," Roxie said. "It's going to be beautiful, Ma."

"Then it'll be perfect. Your enchiladas are my favorite."

Roxie smiled. "Okay, good. I'm going upstairs to see if Claire's around and tell her about dinner. Wish me luck. Can't wait to see the hair when it's done."

She took the steps. Nothing wrong with a little extra exercise. She liked to do squats, leg lifts, and pushups every day to keep things tight. She tried to walk often as well, which reminded her that she hadn't gotten down to the beach yet. Bryan had always appreciated how she kept in shape. She imagined the next man in her life would, too.

She stopped on the landing and just stood there. Would there be a next man? She hadn't intended to have that thought, it had just popped into her head on its own, sort of. But now she really dug into it.

Did she want another man? She wasn't sure. They were a lot of work. Bryan really hadn't been, because he'd been gone so much, but she'd heard enough from her girlfriends about how demanding a husband could be. One who was around all the time.

She'd always counted herself lucky to have a husband who traveled so much. When Bryan was home, it was her pleasure to take care of him and look after him. It never felt like a job or a duty. And he'd done the same for her. When he was gone, she had time to herself, which was also enjoyable. She could spend time with Willie and Trina that way, too.

Maybe she didn't want another man. Although, it would make life easier if there was someone else around to pay the bills. Probably not the best way to approach a new relationship, but wasn't that just the way of things?

Men wanted a pretty face and a nice figure. Women wanted a provider.

Didn't matter about another man. Wasn't like there was one on her radar. She could think about it more if the situation actually came up. She knocked on Claire's door.

No answer.

She walked through the kitchen. Margo was watching television. Roxie was about to ask if she knew where Claire was when the question was answered by the reflection in the decorative mirror on the wall. Claire was on the screened porch.

Roxie went to the sliders, opened them, and went though. "Hi, Claire. Sorry to interrupt. Do you have a second?"

Claire put her book down. "I guess."

Roxie shut the slider and took a few steps closer.

"I want to invite you and your family to join me, Trina, and Willie for dinner downstairs tomorrow night. I'm going to make my Mexican supper. Enchiladas, yellow rice, refried beans, salad, and flan." The dessert had just come to her. She'd seen some at the Winn-Dixie's bakery. Trina was going out to the beauty supply store tomorrow anyway. She could pick one up.

"Um..." Claire bit her bottom lip. "That's very kind of you to offer but...I was already planning on using the downstairs tomorrow night."

"Oh." Roxie wasn't sure what to say to that. But obviously, Claire's plans didn't include them. She shrugged it off like it was nothing. "We can do it some other night."

Claire didn't look happy. She put her book down. "Why don't you all join us? I'm just having the neighbor over to thank him for trimming the palm trees and helping me with some landscaping. You remember, I mentioned it earlier when we spoke?"

Roxie nodded. She'd been unable to sleep in because of it. Maybe she'd start sleeping with an eye mask and earplugs. Too much noise and light in the morning, or at any time, bothered her. "That was nice of him. And it's nice of you. Are you sure you want us to join you? I wasn't angling for an invite."

"I know you weren't but it's fine. You should join us. I was going to do barbeque chicken on the grill, potato salad, baked beans, and cornbread. If you want to add something to that, it would be welcome."

"Okay. Or I could do the baked beans. If you don't mind." Roxie had a pretty good recipe for those. A little bacon, a little brown sugar, some mustard, plus her secret ingredient. It was easy and not too expensive.

"No, that would be great." Claire smiled but it looked strained.

Roxie wasn't sure what Claire was so worried about. The people next door were Roxie's neighbors, too. "Is there a reason you don't want us there? Besides the obvious one, I mean?"

Claire exhaled. "No. I just...it's fine."

Roxie didn't buy that for one second. "You seem pretty bothered by something that's fine."

Claire pursed her lips, then shook her head. "My daughter and my sister think I should ignore the fact that Bryan just died and entertain the thought of dating again. As if the next-door neighbor is a candidate."

"Is he?" Roxie would have to pay more attention to who lived next door.

"*No.*" Claire's emphasis seemed unnaturally heavy. "He's just a nice man who helped me out, that's all. I know they mean well, but..." She shrugged.

"People don't really know how to act around the grieving. It makes them uncomfortable. They think they need to fix things. To offer a solution when all they really need to do is listen."

Claire stared at her, then tipped her head to one side. "Sounds like you're saying that from experience."

Roxie stared back, shocked that Claire seemed to be asking about Roxie's life. Was she trying to make friends? Roxie was probably seeing more than was there. "I've been a nurse most of my adult life and in the last few years, I've specialized in hospice and palliative care. I've been around a lot of grieving people."

"Been around a lot of dying ones, too."

Roxie nodded. "I have."

"That's an incredibly hard job."

"It was. I haven't been doing it much lately. But it wasn't always. Depended on the situation. Some people go into death terrified. Others with a sense of peace, looking forward to seeing all their loved ones who'd gone before them. But the family around them makes a difference, too."

Claire's expression turned gloomy, and Roxie wondered if she was thinking about Bryan. Roxie was. She sighed softly and offered a few more words. "If it's any consolation, he would have gone very quickly."

Claire swallowed. "I don't know if it is or not. I guess that takes me out of the running for Best Widow of the Year."

"Neither one of us is going to win that one." Roxie knew she should go, but this felt like a break-through moment. "I really didn't know he was married. I hope you can believe me, because I might be a lot of things, but 'the other woman' isn't one of them. I would never intentionally do that."

Claire nodded but said nothing.

Sensing the conversation was over, Roxie left.

Chapter Twenty-six

Kat gazed at the slim pickings on display in her closet and dresser.

She had no idea what to wear to a sandcastle-building contest. Not that she cared what she looked like. At least that's what she tried to tell herself. But if she allowed herself to be really, truly honest, she knew she wanted to look nice. Because Alex was going to be there.

That was probably wrong. It probably meant she was vain and disloyal. And yet, she couldn't summon enough energy to chastise herself. What woman didn't want to look nice for an attractive guy?

Most likely a woman who was a better girlfriend and former fiancée than Kat was, that's who. She groaned at the mess of emotions going on inside her heart. Why was her life suddenly so hard to figure out?

Did she love Ray? Yes. That was a definite. The question remained as to whether she was *in* love with him enough to spend the rest of her life with him. And therein lay the real issue.

Maybe seeing Alex would be a good thing tonight. It might help her figure out what was going on. If she reacted to his presence, that could be a sign. Just like if she didn't react, if that little spark she'd felt with him the first time didn't happen again, she'd know Ray was the guy for her.

Seemed logical. And she liked logic. Hard facts and clear data were her lifeblood as an actuary. No reason they shouldn't be part of the rest of her life, too.

She chose a pair of light-washed, rolled-cuff jeans, low white sneakers, and a long-sleeve T-shirt with a band of soft blue hibiscus flowers patterned across the front.

She'd bought the shirt a couple of years ago at one of the local surf shops and it bore the shop's logo entwined with the floral design. She pushed the sleeves up and took a look at herself. It was a fine beach event outfit. Not sexy, but not shlumpy, either. Kind of I'm-too-cool-to-care-what-I-look-like-because-I'm-digging-in-the-sand-anyway. At least she hoped that was the vibe it gave off, because that's what she was going for.

Who knew with fashion? Trina would probably be in something that glowed in the dark or required batteries.

Kat went out to the kitchen, got out the left-over spaghetti, and started fixing herself a plate to heat up. Jules came out of the bedroom. She was in frayed denim shorts, which showed off her tanned legs beautifully, and a vintage-looking lavender sweatshirt with "New York" printed on the front in faded white letters. Aunt Jules was cool without even trying. Kat had no idea how she did that.

Jules came over to the kitchen. "You look cute."

"Yeah?" Kat nodded. "Thanks. I wasn't sure what to wear to build a sandcastle in."

"I think what you have on is fine." Jules got a plate out for herself. "Are you allowed to use tools? Because that could give you a big advantage. Or disadvantage, if you don't have them."

"I have no idea. I haven't really read the flyer, to be honest."

Jules gave her a skeptical look. "If you're not going to try to win, why are you going?"

Kat looked toward the stairs, then lowered her

voice so no one would overhear. "Mostly to keep Trina happy."

"And you care about that because...?"

With a sigh, Kat put her plate in the microwave, set it to heat, then motioned for her aunt to follow her into the bedroom.

When she was in, Kat shut the door. "This is what I wanted to talk to you about earlier. I'm not sure I'm in love with Ray enough to marry him. I don't know if he's really the right guy for me."

"Oh, honey. I could have told you that ages ago."

Kat stared at her aunt in shock. "You could? How?" Anything her aunt knew might help Kat figure out her next step.

"Just from the way you are with him. You treat him like a really good friend. And, not to be unkind, but more like a convenience than a soulmate."

Kat exhaled as she sank down onto the bed, her stomach twisting. "That makes me sound awful."

Jules sat beside her, putting her arm around Kat's shoulders. "I'm sorry, I didn't mean it that way. It's just been clear to me that while I believe you love Ray, I don't see that kind of wild, passionate thing that drives you to be with him. If he disappeared tomorrow, I think you'd miss him, but I don't think you'd feel any deep sense of loss."

Kat studied her hands and the place where her engagement ring had once been. A slight indentation remained, but it was already fading. "My mom says soulmates aren't really a thing for most people."

"Well, I'm going to have to disagree with her on that one. Lars and I were definitely soulmates."

"But you divorced him." She looked at her aunt. "If you were soulmates, why didn't things work out?"

"Because he had issues beyond what I could deal with."

"His addictions?" Kat knew a little about her Uncle Lars, but had never really gotten to know him very well during the time he and Jules had been married. What she did know was that he was a bass guitar player who traveled the world with his band, Alchemy.

As for his addictions, they ran mostly to the young female variety, but also to booze and recreational drugs. He lived the rock-n-roll lifestyle, something Jules had wanted nothing to do with.

Jules nodded. "I give him credit for admitting that he can't stay faithful, clean, or sober. And for not putting up a fight when I went for custody of the boys. Not that he could have raised those kids while hopping from country to country. He never missed a child support payment, either."

"Is that why you're still friends?"

"For all of those things, yes. And we're both adults. On some level, we still love each other. He's the father of my boys. I will always care about him. But we just couldn't be together in a healthy way. It happens sometimes."

"And Uncle Trevor?"

Jules snorted out a breath. "He was a mistake from the beginning. A fun one, at first, but definitely a mistake."

"Do you think you'll ever get married again?"

"I don't know. Probably not. I'm okay being by myself." She grinned. "Or with you guys. But my music is its own kind of company and I'm all right with that."

Kat couldn't imagine being alone the rest of her life. She definitely wanted to get married and have kids, which was the first time she realized how deeply that desire abided within her. The sudden understanding caused her to confess a little more. "I met a guy on the beach, the guy who told me about the contest. Our hands touched when he gave the flyer to me and...I think I felt a spark."

Jules's brows went up. "Yeah? What's his name? What's he like?"

"Alex. He's a surfer dude. And a fireman." Kat bit

her lip. "But it's not like I want to date him or anything, I swear. It's just that I've never felt anything like that with Ray. And apparently, my mom never felt it with my dad, according to what she told me. I was starting to think sparks and fireworks and butterflies were just fairytales."

Jules shook her head. "I can assure you, they are *not*. Also, I think you should date him. At least once. You ought to date a lot of guys. It's not an experience you've ever had."

"True. Not sure how Ray would feel about that."

"Just tell him you need to do it to be sure about you and him. He'll get it. And if he doesn't...the problem might solve itself. But none of this explains why you care about keeping Trina happy."

"Because she saw me with Alex on the beach and I'm worried that she'll tell Ray about him if I don't do what she wants."

Jules rolled her eyes. "Trina is desperate to be friends with you. I don't think she has any plans of upsetting you like that. Just the opposite. But if you think she does, you ought to just tell her what you're going through. She's a woman. She'll understand."

"I'm not so sure." Kat didn't know Trina well enough to make any assumptions, so erring on the side of caution seemed like the way to go.

"Well, I'll be there with you guys tonight. I'll talk to her and see if I can pick up on any nefarious intentions, all right?"

"Okay. Thanks." Kat smiled. Aunt Jules was a pretty good judge of character, Uncle Trevor clearly being the exception. "I'm glad you're going with us tonight."

"I think the distraction will be good for all of us. Maybe I should see if your mom will go?"

Kat laughed. "Yeah, I don't think there's any chance of that."

"Think about what I said. About telling Ray you want to date other guys."

"I will." The microwave beeped that her food was ready. Kat stood up. She was ready, too. Ready to see if Alex could make her feel something again.

illie kept her hands over her eyes. She didn't trust herself not to peek. "Hurry up! I can't stand it."

Trina laughed. "I'm almost done, Mimi, I swear. I have to be. I need to leave soon."

Willie heard and felt one last blast of hairspray, then the metallic clink of the can being set down.

"All right," Trina said. "You can look."

Willie took her hands away and opened her eyes. She gasped at her reflection in the mirror. Her hair was a perfectly curled and coiffed swirl of pale lilac. "It's gorgeous. My girl has done it again."

Trina grinned at her through the mirror. "I'm glad you like it."

"Like it? I love it." Willie held out her arms. "Come here and give me a hug. You are the best stylist in the world, you know that?"

Trina hugged her, laughing. "I don't know about that, but I'm happy you think so."

Willie kissed her granddaughter's cheek before letting her go. She patted the side of her stiff curls. "This is definitely my new color. I'm going to be doing this for a while." She turned her head to see the other side. "I mean it, you've outdone yourself. Your mother is going to be jealous."

From one of the other rooms, Roxie called out, "I heard my name."

Willie snorted in the direction of her daughter's voice. "No, you didn't." She looked at Trina again. "What time do you have to leave for your shindig tonight?"

Trina checked the time on her phone. "Probably in about forty-five minutes or so. I need to eat something and get ready."

"I'd offer to go with you but with this hair, I'll have men swimming around me like sharks. I can't risk it, honey."

Trina snorted. "No, you're right. You'd better stay home. We can't have you married off again."

Willie gave her a wink and climbed down off the stool, her body stiff from sitting so long, but that was the price of beauty. "You get ready, I'll make you a sandwich. It's the least I can do to repay you."

"Ma." Roxie tilted her head to one side. "You know I would never do that to you."

"I know," Willie said, smiling. She was blessed to have a daughter who loved her and cared for her. "But I like to tease. Sure, we could go. That sounds like fun. And if it's not, it'll at least give us something to talk about. How much are tickets?"

"Hang on." Roxie read. "Fifteen bucks."

"I can swing that." Willie layered on the meat and cheese. "Might be dangerous for me at the seniors center, though."

"Why's that?" Roxie turned the page again.

"All those men? And me looking so irresistible? Purple is the color of passion, you know. I'd better take pepper spray."

Roxie just shook her head. "Maybe we can both find a man. Some nice, older guy with money to burn and only a few months left to live."

Willie slapped the top piece of bread on. "*Roxanne.*"

"Just kidding, Ma."

Willie cut the sandwich on the diagonal, the way Trina liked it, then added a handful of chips and a pickle spear and put the plate up on the counter. She added a glass of water, too. "Go tell Trina her dinner is ready."

Roxie put the paper down. "You made dinner?"

"No, I made her a sandwich. She's going to that sandcastle-building contest tonight. You and I can have something else for dinner. You bought enough stuff."

"There's a frozen lasagna. We could have that."

"You want me to put it in?"

Roxie nodded. "Sure."

Willie got the lasagna out, turned on the oven to heat up, then made herself a cup of tea and carried it over to the seating area. She sat in the easy chair, which was her usual spot, and turned on the television to see some local news. As a rule, she never watched the national stuff. Too miserable.

She was about to remind Roxie to tell Trina about the sandwich when Trina came in.

She wore hot pink pedal pushers and a black T-shirt with a sparkly rhinestone tiger on it. She had her black rhinestone flipflops on, too. Her hair was in a high ponytail with a tiger-print scrunchie around it, and her makeup looked fabulous, as always.

Willie had gotten her the T-shirt for Christmas last year. She nodded in approval. "You look like a million bucks."

"Thanks, Mimi."

"Is that why you were looking in the paper?" Willie asked Roxie.

Roxie lifted one shoulder. "They pay better by the beach. Of course, moving here would give us a whole bunch of new expenses."

"True."

The oven dinged, announcing it had come to temperature.

"I've got it." Roxie jumped up.

Willie thought hard. She had a little money put away. Her Rainy Day Fund. Wasn't much, but it would help. And she'd rather spend it on her daughter and granddaughter than herself. Especially when the sky above Roxie and Trina seemed like it was about to burst open.

Chapter Twenty-eight

rina had offered to drive to Carlton Fisk Park where the contest was and Kat had said that was fine, but she was so quiet in the car that Trina thought maybe something was wrong. Aunt Jules, who was in the back seat with her cute little dog, Toby, hadn't said much, either. Trina glanced at Kat. "You okay over there?"

"Hmm?" Kat looked over, brows raised.

"I asked if you were okay," Trina repeated. "You just got so quiet."

"Oh. Sorry. Just thinking."

"About Ray?" Trina figured Kat must miss him.

Kat gave her a long look, then went back to staring out the windshield. "Some of it's that."

"Must be nice to have a serious guy like that." Trina worked a lot, which didn't leave a lot of time for dates. Although she got asked once in a while.

She always said yes. You never really knew when you might click with someone, so she tried not to be too particular if a guy wasn't exactly her type.

"Yeah, it's nice."

Nothing about that sounded convincing. "You and Ray having problems?"

Kat frowned. "Why would you say that?"

Her tone had gotten sharp, telling Trina she'd overstepped. "I don't know. You didn't sound like you really meant it. And you're not wearing your engagement ring. Look, I'm sorry if I said something I shouldn't have but I'm your sister, right? We're family. You should be able to talk to me about anything. I mean, you can if you want to. I hope you know that."

Aunt Jules cleared her throat softly. "I don't think Kat's ready for that yet, Trina. But it's sweet of you to offer."

Trina shrugged. "I get that we barely know each other. I know that's still new and weird, but blood has to count for something, doesn't it?"

Kat sighed. "I guess. But like Aunt Jules said, I'm not ready. I'm not sure I ever will be."

"Oh," Trina said softly. Kat's words hurt, but Trina got it. Some people were just very closed off. Being a hairdresser meant she talked to a lot of people who'd had all kinds of different life experiences. The ones who'd been hurt the most were usually the ones who needed to talk the most, but they were often the most reluctant, too.

Until that dam broke. Then good luck getting them to stop talking.

She figured Kat was one of those. Hurt by something, closed down because of it, but bottling a lot up inside that was going to come out someday when the right time or opportunity came about.

Trina tried a different approach. "What kind of sandcastle do you want to build? Any ideas? I know we probably won't win, but we should still do our best."

Aunt Jules scooted forward. "I agree. I was thinking you should go traditional. A turret at each corner with one larger center turret, a crenellated wall, and a moat."

"Crenellated?" Trina glanced into the rearview mirror. "Is that where the wall has that broken edge to it? Like a serrated knife?"

Aunt Jules smiled. "Exactly!"

Kat crossed her arms over her body. "Sounds like a lot of work." Then she seemed to hear herself. "But I guess that's what we're supposed to do, right?"

"Right." Trina caught Aunt Jules's gaze in the mirror. "What's in that bag you brought?"

"Tools," Aunt Jules answered. "I didn't see anything in the flyer that said you couldn't use them, so I threw together a bunch of stuff in that shopping bag. A couple of small trowels, a flat-head screwdriver, some spoons, a straw, some cookie cutters, cups, a pair of kids' play buckets, and a folding shovel."

"Wow, nicely done!" Trina hadn't even thought about bringing tools.

Aunt Jules laughed. "Thanks. We just need to be sure we clean everything up and put it all back in the kitchen and the storage closet where I found it."

"Absolutely." Trina loved that Aunt Jules was so into it. She hoped that enthusiasm rubbed off on Kat, who was blankly staring out the window.

Trina pulled into the lot at Carlton Fisk Park and found a spot near the walkway to the beach. "Here we are. Ready to go, partner?"

Kat unfastened her seatbelt without looking at Trina. "Yep."

Trina left the car running. Enough was enough with Kat. "If you don't want to be here, just say so. I'll take you home."

Kat gave her a weird look. "Why would you say

that? I got in the car, didn't I? I obviously want to be here."

"You're not acting like it. Are you mad at me for what I said? Or is it something else?"

Kat exhaled and sat still, her bottom lip quivering. "There's just a...a lot going on with me right now."

Aunt Jules reached up to put a hand on Kat's shoulder. "Honey, we're all still struggling with the loss of your dad and the revelation that there was more to his life than any of us knew. You don't have to keep that in. Trina knows. She's going through the exact same things you are."

Maybe, Trina thought. But Kat seemed like she had some bigger issues happening. Even so, Trina nodded. "That's right. I miss him so much it hurts. But I'm also really upset with him for the secrets he kept." She exhaled as a wash of grief and anger went through her.

Kat kept quiet.

"If he'd just spoke up..." Trina's voice caught for a moment, snagged on the emotion clogging her throat. "I could have grown up knowing you. Instead, I missed almost thirty years of having a sister. That's a big thing to get over. Or get past. Or whatever I'm supposed to do with it. Nearly thirty years. That's what he cost me with you."

Kat pushed a strand of hair out of her eyes and looked at Trina, really looked. "That's what bothers you the most? That you and I didn't grow up knowing each other?"

Trina nodded. "Sure. I mean, I miss him and I'd give all kinds of stuff to have him back, but I'm so used to him not being around that maybe it just hasn't sunk in yet. But keeping me from a sibling? That bothers me. A lot. I understand why he did it. Doesn't mean I like it or forgive him for it."

Kat blinked but kept looking at Trina. Finally, she spoke. "You're a better person than I am."

Trina snorted. "I doubt that."

"No," Kat said. "I mean it. What's bothering you and what's bothering me are two very different things."

"Why?" Trina asked. "What's bothering you?"

Kat glanced at her aunt before answering. "What's bothering me is that losing my dad has made me question all sorts of things I never did before. Like..." She dropped her gaze to the console between them. "Whether or not Ray is really the man I should marry."

Trina's brows rose. "That is a huge question. No

wonder you're so mopey. That's got to have you all torn up inside."

Kat nodded. "It does. That's exactly how I feel. Torn up."

"Sure you do. How long have you been engaged to him?"

"A long time. We met when we were still in school—"

"High school?" Trina was mortified. They'd been together that long and still weren't married?

"No, college."

"Oh. But still. That's a long time. Don't you think it means something that you've been together so long and still aren't married?"

Kat took a breath, brows bent in thought. "I don't know. He wanted to get through school and his residency, which was three years by itself, and I was focused on my job and...I don't know. Maybe."

Trina shrugged one shoulder. "I just know that if I got engaged to a guy and I loved him so much I wanted to spend the rest of my life with him, it wouldn't take me ten years to get down that aisle."

"It hasn't been ten years," Kat said. "But I see your point."

"So do I," Aunt Jules said. "And she's right. You've

been looking for an answer and it's been in front of you this whole time."

Kat looked at her aunt. "So you think I should break up with Ray?"

Trina turned the car off, unhooked her seatbelt, and twisted to see both of them better.

Aunt Jules held up both of her hands. Toby panted like he thought something fun was about to happen. "I don't know. I really don't. You've been with him so long, he's like part of the family. But if he's not the right guy for you, you really shouldn't marry him."

Trina knew Kat might not welcome a suggestion from her, but she spoke up anyway. "Can't you talk to him about taking a little time to see other people? Just to be sure you're sure?"

Kat rested back in her seat. "I did. I texted him right before we got in the car. Aunt Jules, you told me to and I did."

"You texted him?" Jules shook her head. "I guess that's what your generation does. What was the result?"

"That you were right," Kat said. "He said he understands and if I want to see other people he's okay with it. Said he doesn't love it, but he knows I need to figure out what's going on."

No one said anything for a moment. Trina had never heard of a guy being *that* understanding.

Kat exhaled. "So I guess we're officially on a break."

Trina nodded. "He had to know something was going on before that text, though, right?"

"He did," Kat answered. "But why do you say that?"

"Because so much time has gone by without you two getting married. He's a doctor, right? He's not a dummy. He had to know you were reluctant, even if you didn't understand why."

Aunt Jules nodded. "She makes a good point."

With that, Trina was on a roll. "Not to mention, if he's that into you, why hasn't he pushed harder to get married? Seems like he's pretty comfortable with the status quo. Personally, that would raise some questions for me."

Aunt Jules's brows lifted but she didn't say anything. Kat slowly turned her head to look at Trina. "I...I never thought about that."

Then she shook her head almost violently. "No. No to whatever you were thinking. He's not like that. Ray is just a very easygoing guy. He's happiest making me happy. That's *all* it is."

Aunt Jules leaned forward again. "He's a

pushover, to be honest. And he's pretty dedicated to his work. Plus, you have to understand that he's not one to rock the boat. At all. Whatever Kat wants, Kat gets."

"That's convenient," Trina said. She pulled her keys out of the ignition.

"What's that supposed to mean?" Kat looked wounded. Like she'd just had a Band-Aid ripped off against her will.

Trina put her hand on the door, preparing to get out. "I guess what it really means is you and Ray need to have a serious talk. If you want to sort this out, that is. Because if you've both been putting off the wedding, sounds to me like it's not just you that's been having doubts."

"Oh," Kat said softly. Her mouth formed a thin, even line. "In a weird way, that makes me feel better. If that's what's going on. Thanks."

Trina hadn't expected that, but she'd take it. She smiled. "You're welcome. Ready to build a sandcastle?"

Kat nodded and looked slightly less miserable than she had just a second ago. "Yeah, I am."

Chapter Twenty-nine

While the girls got registered and were shown their building site, which was marked off by tiki torches, stakes and rope, Jules took Toby for a quick trip to the small grass patches that the park had reserved for dogs so he could do his business.

Once that was taken care of and she'd found a garbage can to dispose of the poop bag, she rejoined them on the beach and quickly found their square of building ground.

All of the entrants had been supplied with a five-gallon utility bucket and a standard-sized shovel. Their patch of sand was about twelve feet by twelve feet and the two girls were standing side by side in one corner, contemplating the blank slate before them.

There looked to be about twenty-five or thirty

spots altogether, and the firemen were going around helping people figure out where they belonged. Jules's gaze jumped from one fireman to the next as she wondered if one of them was the young man Kat had met.

She led Toby over to Kat and Trina. "Are you formulating a plan?"

Trina nodded. "We're going with the classic, like you suggested. Just trying to figure out how big it should be."

"How much time do you have to build?" Jules asked.

"Only an hour," Kat answered. "Which doesn't seem like nearly enough."

Trina shook her head. "It really doesn't. Not with just two of us. But I guess that's what makes it a contest."

Kat picked up the five-gallon bucket they'd been given and brought it closer to where they were standing. "Trina, you sure you want to haul the water? It's going to be heavy filled with water."

She nodded. "I can do it."

Jules glanced toward the water. It was a good distance away. "What's the plan? Wet the sand down so it'll be easier to mold?"

"Yep." Kat nodded. "I'm going to start digging

and getting it into a mound, then Trina will dump the water on and we'll mix the water in as best we can, then start shaping. Might take a couple of buckets, I don't know."

Jules gave Toby a little slack on the leash. "I'm guessing it'll take more water than you think."

Toby let out a little yip and started digging in the sand, making them all laugh.

"Go, Toby!" Kat grinned. "Too bad we can't have him on the team, too."

"He's the cutest thing," Trina said. "I always wanted a dog."

"So why don't you get one?" Jules said.

"Because I work a lot. I feel like the poor thing wouldn't get enough attention. And plus, my mom and Mimi would have to help take care of him, too. Which I'm sure they wouldn't mind, but my mom might have to go back to full-time work now that my dad's gone."

Jules understood. "Well, if you ever want to take him for a walk while you're here, just ask."

Trina grinned. "Yeah? I'd love that."

"Castle builders, if I could have your attention, please!"

They all turned toward the registration table where an older man with a megaphone was speaking. "Thank you for joining us for our night of fun and fundraising. We'll be starting our contest in just a moment, so please get to your assigned spot if you're competing. Also, please don't forget to buy some raffle tickets! You could win some great prizes. We've got a dinner for two at the Flying Fish, a spa day at Ocean Blue Spa, a year's worth of oil changes from Prime Tire, and, last but not least, a basket of goodies donated by Guilford's Fine Chocolates."

Jules grinned at the girls. "I'm going to buy some raffle tickets. Other than the oil changes, I'd be happy with any of those."

Kat dug in her pocket and pulled out a ten. "Here. Get me some, too."

Jules took the money. "What about you, Trina?"

She shook her head and gave Jules a little smile. "I'm good. I didn't bring any money with me. Thanks, though. I never win that stuff anyway."

Jules had a feeling not bringing money with her had nothing to do with it. "Okay, I'll be back in a bit. I'm rooting for you!"

They both said thanks and went back to their planning as she walked up to the registration area. She got in line behind an older couple with a Chihuahua in a red plaid sweater. The little dog was eyeing Toby like he was trying to decide if he could take him.

She did her best to give the little dog a look that said, "Don't try it."

"This must be my lucky day."

She turned to see Jesse standing behind her. "Hi."

"Hi back. Are you competing?"

"No, but my nieces are." It was the first time she'd used the plural of that word and it made her smile. Trina was a lovely young woman, a different sort of person than Kat was, to be sure, but lovely all the same. "Are you competing?"

He shook his head. "No, but some friends of mine are. I'm here for moral support."

Toby sniffed at his shoes. Probably smelling Jesse's dog. "Where's Shiloh?"

He smiled like he was pleased she'd remembered his dog's name. "She's with my friends. I just came up here to get some raffle tickets."

"Me, too." He looked better than she remembered, but who didn't look better by the light of tiki torches? That was an unfair advantage.

"Next."

Jules went up to the table and got her tickets. Twenty for herself and ten each for Kat and Trina, as a treat. She planned on returning Kat's money. It was all for a good cause anyway.

She hung around while Jesse bought his. He got fifty dollars' worth, which didn't fail to impress her.

He tucked his wallet back into his pocket, the loops of tickets he'd been given dangling from his hand like ribbon. "Have you had a chance to think any more about getting coffee?"

She smiled. "Yes. And I'll have coffee with you."

"Can I persuade you into making it breakfast? My treat, of course. At Digger's Diner? They do the best omelets. As I'm sure you know."

Breakfast was a pretty safe meal. But he didn't strike her as an early riser. "What time?"

"Ten too late?"

Not if she had a cup of coffee at home first. "No, I can do that. Tomorrow morning?"

He nodded. "Yes. If that works for you."

"It does."

"Great." He leaned his head to the side, his gaze filled with amusement. "You will call or text if you can't make it, right? Because if you ghost me, I don't have your number."

She grinned. "No, I guess you don't. I'll show, I promise. But I'll text you now so you have my number, too."

"Thanks."

She got her phone out and did exactly as she'd said. "There. Now you have my number. Don't go posting it on bathroom walls."

He laughed. "I won't, I swear. Hey, would you mind meeting my friends? They're fans of your music, too, and I know they'd get a kick out of it."

"Sure." She was never one to turn down an opportunity like that. Fans were the people who kept her in business and paid her bills. And would continue to do so, if she could get another album out.

Jesse led her over to their patch of ground. "Mike, Liz, this is Julia Bloom."

The pair came over to her, the man sticking his hand out first. "It's a real pleasure to meet you. My wife and I love your music. Are you playing anywhere locally?"

Jules smiled as she took his hand. Toby and Shiloh were busy sniffing each other. "No, just here with family. It's lovely to meet you both." She shook his wife's hand after his.

The older man with the megaphone spoke again. "All right, contestants. When I say go, you can start building those sandcastles. Three. Two. One. GO!"

All across the beach, people began to work and the cheers from the audience went up.

Jules glanced toward the girls. They were hard at work. She returned her attention to the couple she'd just met. "Best of luck, Mike and Liz!"

They gave her a nod, but they were already busy digging. A fireman was bringing them a bucket of water. Apparently, that was not the contestants' job. Nice of the fire station to help out like that.

She looked at Jesse. "I really do hope your friends do well in the contest. Not as well as my nieces, but you know, close. Anyway, I should get back to them."

He snorted. "Thanks. Looking forward to breakfast tomorrow."

"Me, too. C'mon, Toby." She headed off to where Kat and Trina were digging away.

They were working together to make a big mound of sand first, both of them shoveling, Kat with the provided shovel and Trina with the folding one Jules had found in the storage closet.

Jules looked to see if they had someone bringing them water. They did. And he was headed toward them now, a fireman who just happened to be a handsome young man who looked very much like he could also be a surfer.

Chapter Thirty

Margo sat on the end of her bed, holding the ridiculous black crystal-covered sunglasses Willie had given her. They were hideous and tacky and about the last thing she could imagine wearing. Maybe to some kind of costume contest. But that wasn't something she was likely to attend, either.

She got up and went to stand before the dresser mirror. She put them on. Just as she'd suspected, they looked even more foolish on than they did off.

"Those are snazzy. Not something I'd ever expect to see you in, but I like them."

Margo whipped the glasses off her face at the sound of Claire's voice. "They're not mine. I mean, they are, but they're not something I bought."

"You didn't steal them, did you?"

"The very idea." Margo rolled her eyes. "Willie bought them for me when we went shopping."

"That was nice."

Margo looked at the glasses. It *had* been a nice gesture. She glanced at her daughter again. "You don't really like them, do you?"

Claire shrugged from her spot by the door. "They're not my style and they're definitely not yours, but I could see them on Willie. Or Roxie. Or Trina." She laughed. "We aren't sparkly sunglasses kind of people, but they are. Very much so."

Margo turned the glasses slightly, watching as the crystals caught the light. "We aren't fun, are we?"

Claire didn't answer right away. "I don't know. What's the definition of fun? Rhinestone sunglasses? If that's it, then no, we aren't. But we're fun in our own way."

Margo looked at her daughter. "Are we? Because I don't think we are. And I'm not sure I remember how to be fun." She put the glasses on the dresser and went back to sit on the bed. "I've gotten so used to being a widow that I've forgotten how to be anything else. It's become my identity."

Claire came in and sat across from Margo on Jules's bed. "What's brought all this on? Bryan's passing?"

"No." She thought about that. "To be truthful, I'm so used to being in a perpetual state of grief that his death just gave me another reason to keep on being me."

"Then what's going on with you?"

"They are. They're going on with me." She looked up. "They're so different than we are. So..."

"Happy? Carefree? Unencumbered by what anyone thinks of them?"

Margo nodded, a little surprised that Claire saw them so clearly. "All of that. Are those the qualities that drew Bryan to Roxie? Did he need them to balance us out? Are we that bad?"

Claire put her hands up. "First of all, we're not bad."

"I didn't mean bad. I meant..." What did she mean? "Are we hard to be around?"

"No." Claire shook her head so hard her hair swung. "I refuse to believe that. We're good people."

"I'm not saying we aren't. But he was married to you and a part of our family, and he decided it wasn't enough. Or at least that he needed more. And look at the direction he went in. That has to say something about us."

Claire sighed. "It makes me feel a little better that you don't think it was just me." She sat back on the bed a little more. "Do you really think we pushed him into a second marriage, though? That's a pretty big decision. If he was that unhappy with me, why not just get a divorce?"

"Because of Kat." But Margo wasn't really sure if that was true.

Claire seemed to agree. "He *was* a devoted father when he was around. He never seemed unhappy to me, though."

"Of course not. When he'd had enough of us, he went back to them. He never let himself get unhappy." A desperate bleakness rose up in Margo. "We have to change. We can't keep on like this. But how?"

Claire frowned. "I feel no need to change."

"You honestly don't? You can be around those people and not feel like they've got some secret to living life that you don't? Because that's how they make me feel. Like I'm missing out."

"Really?"

Margo nodded. "I always thought I was just fine the way I was. That I was happy, in my own way. I have you and Jules and Kat, and even Jules's boys, although they're off living their own lives. Anyway, it felt like being around the three of you was enough. Now, I think...maybe I'm a burden on all of you. Maybe I'm the reason you are the way you are."

"Mom, I think you're just having a bad day. I don't know what you're trying to say but we three are fine."

She snorted. "No, you're not. Jules is all right. She's had a couple of bad marriages, but she's got her music as an outlet, and I think that's probably saved her. She's got her boys and Toby, too. Something more to focus on than herself. But you and Kat are just like me. Or you will be if you don't do something differently."

Claire stood and put her hands on her hips. "Just like you? How do you mean?"

Margo could only tell the truth at this point. There was no energy left in her for anything else. "You're rule-followers. You live the life you're given, not a life you make for yourself. You absorb all the negative energy that comes your way like it's your job, never seeking to do anything that might lift you above it."

She got to her feet. "I'm done living that way. I don't know how exactly I'm going to change, but I am. Whatever years I have left, I want to spend them taking chances, seeing what the world has to offer, and not being afraid of what other people think."

"Mom, I—"

"No, Claire. I mean it. Bryan did us all a favor by

marrying that woman. Maybe he knew this day would come. Maybe he knew just how much we needed things to be shaken up around here. Whatever the reason things happened the way the did, I'm not letting this moment pass me by. I'm going to spend the rest of my life figuring out how to have fun again."

Before Claire could say another word, Margo marched out of the room and through the kitchen. She didn't have time to wait for the elevator. She took the steps downstairs. "Willie? Are you here? Where are you?"

"In the living room," her voice called out.

Margo went on through and found Willie and Roxie there, Roxie on the couch, Willie in the chair, each of them with a partially eaten plate of lasagna in front of them. Store-bought, premade lasagna, no doubt, something Margo would never think of buying or eating in a million years.

How did they live such a carefree life?

Willie looked up at her with trepidation in her eyes. "What's wrong? Did something happen to Trina?"

"Your hair is purple." Margo shook her head, ignoring that change. She was touched that the first thing the woman thought of was her granddaughter.

Maybe they weren't so different after all. Maybe there was hope for Margo yet. "No, nothing's wrong, she's fine."

Willie exhaled. "Good. And my hair is technically Lavender Ice. What's got you on fire, then?"

Margo took a breath. "I need your help. I want you to teach me how to have fun. How to be...happy."

Chapter Thirty-one

Claire felt like she'd had a bucket of cold water thrown on her. Was that really what her mother thought? That they were all a bunch of boring duds?

Worse, did her mother genuinely believe that Claire was the reason Bryan had sought out a woman like Roxie? The reason he'd been drawn to her?

That hurt. And Claire was already in a dark place. Her mother's words threatened to send her spiraling.

She needed to get out of the house. Even if it was dark outside. She'd use the flashlight on her phone and walk on the beach, although she probably wouldn't need the extra light. The houses along the shore usually provided enough, even if the moon wasn't bright.

But she had to walk and be near the water and hear the waves. It was the best way she could think of to soothe herself.

She put on some long leggings and a tunic-style sweatshirt that had a front pocket. Her phone went in there, although no one would be calling her. She slipped her feet into some laceless sneakers. There was nothing else she needed.

She went out the sliders and down the circular stairs, skirted the pool and followed the path through the dunes but went no further.

The breeze was cool but gentle, passing over her like a quiet caress. She almost felt like crying again, but even the thought of that exhausted her. She was so tired of crying. It accomplished nothing, except to make her eyes puffy and her nose red.

She took a few steps toward the water, giving her eyes a moment to adjust to the dark. Wasn't really that dark, just as she'd known it would be.

The moon was a fat slice in the sky and a few stars twinkled here and there. A beautiful night. A night very much the opposite of how she was feeling.

Was she boring? Dull? Hard to take in long stretches? Was that what Bryan had thought? Why he'd needed Roxie and Trina?

She sniffed and lifted her chin. Did boring people go for walks on the beach in the dark?

Maybe she should go back inside, fill the tub, pour herself a glass of wine, and do her best to ignore her mother's words.

Except...she couldn't. They might as well have been on a neon sign emblazoned in the sky.

Boring. That really was the kiss of death, wasn't it? Sure, there were worse ways to be described. Bryan was an adulterer and a bigamist, for example. Those were definitely worse. But those were adjectives that would never be applied to her.

For some reason, boring cut her deep. She sniffed again. "Get ahold of yourself, Claire," she whispered. "No more crying. Not over him. He doesn't deserve it."

If she'd been the one who'd had the heart attack, she knew full well that Bryan wouldn't have cried over her. If anything, he would have been relieved that his complicated life had just worked itself out.

She sighed and tipped her head back to look at the sky. She didn't want to be boring. But she didn't know how to change, either. She wasn't sure she could. What would she do differently?

She honestly didn't know. Which probably proved her mother right.

Her desire to walk the beach had left her like air leaving a punctured balloon. Now the only thing that sounded good was going back inside and going to bed. Which definitely meant she was boring. But she was too upset to care.

Coming to the beach house was supposed to be her path to healing. All it had done so far was make things worse, rubbing salt in her wounds and ruining the happy memories she'd once had of her husband.

Selling this place could not happen fast enough. Once she got the word from Charles, that was exactly what she was going to do. Let it be someone else's escape, because it sure wasn't hers.

She turned to walk back to the house and saw flickering light coming from the backyard of the house next door. The dune grasses made it hard to see exactly what was going on. Then the breeze shifted, and she smelled smoke. *Fire.*

That was Danny's house. Were he and his dad in trouble? Or maybe Danny wasn't home, meaning his dad might be alone. Panic sluiced through her, erasing all other thoughts. She raced toward his house and along the path that led between the dunes.

Only to find Danny sitting by a firepit with a beer in one hand.

She was panting slightly from the exertion.

He lifted the brown bottle. "Hi, there."

"Hi." She felt like an idiot. "I just saw the light from the fire and smelled smoke and I thought..." She frowned. She was about to sound like an idiot, too. "I thought your house was on fire."

He grinned like he was trying not to laugh. "And you came running up here to save me. That is highly commendable behavior. I like knowing I have a neighbor willing to risk their life for me. Thank you."

"Actually, I thought your dad might be alone and...never mind."

"You just missed him. He went up to bed."

"I'll meet him tomorrow night. I'm glad you're okay." She turned to go.

"Maybe you should sit and rest for a minute."

She stopped and faced him again. Was her lack of fitness that apparent? She really needed to do something about that. "Do I look like I need a rest?"

"Just saying that sort of effort deserves a drink. If you want one."

She didn't drink beer. It was so not her thing. Although it had been a long time since she'd tried one. Probably since...college? "I don't think I like beer."

He reached into the cooler beside him and picked up a bottle. "This is ginger beer. Have you ever tried it?"

She shook her head as she took a few steps closer. His backyard and the area under his house was beautiful. It was clear he lived here full-time and took great pride in his space. Whoever he'd paid to do this had done an outstanding job. "Is it alcoholic? Not that I'm opposed to that."

"Nope. Just crisp and sharp and a little spicy. You have to like ginger to enjoy it, which is probably easy to figure out, given that it's called ginger beer."

"I like ginger." Gingersnaps. Gingerbread. Ginger chicken. Those were all things she made on a regular basis, depending on the time of year.

He held the bottle out to her. "Then give it a try."

She came over and sat in the chair next to his. The warmth from the firepit felt nice. She took the bottle. "Do you have an opener?"

"Here, let me get that." He took the bottle back from her, twisted off the top with his bare hand, and returned it. "There you go."

She took a sip. "That is spicy. And gingery." She nodded. "I like it." Boring people probably did *not* drink ginger beer. It seemed like a very interesting beverage.

"Great." He leaned his bottle toward hers. "Thanks for being willing to save my life. And my dad's."

She laughed. "You're welcome." She clinked her bottle against his and they both drank. A little heat from the ginger built in the back of her throat, but it was pleasant and warm and she enjoyed it. She settled into the chair a bit more. "Do you sit out here a lot? It's really nice."

"Not as much as I'd like, except during the winter months when it's slower."

She twisted a bit to look over her shoulder and really take in his backyard. Lattice divided the front parking area from the part dedicated to leisure where they were now. His pool was tiled with bright blue tiles that look fresh and modern, the lights within slowly shifting through various colors, a sure sign that he'd upgraded to LEDs.

The whole area around the pool was tiled, too. Big terracotta squares that gave the space a much warmer feeling than the painted concrete at her place. There were string lights, large, comfortable pieces of furniture, an outdoor speaker system and television, a hammock, and lots of hanging plants.

"Your space out here is incredible. It's so much nicer than ours. Who did it?"

"I did. With some help from my dad."

She looked at him, incredulous. "You did all of this?"

He nodded and took a sip of his ginger beer. "Took me a while. Wasn't like I did it all in a week, but yes."

"I'm really impressed. It looks great. I never would have guessed you did all this."

"Wasn't that hard."

"I think you're underselling it."

He smiled. "Anything can be learned."

"I suppose that's true." Could she learn to be more interesting? That seemed a lot to ask. "I really like the lattice separating the parking area. Was that hard?"

He shook his head. "A few sheets of lattice, some reinforcing timbers and lag bolts to secure the panels into the concrete, and a gallon of stain. It's a weekend job."

"Maybe for you."

His slouched in his chair, his expression making him look very amused. "Are you asking me to put up some lattice panels at your place?"

She blinked. "No! I was just admiring them and —no, I didn't mean to imply that at all."

He seemed disappointed. "Oh. Well, I could. If you wanted."

She intended to sell the place, not spend more money on it. But maybe a thing like that would help it sell? "That's nice of you. I really appreciate the offer, but I don't think it's something I should do right now."

"Well, if you change your mind, let me know."

"I will. Listen, there's something you need to know, since you're coming to dinner." Claire had been dreading telling anyone, but there was no way she could have Danny over to her house without explaining the presence of Roxie and her family.

"What's that?"

Claire took a breath. "Unbeknownst to me, my husband, the one who just passed away, had a second family. Another wife and another child. And as it happens, they're also at the beach house right now, along with the wife's mother. They're coming to dinner, so I figured I should tell you." She explained how they'd come to remember good times, just like Margo and her daughter had.

His eyes widened. "I can't imagine how you're

coping with a bombshell like that. You must have been knocked for a loop."

"You can say that again. It's part of why I've been in such a strange place. It's a lot to deal with."

"It's more than anyone should have to deal with. How are you—" His pocket buzzed. He set his ginger beer down and pulled out his phone. He glanced at the screen and sighed. "I'm sorry, I have to go. One of the poppers at the store broke down. I need to run over there and see if I can get it going again." He looked over at her. "This is why I don't get to sit out here as often as I'd like to, but it was nice having company. I'd like to do it again sometime."

She nodded. "So would I."

They stood at the same time, putting them nearly face to face, just inches away from each other. She moved to let him by just as he moved to give her the same opportunity, but they both went in the same direction.

They laughed and the lightness of the moment emboldened her, as had his compassionate reaction to her news about Bryan's infidelity. She took a breath. "I know you have to go but could I ask you a question?"

He nodded. "Of course."

"Do you think I'm boring?"

His brows bent. "Boring? I wouldn't say that. Although I don't think I know you well enough yet to be an expert."

That felt like him trying to spare her feelings, which was nice. But not the answer she was looking for. She did *not* want to be boring.

So she leaned in and kissed him.

Chapter Thirty-two

*R*oxie stared in amazement at Margo and her unexpected declaration. She looked like she meant it, too.

"Please," Margo said. Her hands were clenched as she spoke to Willie. "I know you don't like me, and you think I'm an awful person. I'm sorry I'm who I am. I mean it. That's why I'm here. I want to change. I can't live like this anymore."

Willie's mouth gaped. "I don't think you're an awful person. Maybe not the easiest to be around, but you're not awful. And I like you just fine. But I do think you've let your grief get the best of you."

A shuddery sigh of agreement slipped from Margo's lips. "I know I have. But I don't know how to get out from under it."

Roxie got up and pointed at the spot she'd just vacated. "Sit."

Margo seemed like she might refuse, then she nodded. "Thank you."

Roxie took a few steps toward the kitchen. "You want something to drink?"

Willie held up her finger. "Gin and tonic. I need the strength."

Under normal circumstances, Roxie would have rolled her eyes. These were not normal circumstances. "Margo, would you like one?"

Again, she sort of hesitated. "Okay, yes. Thank you."

Roxie went into the kitchen, took out two old-fashioned glasses, filled them with ice, then got the gin from the upper cabinet where they kept a few bottles of spirits for certain occasions. Like when the uptight matriarch of your late husband's secret second family came for a visit.

She added a splash of gin in each before topping them off with tonic and a wedge of lime from the fridge.

She carried the drinks over, handing one to each woman, then she went back to the fridge for a Diet Coke for herself. Caffeine didn't really affect her, unless she hadn't had enough of it. Too many pots of coffee guzzled on too many overnight shifts at the hospital.

She rejoined them, grabbing the remote so she could turn the volume down, and sitting in the chair on the other side of the couch, giving them plenty of space to chat. She wasn't about to miss a second of this.

Willie lifted her glass. "Bottoms up."

Margo took a small sip.

Willie did better than a sip. She swallowed the mouthful she'd taken and set her glass on the side table. "Do you think you've ever been happy in your life?"

Margo got a faraway look in her eyes. "Yes. When I was married to Mitchell." She smiled. Actually smiled. "Mitch and I were so in love. Poor as church mice but that didn't matter, because we had each other. We lived in a one-room apartment three flights up. Claire slept in a dresser drawer for the first six months of her life. We moved right around then, because he got a promotion and a nice raise a couple months after she was born. He worked at a research center. He was incredibly intelligent. A mind like you wouldn't believe."

Willie grinned and nodded. "So you were happy even though you didn't have much."

"Yes," Margo agreed, her gaze still sparkling with the joy of her memories.

"Now you have a lot but happiness is no longer a part of your life."

The sparkle disappeared. "No, it isn't. And I don't know how to get that happiness back. I don't even think I know how to feel that way anymore."

"Of course you do and you can," Willie said. "And you will. If you want to. You can do anything you put your mind to. Including overcoming grief and reclaiming your ability to be happy."

Margo slumped back against the sofa as though a thousand pounds of weight had just been dropped on her. "Not like this. It's too much. Whatever space I had for happiness has been taken over by grief."

"Have you tried therapy? Or counseling?" Willie asked.

"No." Margo picked up her gin and tonic and took another sip.

"Why not?" Willie asked. "I thought rich people were really into that."

Margo made a face. "I'm not rich. I'm comfortable."

"Call it whatever you want, but you've got money," Willie said. "More than I've got, so that makes you rich in my book. Back to therapy. Why haven't you done it?"

Margo studied the slice of lime in her drink. "Not sure I believe in it."

Willie made a little noise. "Not buying that. I'm guessing it's more like you're worried what people might think if they found out. Is that it?"

Margo let out a sigh that sounded like agreement.

Roxie smiled. Willie was so sharp. The only people she couldn't read with such clarity were men she was in love with. It was her tragic flaw.

Willie wasn't done. "What about a group session? Maybe that would be an easier way to start. You could just go and listen the first time so you could see how it works and what people talk about. That's what I did."

Margo's head came up. "You went to therapy?"

"Sure. After the death of my Ronnie. I told you about him. Losing him just about broke me, but grief counseling helped a lot. And it was free at the church. They had a group there. They have one here, too, at the Presbyterian church."

"How do you know that?" Margo asked.

"Because I still go once in a while," Willie said. "Whenever I get low or a little too much in my own head. Keeps me in a good place."

Margo shook her head. "I don't know."

"I'll go with you," Willie said.

"You would?"

"Sure."

Margo did nothing for a moment, then she gave a little nod. "Okay."

Willie drank more of her gin and tonic. "I'll find out when the next one is and let you know. In the meantime, what kind of activities do you like?"

Margo's blank expression prompted Willie to elaborate. "You know, what do you do with your day? I already know you don't hate shopping. But what else?"

"I usually just watch TV or read."

"So you keep to yourself. You isolate yourself in your own world." Willie gestured as she spoke, using her hands to add emphasis. "Nothing wrong with those things, mind you, but if that's all you do, it's not healthy. Not with everything you're dealing with. You need to get out more and interact with people."

"I don't like people."

"You like people just fine. What you don't like is the thought of starting to care about someone and then losing them."

Roxie shook her head, amazed by her mother's understanding of what was going on.

"Maybe," Margo said.

"If you like to read, why not join a book club? Then you can read and have people to discuss the book with. Two birds with one stone and all that. The library might even have a group."

"I'm not sure."

Willie rolled her eyes. "Do you want help or don't you?"

"I do." Margo frowned but it seemed aimed at herself. "Okay, I'll find out if the library has a group."

"Changing isn't easy. If you thought it would be, you need to rethink." Willie swirled her glass to move the ice around. "And if you're not willing to do the work, to put yourself out there, change will never come."

"I understand that. I really do," Margo said. "But it's hard to do things that are so outside of my comfort zone."

"The more you do them, the easier they'll get." Willie grinned. "Which is why your schedule is about to get full."

Margo looked slightly terrified. "Meaning?"

"Meaning I'm now in charge of your social calendar." Willie glanced at Roxie. "Get an extra ticket for that play at the seniors center."

Roxie nodded. "Will do."

Willie wiggled a finger at Margo. "Give my daughter fifteen dollars for your ticket."

"For a play at the seniors center?" Margo made a face. "It had better be starring George Clooney for that kind of money."

Willie cut her eyes at Margo. "Another thing—happiness doesn't come from that kind of attitude. Every time I hear you complain about something, you owe me a dollar." She stuck her hand out. "Starting now."

Margo pursed her lips. "What? That's the most ridiculous thing I've ever heard."

"And now," Willie said. "You owe me two."

Chapter Thirty-three

*K*at couldn't believe it. She stared at the little trophy. Trina and Aunt Jules had picked the wrong time to go to the bathroom. They'd both had to go and Aunt Jules thought Toby should try again. "Are you sure about that?"

Alex laughed. "Yes, you really did win third place."

"I don't know how. There were a lot of other entries that looked better than ours."

"You had height, though," Alex said. "That really won the judges over."

Kat glanced back at the castle she and Trina had made. Thanks to Trina, the center turret was remarkably tall. Probably two feet or more. And because the castle was already built on a mound of sand, it looked even more impressive. "That was all

Trina's doing. I really don't know how she did it, either."

Kat brushed the sand off her hands, although she was covered with it and probably wouldn't feel completely clean until she could shower. She took the trophy, hoping her fingers would touch his again, but they didn't. "I'm giving this to her when she gets back."

Alex smiled. "Well, you did also get a consolation prize."

"I did?"

He nodded. "Dinner with me."

She wasn't quite ready to smile back at him. She crossed her arms as best she could while holding the trophy. "So you're saying I'm a loser then?"

He shook his head, obviously amused. "Not to sound full of myself but seems more like a win to me."

He was right, it was. He was a handsome fire-fighter, and he was offering to buy her dinner. And Ray had given her the green light to date other people. She no longer had a reason to turn Alex down.

Trina returned. Kat, happy for the distraction, held up the trophy. "We got third place!"

"What? No kidding! That's awesome!" Trina

pumped her fist into the air. "I can't wait to tell Mimi."

"Here," Kat said as she put the trophy into Trina's hands. "You earned this."

"I did?" Trina clutched the little gold statue. "Thanks."

"You're welcome." Kat gestured to Alex. "He brought it over."

"That was nice of you," Trina said. "Nice of you to get us water during the contest, too."

"That's what firemen do." He pointed to their sandcastle. "I understand you were responsible for that impressive center turret."

Trina grinned. "Yeah, go big or go home, you know?"

Alex nodded. "Love that. Totally agree."

She smiled at Kat. "I didn't want to let my sister down, either."

"That's right, you're sisters. I'd forgotten that."

"Half," Kat corrected. She hadn't explained that to him earlier. "We share a father. Or we did. He's...passed on."

Alex's smile disappeared. "I'm sorry to hear that."

"Thanks."

He shifted slightly. "Look, if this is a bad time for dinner..."

"No," Kat said. "I'd like to go." She'd never know if Ray was the right guy for her if she didn't at least see how dinner with Alex made her feel. As weird as it would be to date someone else.

"Okay. What night is good for you?"

"Not tomorrow. We have a family dinner thing. Night after that?"

"I can do that. Pick you up at six?"

She hesitated. He already knew where she lived. He'd seen the house from the beach.

"Or if you want to just meet me—"

"That might be better."

"Flying Fish okay?"

She nodded. "Sure. That was my dad's favorite place. Lots of happy memories there."

His smile returned. "Maybe we can add a new one."

Someone called his name. He glanced toward the sound. "I'd better go. I'm on the cleanup committee. Flying Fish at six, two nights from now."

"Right."

He took off.

Trina's arm was suddenly touching hers. "He's hot. Like, without even trying."

Kat's eyes were still on him. "Yeah, I know. It's a little scary."

"Why?"

"Because I have no idea what I'm doing with a guy like that. Ray is so...he's just not..."

"I know exactly what you mean."

Kat looked at her. "You do?"

"Sure. You don't feel like you're up to Alex's level. Whereas Ray is a known quality."

"Quantity. But yeah, that's it." That was exactly what Kat was feeling. Ray was comfortable. Alex was...exciting.

Trina continued. "You are, you know. Up to Alex's level. Even if you don't realize it. But you're also in your own way."

"What does that mean?"

Trina shrugged as her gaze ran over Kat. "You look all right tonight, considering the activity, but for a date, you need to bring it. You need to make the most of your assets and not be afraid to let them shine."

"I have no idea what you're talking about."

Trina laughed. "I know. I can help you, if you want. Give you a little makeover."

Kat had visions of being dressed in head-to-toe leopard print. "I don't know."

"Nothing crazy, I promise. But you could use a little more makeup and if I'm being super honest, your hair is too heavy at the bottom. It's dragging you down. Some face-framing layers would work wonders. They'd give your hair body and movement and add cheekbones."

"A haircut can give me cheekbones?" Kat was sure she looked skeptical, because she was.

"You *have* cheekbones. They're just not being highlighted because of all that hair. Shaping up those eyebrows wouldn't hurt, either."

Did she need a makeover? Kat didn't think so. But then again, if she was going out with a guy like Alex, maybe a little something extra wouldn't hurt. "Could you show me a picture of what you're talking about with the hair?"

"Sure."

"Okay. Maybe if I can see a picture."

Aunt Jules came back with Toby. "Was that Alex? And is that a trophy?"

Trina lifted the little gold statue. "Yes and yes! Isn't he hot? And can you believe we got third place? I'm so stoked."

"That's great." Aunt Jules looked toward Alex. "So what's the deal with him?"

Kat shrugged. "We're going out to dinner the night after tomorrow."

"You are?" Aunt Jules sucked in a breath, her eyes

twinkling in the light of the tiki torches. "Wow. Good for you."

"I'm going to give her a makeover," Trina volunteered.

"Maybe," Kat said.

Aunt Jules smiled. "Go for it. You could use a change. And it's only hair. It grows back."

"Not in one night it doesn't," Kat countered. "Do you really think I need a new look?"

"It couldn't hurt," Aunt Jules said. "You're a beautiful woman but you don't make the most of what you have."

Trina nodded. "That's exactly what I was saying. See?" She poked Kat in the arm.

"All right, I get it," Kat said. "I need an update. I told you I would, I just want to see pictures."

Trina tapped away at her phone for a couple of seconds, then held the screen out for Kat to see. "Like this."

Kat blinked at the image before her. She almost said wow, but then realized the haircut looked so good on that woman because the woman was a model and naturally beautiful. She focused on just the hair. "That would be all right."

Aunt Jules leaned in. "That would look great on you. It would change your whole face."

Kat looked at her. "You think so?"

Aunt Jules nodded. "So long as you did something with those eyebrows."

Trina went smug. "I did mention that."

"What's wrong with my eyebrows?" Kat huffed out a little breath. "I thought natural was in."

Aunt Jules pursed her lips. "They need some refining."

Trina snorted. "She's right, they do. A little shaping would fix them right up. Nothing wrong with the natural look, but..."

Kat gave up. "Fine, make me over. But I draw the line at glitter."

Chapter Thirty-four

Jules wasn't exactly nervous about having breakfast with Jesse, but she also wasn't completely calm. It wasn't because of the coffee she'd had at the house, either. She'd only had one cup and she could drink half a pot in a day without side-effects.

Realizing that he'd only seen her in shorts so far, she'd chosen an outfit that reflected her true style. Her favorite dark-washed jeans, a long-sleeve top in teal with a long, lightweight Aztec-print cardigan over it in tan, rust, and deep turquoise. She'd accessorized with some of her favorite turquoise and silver jewelry. Her shoes were brown ankle boots that she'd picked up on a tour through the Southwest.

If she didn't love the beach so much, she could have easily lived in that part of the country. Maybe she should buy a place out there. Like Sedona. Spend the hottest months of the summer there. But to really feel comfortable about affording something like that, she'd need her next album to do well.

And she was so stuck creatively, she wasn't currently sure there would *be* a next album.

She parked her Jeep in the Digger's Diner lot and looked around. She had no idea what kind of car Jesse drove, but she was early, and he probably wasn't here yet.

That was all right. She'd go in and get a seat, then he could join her when he arrived. She got out, locked the car, and went inside.

Jesse waved to her from a booth at the far end.

She smiled and went to join him. "I didn't expect to see you."

"I had a feeling you were the kind who showed up early, so I got here sooner than I normally would. Do I get points for that?"

She laughed as she slid into her side of the booth. "Yes."

"You look great."

"Thanks. So do you." She wasn't just saying it. Jeans and a soft heathered sweater looked good on him.

A middle-aged woman in a Digger's Diner polo shirt and khaki pants came by with a pot of coffee.

Jules and Jesse both flipped their cups over, indicating they wanted some. The server filled the cups. "I'm Betsy. I'll be right back with menus and creamer."

She was, returning just moments later with a small metal pitcher of cream and two menus. "Special today is strawberry pancakes. Comes with bacon, sausage, or ham. I'll give you a minute."

As Betsy left, Jules perused the menu. "It's been a while since I've eaten here."

"It's all good, I promise. I eat here way more than I should."

She looked at him over the top of her menu. "Does that mean you don't cook?"

"It means they're open until two a.m., and I tend not to have time to eat when I'm at the club, so even though we have a full kitchen, on most nights, I have my dinner here before I head home."

"How are you not..." She looked at him and at his body. She still wasn't sure how old he was, but he was definitely younger than her. "I mean, you're in decent shape for someone who eats that late."

He grinned. "I run, I work out, and I try not to overdo it on the carbs or alcohol."

The more he talked, the better he was. She nodded. "That's a smart way to live."

"It's the only way to live. I work too hard not to stay healthy. You're not exactly in bad shape yourself."

"It's kind of the same thing for me. Being in the public eye makes me pretty aware of what I look like. And getting older means working even harder."

"You look great. And I don't mean just for your age. You look phenomenal, period, dot, end of sentence."

Hard not to smile at a comment like that. "Thank you. That's very kind."

"Just being truthful."

She lifted her coffee cup. "You might be a tiny bit biased, though."

He put his menu down. "Guilty as charged. I'm already a fan, so yes, I am biased. Is that so bad?"

She swallowed the sip she'd taken, then shook her head. "No, it's not." She went back to the menu for a moment, finding something that looked good and healthy, then set it down on the table. "How did you end up with the Dolphin Club? I know you're not the original owner. It's been around too long."

"I was in a bad motorcycle accident when I was in my late twenties. I'm fully recovered now, but I'll never get on a bike again, I can tell you that much. Anyway, I ended up with a pretty big settlement because of the accident and since I didn't know what to do with the money, I let my dad help me invest it."

"Smart. Uncommonly so, maybe."

"Probably. But I was also on a lot of painkillers and had enough sense to realize that my dad was in better shape to handle the money than I was at the time. Another ten years roll by and the Dolphin Club comes up for sale. It was a wreck, to be honest. Rundown, bad rep, not much in the way of regular income, but I've always loved music and always thought this area could use a real, honest venue."

"So you bought it."

He nodded. "And fixed it up. Then I spent another insane chunk of money booking some quality acts to bring people through the doors and help rebuild the club's reputation."

"It worked."

He smiled. "I'm really grateful, too. Otherwise, I'd probably be living over my parents' garage."

She laughed. "Good for you. You took a risk, and it paid off."

He seemed to be staring directly into her soul when he answered. "Yes, I did."

Their server came back. "Are you ready to order?"

They both nodded. Jules went first. "I'll have the bacon and avocado omelet with tomato slices and fruit."

Betsy jotted that down. "White, wheat, rye or a biscuit?"

"None, thanks." She slid her menu to the end of the table.

Jesse did the same with his. "Steak and eggs. Medium rare and over-easy. No bread for me, either."

Betsy picked up the menus. "You got it."

He leaned toward Jules. "Do you always order that way?"

She shook her head. "Pretty much. That's just how I eat."

He sat back and nodded. "Is it too forward of me to ask what you're working on? I don't want to turn into some raving fan, more than I already have, but I've told you how I feel about your music."

She smiled and played with the spoon on her saucer. "I don't like to talk about current projects much. Feels like it steals some of the magic, especially if they turn out differently than expected. I hope that makes sense."

"Sure." He didn't look bothered. "I would never want to interfere with the creative process. I've been around enough musicians to know that they each have their own way of doing things and it's no one's business but theirs."

"That's about right." She felt bad, because she wasn't usually that secretive about her work, but her creative block meant she really had nothing to talk about and the last thing she wanted to put out into the universe was that she was stuck.

She doubted Jesse would share that kind of information, but then again, she really didn't know him. And he was undoubtedly better connected in the music industry than the average person on the street.

It just wasn't a good idea to share the reality of what was going on with her music.

"You have a sister? I think you said you were staying with her?"

"That's right," Jules said. She was pleased with the change of topic. "Her husband recently passed away and she wanted to come to their beach house one last time before she puts it up for sale."

"I'm sorry to hear that. Especially about your brother-in-law but also that you won't have a place to stay around here anymore."

She toyed with her spoon again. "I'm sorry about that part, too. I've been coming to Diamond Beach with them since he bought that house. It'll be strange not to come here." She hadn't really thought about that until now. It made her sad.

Betsy refilled their coffees, then brought their food over and they dug in, the conversation shifting to how good it was, then favorite meals they'd had, and, eventually, Jesse brought up a new request. "How about you swing by the club sometime and share dinner with me?"

"You just told me you never have time to eat when you're at work."

He laughed. "True, but for you, I'd make time. So long as it's not on a major performance night."

"I'll think about it. It's been ages since I've been in there. I would love to see what you've done to the place."

"I would be happy to give you a tour. If you decide to come."

"Thanks." She changed the subject. "How did Mike and Liz do at the sandcastle contest, by the way?"

He groaned. "Don't ask."

"Why?"

He shook his head. "Because ten minutes before

time was up, Shiloh ran through their site and destroyed their work. I promised them tickets to the club for whatever show they wanted to see next."

She laughed. "Oh, no—that's awful!"

"I love that dog, but she's a handful." He sighed, chuckling softly. "I wouldn't change her for the world, though. I mean, nobody's perfect, right?"

"That's for sure." How could she not want to spend more time with a guy like that? Jules was still grinning when she nodded. "Okay, I've decided. I'll come to the club and have dinner with you."

Chapter Thirty-five

Claire returned from her brisk walk on the beach to find that Trina and her mother had turned Margo's bathroom into a hair salon. She could see through the door that opened onto the living room that her mother was wearing a cape and sitting on a kitchen counter stool in front of the mirror, while Trina had a smock on and was mixing things in a black plastic bowl with what looked like a hot pink paintbrush.

Kat was sitting on the sofa, drinking a cup of coffee and watching through the open door like it was a new episode of her favorite show.

Claire turned to her daughter. "What's going on here?"

"Grandma's getting highlights, then I'm next."

"You're getting highlights?" Claire wasn't sure

she'd heard right. Kat wasn't the high-maintenance sort.

"And face-framing layers. And my eyebrows shaped."

Claire frowned. "I've been trying to get you to do your brows for years."

"Well, I'm doing it now."

Claire felt like she'd walked into the wrong house. She gestured with her thumb toward the bathroom but did it in front of her body so neither Trina nor her mother could see. She kept her voice down. "How did that come about?"

Kat shrugged. "She offered. Grandma took her up on it."

Claire shook her head at the strange and out-of-character behavior. Trina was the last person she'd have thought would be allowed to touch her mother's hair. "I haven't had enough coffee for this."

"There's half a pot left. I can make more if you want."

"I can do it when I'm ready. I need to shower before I eat anyway." Claire poured a mug full, added some sweetener and a splash of half and half, then took the cup into the bathroom with her, closing the bedroom door as she went.

She had worked up a good sweat during her two-mile hike, which had been the idea. Leisurely walks were all well and good, but she needed to burn some calories and work her muscles a little more. The sand was perfect for that when she walked with purpose.

She set the coffee on the bathroom counter, then stripped out of her walking attire and took a long look at herself in the mirror. Her body was not the body it had once been. There was more of her than there should be. The firm places had gone lax. There were stretch marks. And cellulite.

Some of those things were out of her control, but some of them she could have prevented. Or at least lessened. But she'd spent so much of her life caring for others and putting their needs before her own that she'd come last in her own life.

Bryan was gone, Kat was grown, and Claire's mother was more than capable of looking after herself, obviously.

There were no more excuses for not treating herself better. Today's walk was the start of that. Of putting herself first. Or at least as close to first as she could. That was going to take some practice.

She deserved a stronger body, better health, and all the self-care she could manage. The sacrifice of her time hadn't earned her the loyalty of her husband, had it?

With a sigh, she went out to get clothes to change into. The box of Guilford's rum truffles on the night-stand caught her eye.

If left to abandon, she could easily polish off half that box in a sitting. Which meant those needed to go. She couldn't allow herself to be upset by the state of her physical fitness and yet still indulge in food she knew wasn't good for her.

That was self-sabotage and would only lead to her feeling bad. She had to make herself a priority for once in her life.

Or Danny wouldn't want to kiss her again. No man would. And while she didn't really care much about having another man in her life, Danny wasn't just any man now. He was the first one in a long time to show her true friendship and generosity.

She closed her eyes and sank down onto the edge of the bed. She could still feel his mouth on hers and taste the ginger beer on his lips. He'd been warm and willing, and not nearly as shocked by her actions as she'd been.

He could have pushed her away or broken the kiss off immediately, but he hadn't. He'd kissed her back, his hands gently on her shoulders.

And he hadn't once asked what she'd been thinking. She'd asked herself that plenty of times since last night, though.

He had, however, commented after the kiss that he no longer thought there was any chance she was boring.

She smiled and lifted her head, staring at the back of the bedroom door but seeing Danny. Last night, she'd been thinking that she needed to do something for herself. Something to prove she wasn't boring, a word that had sent her reeling with self-doubt and pity.

And boy, had she ever proved that word wrong. Boring women didn't just kiss strange men out of the blue, did they?

Except Danny wasn't exactly a strange man. He was her very attractive, very kind, super-generous single neighbor. He was a widower who understood what she was going through and knew how to offer quiet, understanding support just by being there.

He was amazing, actually.

She exhaled, the memory of last night making her warmer than she'd already been.

A new thought occurred to her. One almost as crazy as what she'd done last night. She went into the bathroom, took a long drink of her coffee, pulled her robe on, then went back out to the living room and straight to her mother's bathroom.

Her mother now had foils in her hair and looked a little like a space station antennae.

Claire leaned in. "Trina?"

"Yes?" She glanced over, pausing with the bowl of what must be bleach in one hand and the hot pink paintbrush in the other.

"Do you have time for me, too? I'll be happy to pay for your supplies."

"Really? What do you want done?"

Claire nodded before she lost her nerve. "Yes, really. I want to look...younger. More alive. More modern or current or whatever you call it. Anything you think I need to make that happen, I'm willing to let you do it."

Trina's eyes lit up. "Heck, yes. I can totally do that. It would be a drastic change. Your hairstyle right now is aging you, but that's easy to take care of. As for the rest, are you open to color?"

Claire hesitated. "You mean like pink?"

Trina laughed. "No, I mean going darker. The blond works well to hide the gray but it completely washes you out. A rich caramel brown with honey highlights would make your eyes pop."

Claire gave it a second of thought. She liked the

idea of her eyes being more of a feature. She'd always thought they were nice. "I was sort of that color when I was a kid."

Trina went back to painting bleach onto Margo's hair. "Your childhood color is usually a pretty good indicator of what works best for you."

Claire took a breath. "Let's do it."

"I'll have to run to the beauty supply store again, but that's no big deal. We'll do it early this afternoon, okay? You'll be all done well before the dinner tonight."

"Okay." Claire smiled. She loved the idea of being able to debut her new look at tonight's gathering. She hoped she liked it.

Even more, she hoped Danny liked it.

Chapter Thirty-six

Margo stood in the bedroom, examining the work Trina had done. It was, in a word, astonishing. Margo had expected to be underwhelmed, but that wasn't the case at all. Trina was good. She was better than good; she was gifted.

The highlights she'd added, especially around Margo's face, really had brightened her up. Trina had given her a little trim, too, and done something called texturizing. There hadn't been a whole lot of hair on the floor when Trina had finished, but the shape of Margo's hair was different now in a subtle way that made the cut seem more natural and care-free instead of planned.

Her whole face looked lifted. Her eyes more noticeable. Her cheekbones defined in a way no blush had ever accomplished. Somehow with a few snips and a little color, Trina had made Margo look more like herself than she had in years.

She smiled at her own reflection, something that hadn't come easy in a very long time. She looked like the woman she'd been when happiness had still been a part of her life.

It was high time to find her way back to that person.

She'd changed into white pants, a flowy blue and white top, and white sandals. She slicked on a bright coral lip, then grabbed her purse and dug into her wallet for money. She found a fifty, folded it, and kept it in her hand.

She put her purse strap on her shoulder and went into the bathroom. Trina was in the midst of working on Kat's hair. Highlights again, and a more drastic cut this time.

Margo pressed the fifty into Trina's hand. "I love everything you did. I'm sorry I underestimated you. You're a very talented young woman."

Trina glanced down at the money in her hand, her mouth coming open. "Thank you, but I didn't expect—"

"I know you didn't. But you more than earned it." Margo patted Kat's caped shoulder. "You're going to be amazed when she's done."

From there, she went back into the bedroom and out through that door and into the kitchen. Claire was at the counter, making up a shopping list for the dinner she was throwing later.

Margo paused. "Do you think it would be all right if I used the car?" She'd ridden with Jules, while Claire and Kat had come together. Ray had come separately, since he'd only been able to stay for the weekend.

Claire looked up. "I don't think Kat would mind, but Jules is back."

"She is? I didn't hear her."

"She took Toby out, then she was going to sit by the pool and write." Claire smiled. "Your hair looks amazing." She lowered her voice. "I can't believe Trina did that."

"I feel the same way." Margo nodded. "I am very pleased." She pulled out her phone. "I'll text Jules about the car. I know you have to go to the store, and I don't know how long I'll be gone." She didn't love driving Jules's Jeep, but it was definitely a more fun car than Kat's sedan. And Margo was trying to be fun.

"Where are you going?"

"The library." Margo sent her younger daughter

a text. *Can I use your car? Need to run into town for a bit.*

Sure, came Jules's quick reply. *But I still have the keys on me. I'm by the pool.*

I'll come get them, Margo responded. She looked at Claire again. "Need me to pick anything up while I'm out?"

"No, thanks. I have to go out later anyway to get everything I need for the dinner."

"What are you making for dessert?"

Claire shrugged. "Nothing. We're just going to have that key lime pie Kat picked up from the bakery."

Margo made a face. "That's fine, but I'm a little surprised. You're an excellent baker, as good with sweets as Trina is with hair. And I thought you were trying to impress these people."

"I just haven't had it in me lately." Claire tapped the end of her pen on the counter. "But maybe this would be the perfect chance to see if I can find some joy in that again."

"Your lemon squares would be the perfect thing for a barbeque."

Claire smiled. "They are good."

Her daughter was being humble. "They're incredible. They won the church's bake-off two years in a row. It's the lemon zest in the shortbread crust. My mouth is watering just thinking about them."

Claire seemed undecided. "I guess I could make a pan of those."

Margo wasn't usually one to push, but since she was doing things differently, and Claire had been a bit lost since Bryan's death, a little push couldn't hurt. "Do it. Think about how nice it will be to hear that handsome man next door praise your work. You'll impress him."

"Mom, I'm not trying to—"

"I'm just saying it'll make you feel good to be appreciated." Margo wanted to be happy again, but she wanted that for her daughters, too.

"You're right. It would. Okay. I'll make them."

"Excellent. Now, I'm off. Text me if you want me to pick anything up."

"The only thing I could use is about half a dozen lemons."

"I'll get them." Margo gave her daughter a nod, then took the elevator straight down to the ground floor.

Jules was sitting on a chaise lounge by the pool, under an umbrella, a notebook and pen in her hands. Toby was sprawled on the pool deck, one ear flopped over his eyes. Jules looked up as Margo walked toward her. "Your hair! It looks fabulous. Those highlights are great."

"Thanks."

Jules dug the keys out of her purse. "Sorry. I should have left the keys on the dresser, but I didn't think about it."

"It's not a problem. I had to come down here anyway." Margo sat on the lounge next to Jules's and took the keys. "How was breakfast?"

Jules smiled, then quickly squashed it. "It was really nice."

"But?"

Jules shrugged. "We're going to have dinner sometime. At the Dolphin Club."

Margo frowned. "Then why am I still hearing a 'but' in there?"

Jules let out a long breath. "He's young, Mom. And he looks at me with stars in his eyes."

Margo laughed. "And that's a bad thing?"

"It might be." Jules frowned and stared at her notebook, which Margo could see was blank.

She stopped laughing. "What's wrong, sweetheart?"

Jules's lower lip trembled, and she sniffed. "I wish I knew." She sighed and tipped her head back, looking up into the umbrella. "I've lost my mojo,

Mom. Nothing I write is any good. And I'm supposed to be recording soon. People expect another album from me. I've been talking about it. And I've got *nothing.*"

Margo didn't need to hear the panic and suffering in her daughter's voice to realize how much Jules was hurting. It was written all over her. Jules was usually so good at hiding her real feelings. It was the performer in her. No matter what was going on in her real life, she could put on a smile, go out on stage, and give people their money's worth.

"Sweetheart, I'm sure it's not gone. You're just going through a dry spell, that's all. Happens to everyone, right? You'll get through this, I promise."

Jules shook her head. "I'm not sure."

"Bryan's death has upset us all. So has finding out he had a second family. Regardless of how you feel about it, it's still a stressor. That's bound to wreak havoc on your creative mind."

Jules made eye contact with Margo again. "This started long before Bryan died. I thought coming here would spark something. Be the inspiration I need. This place has never failed me before, but this time...nothing."

Margo did her best not to let her reaction show

on her face. "What's the longest you've gone before without writing anything new?"

Jules sighed. "Never. I've always been able to write. Now the only thing that comes out of my pen is dreck."

"I'm sure it's not that bad."

Jules gave her mother an argumentative look.

Margo held her hands up in surrender. "You know better about this than I do. I'm sorry you're going through it all the same. If there's anything I can do to help, just say the word."

"Thanks. I will." Jules sighed. "I do appreciate the offer. Thanks. And have fun."

"That's my plan." Margo leaned in, kissed her daughter on the cheek, and took the keys as she got to her feet.

"Oh, and Mom?"

"Yes?"

"Please don't say anything about this to anyone, okay? I really don't want it getting out. Not that I think you would, but please, keep it between us."

"Of course." It hurt Margo to see her daughter hurting. Not being able to do anything about it only made her feel worse, but Julia wasn't a quitter. She'd struggled through years of rejection in the early days of her career, and that struggle made her stronger and tougher and capable of withstanding all sorts of slings and arrows.

She would survive this. Margo knew that without hesitation. But as she walked to the car, she couldn't keep her mind from turning over all sorts of possibilities that might offer some help or inspiration. It was just a mother's way, she supposed.

She got in the car and drove into town, headed right to the library. She had a card. She kept one current so that she could get books when they came every July. She parked and went in, going up to the information desk.

The woman at the desk greeted her with a smile. "Hello. How can I help you?"

"Hi. I have two questions. First, I'd like to look at some books on finding creative inspiration or how to unlock it, that sort of thing."

The woman nodded. "I can direct you to those. What's the second question?"

"Do you have any book clubs or book discussion groups?"

"We have four, as a matter of fact. We have a historical group, a women's group, a bestsellers club and a children's book group."

"More than I expected. When do they meet? Not the children's group. I think I'll pass on that one."

The woman smiled and pulled a schedule from a rack of papers on the desk. "Here are all the library activities for this month. The historical group meets on Monday nights, the women's group on Wednesday afternoons, and the bestsellers group starts in about twenty minutes."

"Today?" Margo hadn't anticipated joining one immediately, but it was hard to resist with how good her hair looked. "Do you know what book they're discussing?" She read a lot of bestsellers.

The woman nodded. "*Last Sunset*, by George S. Mathers."

"How about that. I just finished that last week. Do you think it would be all right if I sat in?"

"Oh, sure. The more the merrier. Let me show you where those creative inspiration books are and I'll point out the book clubs' meeting room, too."

"Thanks."

Margo perused the creative inspiration books, choosing two that had the best reviews on Amazon when she'd looked them up on her phone. She checked them out, then went over to the meeting room to see about the book club. There was no one in the room yet, and she started to get cold feet.

Maybe another time would be better. Maybe no one was going to show up. As much as she loved reading and talking about books, she'd begun to think this was a silly idea. How was talking about a book going to help her be happier?

"Hi, there. Are you here for the book club?"

She turned to see a young woman with glasses and her black hair in two braids. She was in denim overalls with a tie-dyed T-shirt underneath and had what looked like an old army bag slung across her body. She had a nose ring and a tattoo of a cat on her wrist. Just the nose, ears, and whiskers.

Margo nodded. "I am. Is that okay?"

The woman smiled. "That's great." She stuck her hand out. "I'm Greta."

"Nice to meet you, Greta." Margo shook her hand. "I'm Margo."

"Wow, cool name. So main character, you know?"

Margo didn't know, but she smiled anyway. "Thank you. Do you, uh, run the book group?"

"No. Conrad Ballard runs it. He's nice, you'll like him. I've never met anyone who's read more books than he has. He's a writer, too."

"He is? Has he written anything I might have heard of?" The name sounded vaguely familiar.

Greta shrugged. "I don't know. Maybe. He writes for the *Gulf Gazette*. Do you read the paper?"

She nodded. "Yes, of course. I knew I'd heard the

name before." She was pretty sure he wrote the
Garden column and the Beach Report.

A few other people filtered in, an older man
among them. Greta waved at him. "Hi, Connie. We
have a new person!" She pointed at Margo.

Margo didn't know what she'd been expecting,
but it wasn't the man walking toward her. Conrad
looked like retired ex-military, with a cropped buzz
cut and the kind of lean, muscled form that meant
he still kept in shape.

He smiled and something turned over inside of
her. "Hello, there. Always nice to have new people
join our group."

He had the gravelly tone of a man who smoked
cigars and drank whiskey.

She nodded, feeling oddly light-headed. "Hello."

"Connie," Greta went on. "This is Margo. Isn't
that the best name?"

Conrad held Margo's gaze with a kind of
magnetic pull. "It's lovely. Nice to meet you, Margo."
He held his hand out.

She slipped hers into his grasp. His hand was
warm and calloused, his grip firm and self-assured.
Not at all like a man who sat behind a desk all day
working on a computer. She got ahold of herself as

he let her hand go. "I understand you write for the *Gazette*."

"That's right. I like to keep busy."

"You don't look like what I expected. For someone who writes the Garden column, that is."

His smile grew and his eyes glittered with amusement. "You know what they say, once a Marine, always a Marine. Even when it comes to flora and fauna."

She laughed. "I suppose so. It's nice to meet you, too."

"Have you read the book?"

She nodded. "I finished it last week. I sort of impulsively decided to join a book club and it just worked out that your group's meeting was about to start."

He looked at his watch. "We're about five minutes out. I just need to get our chairs situated and we'll be good to go. If you'll excuse me." He rubbed his hands together as he headed for the supply closet.

Margo watched him go. So this was book club. Willie had obviously known what she was talking about. Margo felt happier already.

Chapter Thirty-seven

Trina folded the last foil she'd just added to Kat's hair. "All right. Time to just hang out for a bit. I'll be right back, okay?"

Kat nodded, causing the foils to rustle against each other. She was scrolling through social media on her phone. "Okay."

Trina went downstairs and made herself an iced coffee with the good creamer. She took her time before coming back up. Kat would be processing for a while, although virgin hair like hers lifted fast. Trina knew she'd soon need to start checking it every few minutes.

She went back into the bathroom where Kat was sitting, now playing a game on her phone. "How are you doing?"

"Just fine," Kat said. "How long do you think I'll have to sit here? I'm not in a rush, just curious."

"I'll start checking at twenty minutes, then I'll be able to tell you a little more. It all depends on how fast your hair lifts to the right shade of blond."

"Sounds good." Kat tapped away at her screen. "You're the expert."

Trina grinned as she sipped her iced coffee. It was nice to be called that. Amazing how Trina and her family had changed their attitudes toward her recently. She wasn't sure what exactly had brought that about, but she was thrilled all the same. She'd known Margo had doubts from the second she'd sat down, but once Margo had seen the finished product, she'd become a believer.

Trina had exhaled in relief at that moment. There was always a chance Margo could have hated what she'd done, no matter how pretty it had turned out. She'd prayed that wouldn't happen and it hadn't. She really needed to get to church on Sunday and keep herself in good graces.

Kat's hair wasn't going to be nearly so tricky. It was long and untouched. A blank canvas, really. Trina wished every client was like that. Kat's hair would take the bleach nicely, then Kat would wash it, condition it, and add in the face-framing layers that would give Kat a real boost.

Trina would do her eyebrows, too. They had a

nice natural shape, but they were unplucked and a little out of control, even considering the current trend of full brows.

Working on Claire's hair would be harder. She already had blond highlights, and grays on top of that, which could be stubborn. But Trina wasn't too worried. She had a lot of confidence in her abilities and a lot of experience with all sorts of hair

Having Margo slip her a fifty had given Trina a pretty nice boost, too.

Not only was that totally unexpected, but it would definitely help cover the cost of the supplies she'd need for Claire. With a little left over. She thought a moment. Maybe she'd make a list of what she needed and have her mom pick the stuff up, since she was going out anyway. That made more sense. Then Trina could pay her back when she returned.

She sent her a mom a quick text to see if she was willing. She was, so Trina spent the next couple of minutes making up a list of supplies.

Twenty minutes slipped by and Trina opened one of the first foils she'd done on Kat and took a look at how the hair was processing. Not quite there. She refolded the foil and took a sip of her iced coffee. "Another ten minutes, maybe. Still very warm."

"Okay." Kat put her phone down to examine herself in the mirror.

Trina took the opportunity to have a little chat. "Why don't you invite Alex to come over for the barbeque tonight?"

Kat made a face into the mirror. "And introduce him to everyone? Yeah, no. I don't need him thinking I'm serious about him."

"But you agreed to go out with him."

Kat nodded. "Yes, but that doesn't mean anything's going to come of it. Plus, I don't need Ray finding out I had a guy over while he was gone. It's one thing to date somebody else. It's another thing to bring them here."

"So you think you'll get back together with Ray?"

"It's not like we're broken up now. We're just... figuring things out." Kat set her phone on the bathroom counter. "It's weird, I know, but how can I commit to forever with him when I don't know what's going on with my life. Or what I should be doing. Everything is such a question right now. And Alex seems nice, which I'm sure he is, but that doesn't mean I've suddenly stumbled onto Mr. Right. For all I know, that man is still Ray."

Trina leaned against the doorway. "Ray is nice. But your eyes light up when you look at Alex and they don't do that when you look at Ray."

Kat glanced over as best she could with a halo of foils impeding her view. "Trina, I know you mean well, but Ray and I have a long history. That's not something I can just throw away. I can't just end things with him."

"And I wouldn't want you to. But I do want you to be happy. Everyone deserves that." Trina had already said what she thought about Ray being awfully understanding and not pressing for the wedding. More understanding than she thought most guys would be. Was he really that nice? Or was he questioning their commitment to each other like Kat was?

Kat got a curious gleam in her eyes. "So why aren't you dating anyone?"

Trina shrugged. "No one's asked me lately."

"Have you ever seriously dated anyone? Been engaged? Been close?"

Trina went still for a minute, thinking about all her previous boyfriends. Then she shook her head. "Not really. I work a lot."

"So do I. So does everyone. That's not much of an excuse."

Trina frowned. "I don't know. I've dated a lot, but it never seems to turn into anything. Men don't really see me as a serious girlfriend, I guess."

Kat nodded like she understood. "Do you ever think it's because you dress like you're going to a costume party?"

Trina frowned. "I do not. I just have personality." What was it that Mimi always said? "And a unique sense of style."

"It's unique all right. And okay, you have personality. I'll give you that. But it might be too much style and personality for some guys. Like the kind who are looking toward their future."

Trina felt like she'd been cut to the bone. She shook her head and mumbled, "I don't think that's true."

Kat seemed to understand she'd hurt Trina's feelings. "Hey, listen, I'm sorry if that came out harsh. I didn't mean it that way. I really didn't. I just thought we were doing that whole honesty thing. The truth is, you're really pretty, you're upbeat, which is a great quality, and you're about the nicest person I've ever met. But I think that gets lost sometimes behind all the leopard and the glitter and the eyelashes."

Trina swallowed but said nothing.

"I'm serious," Kat went on. "I know you're a hairdresser and there's a lot of look going on in most salons, but you don't need all of that stuff to shine outside of the salon. You'd light up a room even in a burlap sack."

Trina smiled a little. That was a nice thing to say. "Yeah?"

"Yeah. You're really happy and bubbly and that's enough on its own."

Trina felt better. "Thanks."

Kat nodded. "How about I see if Alex has a friend that could double-date with us? And then you let me help you with an outfit. Which is only fair, since you're giving me a makeover."

Trina grimaced. "Are you trying to put me in khakis?"

Kat laughed. "No, I swear. Just a toned down, more accessible version of you."

Trina took a deep breath. "Accessible?" She wasn't sure she liked the sound of that.

"Come on," Kat said. She pointed to the foils on her head. "Look what I'm letting you do to me."

Trina let out a little chuckle. "Yeah, all right. It's a deal. But no khakis. And I'm not wearing sneakers. Unless they're cute and sparkly."

"Do you even own normal sneakers?"

"Sure, for the gym." But even they were hot pink.

"Do you really think Alex might have a friend for me?"

"Why not?" Kat said. "He knows you're cute. He should be able to get you a date no problem. I'll text him right now." She grabbed her phone.

"That would be awesome." Trina checked a different foil. "Almost there. Five more minutes maybe."

"Okay." Kat bent over her phone, typing away.

Trina hadn't loved what Kat had said about the way she dressed, but she'd been blunt with Kat about a few things herself, so if she was going to dish it out, she had to be able to take it. Fair was fair. That was kind of what sisters did, right? Be brutally honest with each other? That made Trina smile.

But not as much as the thought of double-dating with Kat and Alex.

Although what would a guy think of her if he met her wearing an outfit Kat had put together? He might think Trina dressed like that all the time. He'd get the wrong idea about her for sure.

Trina wondered if she should hide a few emergency accessories in her purse. A leopard scarf, hot pink lipstick, and some bright tassel earrings might be just the way to rescue a Kat outfit.

Chapter Thirty-eight

illie loved her lilac hair so much she decided to take a new selfie. That required a little work. First, she had to pick out the right outfit. To compliment the gorgeous lavender of her hair, she chose a sparkly purple top with cutout on the shoulders. A little skin never hurt.

Then she did her makeup, her eyes in more shades of purple but with a little glitter. She did a nice black eyeliner on the top lid and added a pair of the magnetic eyelashes Trina had given her for Christmas.

Trina had taught her how to use them, too. They were so easy. Just swipe on the special eyeliner, let it dry, then the lashes stuck to the liner with the tiny magnets attached to them. So clever! Trina knew all the tricks.

Willie finished putting herself together, then

decided to take advantage of her location and do the picture outside. She went down the elevator to the ground floor and looked around. The pool would make a nice backdrop, but so would the beach. The problem with the beach was it was windy and while Trina had sprayed Willie's hair into place, the wind might still mess up the loose pieces around her face.

The pool it was. She went over to find the right angle. Jules was sitting under one of the umbrellas, staring at a notebook propped on her knees.

She looked up. "Hi."

"Hi, there. I didn't mean to bother you. I just wanted to get a picture of my new hair."

Jules smiled. "Did Trina do that for you?"

Willie nodded. She wasn't sure what the younger woman would think. Probably that it was silly. Not that Willie gave a fig.

Jules shook her head. "She is so talented. You look fabulous."

"You think so?"

"I do." Jules rested her hands on her notebook. "You must be so proud of your granddaughter."

"I am," Willie said. She was touched by Jules's kind comments. "She's a real blessing in my life."

Jules pointed to Willie's camera. "Do you want me to take your picture for you?"

"That's so kind of you to offer. I'd love that. My daughter went to the store to get what she needs to make the beans for tonight, otherwise I would have asked her."

Jules got up. "No problem. I'll even teach you a little trick I learned at a photoshoot years ago. When you smile, press your tongue to the roof of your mouth. It lifts your whole face."

"Really?" Willie had never heard that. "I might just start walking around that way."

Jules laughed as Willie handed her the phone. "Yep."

"What did you do a photoshoot for?"

"I was having some new headshots done for publicity purposes. I'm a musician and a singer."

"You are?" Willie loved music. "I had no idea. What kind of music do you do?"

"Mostly a folksy kind that's a little rock-n-roll, a little country, even a little bluegrass sometimes. I usually tell people if they like James Taylor, they might like me."

"Oh, I love him. I'm going to look you up on my music app right away. What name would you be under?"

"Julia Bloom," Jules replied.

Willie's mouth came open. "I know your music.

Your song, *Finally Home*, was our first dance at my fourth wedding."

"Fourth?" Jules blinked in surprise. "How many times have you been married?"

"Just four." Willie shrugged. "So far."

Jules laughed. "You are something else."

"That's what most of my husbands have said, too." Willie gave her a wink.

Still snickering, Jules lifted the phone to frame the picture. "You want the pool in the background? Or the dunes? Or the beach?"

"I don't know. Whatever you think is best." Willie let out a little sigh. "I can't believe you're Julia Bloom. You have a lovely voice."

"Thank you, Willie. Very kind of you." Jules smiled. "How about we take a few different backgrounds and then you can look through them and decide?"

"Sure," Willie said.

She pressed her tongue to the roof of her mouth and smiled. Jules directed her a little, telling her to lift her chin a bit or turn her face slightly. Willie had no problem doing as she was told. She figured a person in the showbiz industry would know better than she about what looked good in a picture.

Jules took tons of pictures with all kinds of backdrops and made Willie feel like she was a celebrity herself.

When they were done, Willie was impressed with the woman's kindness. "Thank you so much. That was above and beyond what I expected."

Jules glanced back at her abandoned notebook. "Wasn't like I was getting anything done anyway. Might as well do something useful, right?"

"Well, I certainly appreciate it." She noticed a look of frustration in Jules's eyes. Just a brief flash of it. Aimed at the notebook. Something was bothering her.

"You're welcome." Jules was smiling again. "I can't wait to see which one you pick."

"It's going to take me an hour just to look through them all." Willie hesitated. "You were so kind to me, I hope I'm not intruding somewhere I shouldn't, but you seem bothered by something. Is everything all right?"

Jules took a deep breath. "I'm just working on something that's not quite going the way I'd like it to."

Willie nodded in understanding. "My second husband, Jim, was a carpenter. A woodworker, really. He made the most beautiful furniture you've ever seen. He used to have times like that, too. A piece wouldn't come together the way he'd seen it in his head. He'd get so frustrated."

Jules nodded slowly, like she could relate.

"Whenever that happened, he'd work on something else that meant nothing. A throwaway piece, he'd call it. He'd make a shelf or a trinket box or something really simple like that, so simple he almost didn't have to think about the process. Somehow, that always seemed to sort things out for him." Willie lifted one shoulder. "Not sure if something like that would help you, but just thought I'd mention it, since you were so kind to me."

"Thanks," Jules said. "But I'm not sure what I could do that would relate to songwriting."

Willie thought for a moment. "What about writing a letter? Wouldn't even have to be to send. Just to get your thoughts and feelings and frustrations out. Or maybe a silly poem?"

Jules seemed to consider those options. "Couldn't hurt. Thanks."

"Thank you," Willie said. "See you at dinner."

"You, too." Jules went back toward her seat.

Willie went upstairs to look through all the pictures Jules had taken. It took her a good twenty minutes to decide which one to use. In the end, she picked one with the pool in the background.

Her new hair color looked great against the blue water.

She used a few filters to make the picture look even better, then swapped it for her old one on Facebook. She couldn't wait to see what her friends thought, but she was especially interested in what any of her ex-husbands might think. She was still friends with all of them, at least on Facebook.

Just for kicks, she went to visit the profiles of her three exes. She liked to see what they were up to.

Frank had remarried to a Polish woman name Luskia. Willie perused his posts. Lots of food pictures. Cabbage rolls covered in red sauce, perogies, pastries, all sorts of good things. Luskia must be a good cook.

Willie sucked in a breath as a photo of Frank came up. He'd gained at least twenty pounds. "You always were an eater, Frank. I guess you found your true love."

Willie wasn't the best cook, but she could get by. She was more a fan of going out to eat and letting someone else do all the work. Especially the cleaning up.

She went on to Jim's page. Looked like he was still single. Lots of pics of new furniture he'd made, including a crib. His daughter from his first marriage had had another baby. Willie smiled. Jim was a grandpa again.

Willie typed out a quick congratulations on his post. Good for him. Willie was in no rush to be a great-grandma, but she did worry about Trina sometimes. Not that Trina needed a man, but Willie didn't want her granddaughter to be lonely, either. Her luck with men wasn't great, though.

Then again, no man was better than the wrong one.

Finally, she went to Zippy's profile but nothing new had been posted for a couple of months. She did a search to find his professional page, since he was a Vegas magician and still working.

She clicked on the link. As soon as the page loaded, her stomach sank. She read the post at the top of the page, skimming through the messages that had been left on it, not wanting to believe what she was reading.

Her heart broke. Zippy had passed away.

Chapter Thirty-nine

*R*oxie made a quick trip to the beauty supply shop to pick up the things Trina had asked for, texting her daughter a picture of everything for final approval before Roxie checked out. With that done, it was on to Winn-Dixie.

She grabbed a cart as she went in even though she only needed a few things to make the baked beans for tonight. Mostly the cans of beans, bacon, and brown sugar. She also planned to get a throw-away foil container so cleanup would be easy.

There was a buy one-get one sale on Trina's favorite mac and cheese, so Roxie grabbed a few of those. She picked up some more paper towels, got the beans and brown sugar, and on the way to the bacon, had a sudden impulse that sent her to the meat department.

It never hurt to see what was on sale, but she decided on a pack of burgers, the nice ones from the butcher counter, as an additional contribution for tonight's dinner. She went to the bread aisle to get buns. She already had sliced cheese to go on the burgers. Bringing some extra meat seemed like a nice way to contribute, since Claire had gone to the expense of buying the chicken and everything else.

Claire might have invited them, but Roxie didn't want Claire to think they were just there to eat her food. Also, the butcher behind the counter was cute, and it never hurt the old ego to do a little flirting.

She checked out and went home. Thankfully, she had few enough bags that she could take them all in one trip.

She stepped off the elevator on the first floor and called out, "Ma, I'm back."

"Okay," came Willie's soft reply.

Roxie frowned as she carried the groceries into the kitchen. Her mother didn't sound right. She put the perishables in the fridge, then went to check on her in her room.

She knocked on the wall, since the door was open. "Hey, you okay?"

Willie was sitting in the chair in the corner,

scrolling through her phone. She looked like she'd been crying. "No, I'm not."

She looked up, her eyes red, her makeup running.

Roxie went into situation assessment mode as she stepped into the room. "What's wrong? Are you hurt?"

"No. It's not me." Willie let out a shuddery sigh. "Zippy passed away. Cancer. Apparently, he found out he had it and two months later...gone."

Roxie put her hand to her heart. "Oh, Ma, I'm so sorry. I know you had a great affection for him."

Willie nodded. "I loved him. Even if we weren't right for each other, he was a wonderful man. No one made me laugh quite like Zippy." She sniffed and let out a little sob. "I wish I could have spoken to him one more time."

Roxie sat on the edge of the bed. "I know he loved you, too. It was so clear when you were together that he was crazy about you. I think you really made him happy."

Willie set her phone down to unravel the wadded-up tissue in her hand. She dabbed at her eyes and nose. "I think, deep down, I always thought maybe we'd have a chance to try it again. Silly, I know, especially considering our ages, but the heart never really grows old, does it? Not when love is involved."

"It's not silly. It's romantic." Roxie wished with everything in her that she could give her mom one more day with Zippy.

Wille sighed. "Love is the only true fountain of youth."

Roxie nodded. "He would have loved your new hair."

Willie smiled. "Yes, he would have."

"Do you want to go to the funeral?"

"It's already happened, apparently. But I would have gone if I'd known."

"I know you would have."

"I left a message of condolence on his Facebook page." Willie took a deep, shuddering breath, then let it out. "I'll be all right. Just needed to have a little cry. You know."

Roxie definitely did. "Is there anything I can do for you? Anything I can get you? A cup of tea? A gin and tonic?"

Willie just smiled. "Thank you, sweetheart, but I'm good. I'm just going to sit here and look through some old pictures."

"Can I get you something to drink? Or a snack? Or both."

Willie hesitated. "I could have some sweet tea. Maybe with a few cookies, if we have any."

"We have shortbread. I'll bring you a few of those." Roxie poured them both a glass of tea, put a handful of cookies on a plate, then took it all over. Willie loved shortbread, on account of her Scottish heritage. "Here you go."

"Thanks." Willie sipped her tea then set the glass on the side table by her chair and picked up a piece of shortbread. "How did you get to be such a good cook? I'm not that great. Who did you learn it from?"

Roxie laughed softly as she sat on the couch. "I guess I just watched a lot of cooking shows and learned from that. Plus, trial and error. It didn't hurt that Bryan loved to eat. He always encouraged me by his compliments, too."

Willie sighed. "I guess he wasn't all bad."

"I know you didn't like him, but he really wasn't a bad guy."

Willie snorted. "Outside of being a bigamist, you mean?"

"Ma."

"I know you loved him, but have you found out yet if he's left you anything? We can't live here forever, you know. This is all make-believe. La La Land. There's a whole other house with a mortgage and insurance and a power bill to pay that we have to go back to."

Roxie exhaled. "I know. It's been on my mind, trust me. I guess I'm just going to have to call his attorney and see what I can find out. I promise I'll do it first thing tomorrow."

"Do it now," Willie said. "You never know what will happen tomorrow."

Roxie understood. Her mother was understandably upset because of Zippy. Roxie wasn't going to argue. She didn't have the energy, but she also didn't want to upset her mother further. She got to her feet. "Tell you what—you find us a movie to watch, and I'll go make that call. It's going to take me a minute to find the guy's number anyway."

"All right." Willie picked up the remote as Roxie left the room.

She knew Bryan had an attorney. He'd talked about the guy all the time. They were friends. Golfing buddies. They'd gone on a fishing trip together once, too. Bryan had always said if anything happened to him, to talk to...what was the guy's name?

She had all of that written down in the emer-

gency file at home. She just hadn't reached out to the
man yet, because she'd been too sad to have that
talk. Doing that would make it real that Bryan was
gone, and she hadn't been ready for that kind of
finality.

She hadn't known then that she was Bryan's
second wife, either.

What *was* the man's name? Hadn't Bryan
mentioned him in an email once upon a time? She
opened up her email app and did a search for the
phrase "fishing trip."

She found it. Charles Kinnerman. She did
another search, this time for his phone number. It
popped up. All she had to do was tap the number
and hit Dial.

She stared at it. The thing she hadn't mentioned
to Willie was that she was a little scared to find out
the truth.

Bryan had died so suddenly. There was every
reason to think he hadn't had a chance to set things
up the way he'd wanted. Roxie might be getting
nothing. She'd look like an idiot. Claire would probably be happy, though.

But Roxie would be devastated. And not just
because she'd have to go back to work. All those
years with Bryan, all those years of being second

best, and to get nothing? For him not to leave anything for Trina?

That would hurt more than anything else. In fact, that would break her heart all over again.

She took a breath and dialed.

Chapter Forty

Kat shook her head back and forth, watching in the mirror how her hair moved. It had never done that before. "It looks so good. I look like a different person."

"Nah," Trina said. "You look exactly like you. The you I knew was in there."

"But I mean, I look...pretty." It felt weird saying that.

"Prettier," Trina corrected. "You were already pretty. You just weren't making the most of it."

Kat nodded, still a little dumbstruck by what her half-sister had managed to accomplish. "I never thought a new hairstyle and some highlights would make such a difference. And the eyebrows, too. Thank you so much."

"You're welcome."

Kat's mom walked in from the kitchen, where

she'd been prepping food for the barbeque. "Can I see?" She gasped. "Oh, Kat. You look beautiful! Trina, outstanding job."

"Thanks." Trina was all smiles now.

Kat's mom touched her hair, running a few strands through her fingers. "You had highlights like this when you were a little girl. All that time in the sun, playing outside. It's just gorgeous."

Kat couldn't stop smiling. "I guess it's your turn in the chair now."

Her mom looked at Trina. "Is it? Are you ready for me? I just took the lemon squares out of the oven, so I'm good."

"Just about," Trina answered. "I need to clean up a little then reorganize with the supplies to do your hair. My mom went to pick up the things I needed."

"That was very nice of her. Whatever it cost, just let me know and I'll reimburse you."

"That's okay," Trina said.

"No, she's right," Kat said. "I want to give you money for whatever you used on me. I know that stuff isn't free. How much do you want?"

Trina looked like she didn't want to say. "I didn't do it to get money from you."

"We know that," Kat said. "But you already put your own personal time into it. The least we can do is pay for the products you used. Then you can buy more to replace them."

"Well..." Reluctantly, Trina said, "How about twenty bucks apiece? Is that okay?"

"It's more than okay." Kat figured it would have been many times that at a salon. "I'll go get my wallet."

"Me, too," her mom said.

"I'll be right here," Trina said. She started cleaning her tools in the sink.

Kat walked out into the kitchen with her mom. "Those lemon squares smell amazing."

"Thanks." Her mom smiled as she looked at Kat's hair again. "She does amazingly good work. I was a little worried about letting her do my hair, but after seeing Grandma and now you, I can't wait."

"Crazy, right?" Kat shook her head. "I was nervous, too, but wow, she's good." She glanced at the wall mirror. It was like looking at a stranger. A very cute stranger. "I might have to take a selfie. But first, I think I'm going to show Aunt Jules."

She started to leave, then stopped. "Where is Grandma?"

"She took Aunt Jules's car into town," her mom said. "Something about going to the library, I think. Probably went to get books."

Kat looked at the time on her phone. "She's been gone a while, hasn't she?"

Her mom shrugged. "Maybe. I've been so busy with those lemon squares and working on the rest of the food that I haven't really paid attention."

"Maybe I'll text her." Kat wasn't exactly worried about her grandmother, but it wasn't like her to be out so long. She was missing her shows, something that was out of character, too. Kat sent her grandmother a text. *Are you still in town? Just making sure you're all right. Can't wait to show you my new hair.*

Then she looked at her mom. "Need me to do anything in the kitchen?"

"Nope. But if you go down to see Jules, tell her the potato salad still needs to be made. I've already boiled the potatoes and six eggs. I think that's how many she uses."

"Okay, I'll go tell her now." Kat's phone buzzed. She glanced at the screen and read the message that had just come in. "Grandma says she's fine and that she ended up sitting in on a book club meeting at the library. She'll be home soonish."

"A book club?"

Kat shrugged one shoulder. "It doesn't sound like something she'd do but what do I know? She does enjoy reading. All right, I'm going to see Aunt Jules. Back in a bit."

Before she headed for the elevator, she stuck her head into the bathroom. "Thanks again, Trina. I love it. Can't wait to see what you do with my mom's hair."

Trina grinned. "I'm excited to do it."

Kat rode the elevator to the ground floor. Aunt Jules was sitting under an umbrella poolside, furiously scribbling away in her notebook. Toby was sleeping in the sun, oblivious to everything around him. Kat walked over and just stood there, not wanting to interrupt whatever creative process was happening.

After a couple of minutes of not being noticed, she cleared her throat softly. Toby whined a little hello and Aunt Jules jumped.

"Sorry," Kat said. "Didn't mean to startle you."

Aunt Jules laughed. "I'm fine. But hello, your *hair*! My word, you look like a movie star. Is everyone getting a makeover?"

"Sort of." Kat laughed. "Mom's up there now having her turn."

"I couldn't be happier about that. Your mom could use a little pick-me-up and I think a new look could be just the thing. Between us, she is long overdue for an update."

"Especially with the potentially cute neighbor coming over tonight."

Aunt Jules snorted. "You know that's the last thing on your mother's mind, right? I mean, I can't imagine her wanting to get involved with another man so soon after your dad."

"I know. But considering that he wasn't faithful to her, I'd be okay with her not waiting some predetermined period of mourning time before getting back out in the world."

A strange look came over her aunt's face. "You're pretty mad at your father, I take it."

Kat sat on the empty chaise. "I don't know if mad is the right word. I feel betrayed. Definitely angry. But I feel distanced from him, too. Because I clearly had no idea who he really was. He was just a guy pretending to be my father. Just like when he was with Trina, he was pretending to be her father."

"He wasn't pretending. He *was* your dad. And her dad."

"I know, but finding out that he had a whole other family just makes me doubt so much about him. What else was he hiding? Which family was his favorite? Which one did he consider his real family?" Kat sighed. "It's really screwed me up inside."

"I'm sorry. I can't imagine how hard this has been for you. Anytime you want to talk, I'm here."

"Thanks," Kat said. "I appreciate that. I'm not sure talking will help me any more right now. I just need to figure some things out for myself, I guess."

"Including with Ray?"

"That's one of the big ones." Kat sat back. The sun felt good. "By the way, mom says you need to make your potato salad."

"Oh, no! I completely forgot."

"Mom already cooked the potatoes and boiled six eggs, so don't freak out too much."

"Still." Aunt Jules got up. "Are you going to sit here for a minute? Probably won't take me but ten minutes to throw it all together. I'd hate to drag Toby up there."

"Leave him. I'll stay until you get back."

"Thanks." Aunt Jules went upstairs, leaving Toby and her notebook behind.

Impulsively, Kat snapped a few pics of herself, then went through them, picked out the best one and thought about sending it to Ray. After a few minutes, she decided not to. It might give him the wrong idea. Like she'd done it for him. She didn't want to give him false hope. Not when she was so unsure about where they were headed.

She couldn't exactly post the picture to her social media, either, not when she was supposed to be on compassionate leave. How would that look? Not great. And she wasn't about to share her father's dirty little secret with the world to justify her own sudden lack of sadness.

She was still sad, but for more reasons than she had been originally.

Kat put her phone aside, adjusted the recline on the chaise, then sat back and closed her eyes, enjoying the sun and the breeze. She'd never been one to spend too much time by the pool unless she brought work down here with her, or a good book. It seemed like wasted time just to lie in the sun, but now she wasn't so sure.

It felt nice. A chance to rest and relax. Maybe she should do more of this. It wouldn't hurt to get a little tan. She'd be less likely to burn that way, which was something she always worried about.

The jangle of Toby's tag against the buckle of his collar opened her eyes. He had gotten up onto the end of Aunt Jules's chaise.

"Hi, Toby baby. It's nice out here, isn't it?"

He let out a big sigh and rested his head on his paws.

Kat smiled. "You're the cutest thing. Maybe before dinner I'll take you for a...you-know-what." She didn't dare say the word "walk." Toby knew that word and just saying it would get him all worked up.

She looked at the notebook her aunt had left behind. Kat wondered what she'd been writing about. Probably a new song. Aunt Jules was always working on new music. It was her job. Whether it was an actual song or a commercial jingle, she never stopped putting her ideas down on paper.

Kat's curiosity got the best of her. She picked up the notebook and opened it to the page she thought her aunt had been writing on. It didn't read like a song so much as a bunch of disjointed thoughts. Kat read a few of them. Almost immediately, she regretted it.

She shook her head and read on. Whatever this was, it was...strange. Lots of dark imagery and weird phrases. Almost like an old-fashioned curse or something.

Her discomfort grew the more she read. What the heck was this? Had Aunt Jules had some kind of mental breakdown? If so, she was doing a great job of hiding it from everyone.

The elevator thunked softly, announcing its return to the ground floor.

With a thumping heart and a racing pulse, Kat shut the notebook and put it back on her aunt's chaise.

She knew she shouldn't have snuck a peek into her aunt's notebook. It wasn't Kat's property, and she had no right to it. But what was done was done. She couldn't unsee what she'd read.

How was she ever going to look her aunt in the eyes again?

Chapter Forty-one

Margo had lingered longer over her late lunch than she'd intended, but Conrad was quite the conversationalist. She hadn't expected him to ask her to join him, but after the stimulating conversation at the book club meeting, she wanted more.

It had been quite the wake-up call to find out that Willie had been right. Margo was starved for companionship, platonic or otherwise. Well, maybe not starved. But definitely hungry.

Lunch had been wonderful. They'd parted with her promising to see him at the next meeting, the assigned book already purchased from Barnes & Noble through her phone.

Before she headed home, she stopped by the florists and picked up two bouquets of flowers. One for Willie, as a thank you, and one for Claire, who was undoubtedly working herself to the bone to get ready for the gathering she was hosting this evening.

Then Margo drove home, a smile on her face. Today had been a step out of her comfort zone for sure, but she had been rewarded for it.

Conrad was quite charming. A great storyteller, which wasn't surprising. He was easy to be around. And not hard to look at with those sparkling hazel eyes.

It didn't hurt that he'd seemed to be showing an interest in her, either. She hoped that hadn't just been her imagination. She wasn't looking for any kind of permanent companionship but seeing him once a month at book club would be very nice.

Maybe once a week, if they sometimes wanted to share a meal. Or was she reading too much into his kindness toward her?

A sudden, painful thought struck her. What was she doing? She didn't live here in Diamond Beach, she lived in Landry, three hours away. She'd be headed home in another week or so. Surely Claire wouldn't stay longer than that.

And three hours was too far to drive just for a book club.

Her bright mood darkened considerably. What had she been thinking? Today had been a terrible idea. There was no point in making friends with Conrad or Greta or any of them. She didn't live here. And Claire was going to sell the beach house, so there was no chance Margo would be coming back.

She was going to miss that house more than she'd expected. In fact, the realization broke her heart in a way that surprised her. She was sad about losing the friendships she'd just begun. Why did she care so much about people she'd only just met? And how had she become so sensitive to such things?

After her second husband had died, she'd made a conscious decision to not get involved with anyone new. Her family was enough. Opening herself up to new relationships wasn't worth it, not when she'd only end up hurt again.

And now she'd done it and was paying the price.

If she'd been someone who cried, she would have pulled over to the side of the road and done just that. As it was, she pulled over anyway, parking in a small public beach access lot. She needed to gather herself before she went back.

The last thing she felt like doing was socializing tonight, but Claire would be upset if Margo didn't show for dinner. It behooved them to befriend the neighbors. Happy neighbors would be more likely to give a glowing report to anyone interested in buying the place. But nothing about being social appealed to her at the moment. She would have much rather spent the rest of the night in her room reading. Or watching a killer being hunted down on one of her favorite programs.

She sighed and stared out across the dunes blocking her view of the ocean. Maybe she'd take a walk when she got back. That would calm her down. Or at least put her mind back together.

After a few more minutes, she drove on home. She went straight to the second floor. There was no one around. She listened. Faintly, she could hear the sounds of a guitar. Jules must have gone upstairs to work on some music. She liked the privacy the third floor allowed.

But where was everyone else?

She set the bouquet of flowers for Claire on the counter, then went to Kat's room and knocked on the door. "Kat?"

A few moments passed before Kat opened the door.

Margo smiled. "Doesn't your hair look nice?"

Kat nodded. "Thanks. Trina did a great job."

Margo frowned, recognizing the slight tension in Kat's face. She knew when her granddaughter was upset. "What's wrong?"

"You mean besides all the standard stuff?"

Margo exhaled. "Sorry, sweetheart. I know this is a hard time for you."

"Yeah. I was just laying down a little before dinner."

"All right, I won't bother you. Do you know where your mom is?"

"Probably in her room. Trina just finished her hair a few minutes ago."

"Very good. Thank you."

"Sure." Kat shut the door.

Margo went to see her daughter, knocking softly.

Claire opened her door with a big smile. "What do you think?"

Margo's chin dropped in amazement. "You look ten years younger and ten pounds lighter."

"Mom, be serious."

"I am. I can't believe it. You know I'm not one to give false praise."

"No, you're not. Thanks." Claire touched her hair. "Kind of insane, right?"

"It reminds me of the color you were born with."

Claire nodded. "Trina said the color you had in your youth is a good indicator of what looks best on you. It's a big change. It's going to take me a while to get used to it."

"Well, I hope you stick with it, because it's the best you've looked in years."

Claire's brows lifted. "Thanks, I guess. Doesn't say much for how I used to look."

Margo was in no mood for pretending. "Claire, you haven't taken the best care of yourself in some time. I know you were busy parenting, I don't fault you for that. You raised an incredible young woman. But I'm glad you did this for yourself now. It was time."

To soften things a little more, Margo held out the flowers. "These are for you."

"They're beautiful." Claire took the bouquet. "Why? What's the special occasion?"

"I knew you were working hard today, and I thought you would enjoy them." She'd been in a better mood when she'd bought them, too. "Do you mind if I come in for a moment?"

"Sure. I was figuring out what I was going to wear tonight."

Margo came in and closed the door behind her. "What are your intentions with this place? Do you still plan to sell it?"

"I do. As soon as I know if I can or not. I really have no idea how things are going to shake out until

I hear back from Bryan's lawyer and the best he can tell me is that he's working on it."

Margo frowned. "What's the holdup?"

"I don't really understand it myself."

"How much do you think you'll ask when you can put it up for sale?"

"I have no idea until I talk to a realtor and get them to appraise it." Claire's gaze grew curious. "Why?"

Margo hadn't been ready to share her thoughts, but there didn't seem to be any other way to explain herself. She chose her words carefully, posing a different question first, just to see what her daughter's reaction would be. "What if you sold your place in Landry and made this your permanent residence?

"Mom, as much as I'd love that, Diamond Beach is expensive. For one thing, everything costs more around here because it's a tourist area. You know what it's like near the beach. Everything gets a little tourist tax added to it. For another, the insurance on this house alone is nearly double what I'm paying now. Again, because it's at the beach. The power bill would be higher because of the square footage, then there's pool maintenance to think about. And the cost of moving? I can't even imagine what that would be." Claire shook her head.

That hadn't gone how Margo had anticipated. She tried another tack. "I'd be willing to sell my place, too, and move in here with you to help out with expenses."

Claire's gaze darkened. "I came here because I was hoping to bask in the happy memories of my life with Bryan. Instead, this is the place where I found out that he'd betrayed me in the most unimaginable way. Why would I want to live here? Why would *you* want to live here?"

Margo wasn't about to tell her daughter that this place felt like a fresh start. That she'd made some friends. Found a group she could belong to. That for the first time in many, many years, she felt like this could be a real chance to heal. To be whole again.

Those words just wouldn't form on her tongue. Instead, she shrugged. "I like being by the beach. And this house is a lot nicer than the one you live in now. There's room for me here. Room for your sister to visit. And you could still rent the downstairs. It makes good financial sense. But I guess you'd rather go back to work at your age."

"You know that's not true." Claire crossed her arms over her body. "Look, I'll think about it, but don't get your hopes up. I can't do anything until I hear back from the lawyer anyway."

Margo just nodded and turned to go.

Before she could open the door, Claire spoke again. "Would you really want to live with me?"

Margo faced Claire again. "You're my daughter. I love you. Of course I'd want to live with you. I've got to think about my future, don't I? I'm not getting any younger. At some point, I may not be able to live alone." She sighed. "Let me know when the attorney gives you some news."

"I will."

Margo left, her mood no better than when she'd first walked in.

Chapter Forty-two

laire got the grill started and when it was up to temperature, she put the chicken on. Danny and his father weren't due for another fifteen minutes, but the chicken would take some time and she didn't want anyone going hungry.

She couldn't believe her mother actually wanted to move here. It was a great house, no question about that, and the location was to die for, but it really would be more expensive. She stared out toward the water. Was there any way to make it happen?

She shook her head to clear out that silly thought. Now was not the time for unrealistic dreams. Not when she wasn't sure who this place was actually going to belong to.

She put the last few pieces of chicken on the grill and closed the lid. She'd enlisted Kat and Jules to help bring down everything they'd need. Not just food but plates and utensils, a cooler filled with ice and bottled water, condiments, all of those things.

She washed her hands at the outdoor sink, then turned on the string lights that illuminated the recreational part of the ground floor. The sun would be setting shortly, so the light would be needed unless they wanted to eat in the dark.

Then she got to work with some paper towels and cleaning spray. She cleaned the big table they'd be eating at, wiping down not just the top but the legs, too. Even if they were putting a tablecloth on it, she wanted it clean. She did the chairs next.

Thankfully, the big table seated eight, which meant she'd only have to squeeze one more chair in to accommodate everyone. She got the chair from the storage closet next to the elevator. It was a simple folding camp chair of heavy-duty canvas, one of her favorites to take to the beach. She opened it up and tried to decide the best spot for it.

While she was doing that, Roxie came down the steps with a grocery bag in her hands. "Hi."

"Hi."

Roxie lifted the bag. "I bought some burgers. I just wanted to contribute something more than beans. This way we won't be eating all of your chicken, either."

Claire hadn't expected that. She nodded. "That was nice of you. But you're welcome to as much chicken as you want."

Roxie gave a quick smile in response. "Thanks. I've got buns and cheese, too. I'll bring them down with the beans. Is there anything you need help with?"

"Sure. Setting the table? Of course, that can't be done until the plates and such are brought down. My sister's supposed to be doing that."

Roxie put the bag on one of the grill's shelves. "I'll run back up and get the beans then. They should stay plenty hot until it's time to eat."

"All right." Claire watched her go, a little envious and a lot motivated. The woman had an amazing figure. There was no telling how much better she'd looked when Bryan had met her. He must have been knocked out by Roxie's pinup-girl body and vibrant personality, especially when compared to Claire's conservative wardrobe and reserved character.

It was no wonder he'd gone for Roxie. But that was on him. Not Roxie. Claire truly believed the woman hadn't had any idea Bryan was already married. She was sure that's exactly how Bryan had wanted it. After all, he'd had nearly three decades to come clean and hadn't.

Claire was slowly getting past her dislike of Roxie. Slowly. Even if she was blameless, it was still hard to accept that thanks to Bryan having a child with Roxie, Claire would be connected to her for the rest of her life. Assuming Kat wanted a relationship with her sister, which appeared to be happening.

She went to check on the chicken and also to have a look at the burgers Roxie had brought down. They looked good. Better than just a box of frozen patties. Was this Roxie being nice? Was she trying to smooth things out between them? Or was there some other motive Claire couldn't guess?

She sighed heavily. She was so tired of all of this. The not knowing about this house and the rest of Bryan's estate, the trying to figure out what Roxie and her family's motives might be, the sense that there was still a shoe left to drop. It was exhausting.

The elevator doors opened, and Jules came out, carrying a big tray loaded with supplies.

Claire went to help, plucking the tablecloth off the tray so she could get the table covered and Jules could set her tray down. "Where's Kat?"

Jules shook her head. "I got on the elevator with her, and she jumped off, saying she forgot something. No idea what. I offered to hold the door, but she said to go on."

"She's been acting a little strange today, don't you think?" Earlier, Claire had asked her to help Jules bring things downstairs and Kat had offered to do it all by herself. Claire had told her that was silly, to which Kat had rolled her eyes and gone back to her room.

Jules nodded. "She has. When I came back down from making the potato salad, she left before I even sat back down. I asked her to hang out for a bit, but she said she had a work email she wanted to answer." She shrugged. "I thought it was strange, since they know she's on leave, but whatever."

Claire unfurled the tablecloth with a quick snap of her wrists, getting it mostly over the table in one go. She adjusted it so it was even all the way around. "Kat's got a lot going on in her head. I guess we just need to give her some space."

"I guess." Jules set the tray down on the table-cloth, then went around adding the clips to keep the thing in place.

Claire started distributing the stack of plates. "Speaking of someone with a lot going on in her head, Mom told me I should sell my house and move here."

"Hey, that's a great idea." Jules followed behind her with the nice paper napkins and utensils.

Claire set the last plate down. "Are you serious? Jules, this place is for people with a nice, steady income. Something I don't have anymore."

"You could get a job, if you really had to. But you'll have Bryan's insurance money soon. That would give you a good cushion. And you could still rent the downstairs. Wouldn't take much to close the steps off with a lockable door, if that's what you wanted."

"Bryan's insurance money isn't a given." Claire sighed. "I don't know if I'm actually the beneficiary. It could be Roxie for all I know."

Jules's mouth came open for a moment. Then she closed it. "Oh. I didn't realize..."

"Neither did I," Claire said. "Until I called our attorney, and he couldn't tell me anything."

"Have you called the insurance company?"

Claire frowned. "I thought the attorney would handle all of that."

"No, I'm pretty sure you have to notify them of Bryan's death and send them a certificate. Then they can process everything and get you a check."

A light came on inside Claire. A light that felt very much like hope. She checked the time on her watch. "There won't be anyone in the office, but I'll call first thing. I'm such an idiot. I should have done that already."

"You've had a lot on your plate. You're not an idiot. You're a grieving widow. Cut yourself some slack." Jules came closer. "You know, if you did make this your permanent residence, I wouldn't mind renting the third floor from you. It's a great creative space. I was up there yesterday working on some music. I guess I kind of forgot how peaceful it is up there. And the views are amazing."

"Are you serious? What about your place?"

"I have a mortgage to pay there, too, you know. It would be cheaper to sell it and rent from you. Besides, that place is too big for me. It has been since the boys moved out and got on with their own lives."

Claire couldn't imagine Jules trading her home in Landry for the third floor. Her home was gorgeous, a sprawling compound with a few acres that all sat behind a gate. Of course, she wasn't at the beach, either. And it was a *lot* of house for one person. And one Dachshund. "Like I told Mom, I'll give it some thought. But until I hear from the attorney, I don't even know if this house will actually end up being mine."

Jules pursed her lips. "You really think he'd leave

this to Roxie?"

"I have no idea. I never thought he'd be married to another woman and yet..." Claire lifted her hands.

"Good point."

The crunch of gravel turned them toward the side yard. Danny and his dad, Miguel, were coming toward them. Danny had a small, soft-sided cooler slung over one shoulder and a potted plant blooming with white flowers in his hands. His father carried a bottle of wine.

Jules shifted so her face was only visible to Claire. Her brows were pegged to her hairline, and she was grinning. "Okay, hello. He's hot. Way to keep that a secret."

"I wasn't—" Claire smiled at Danny, who was now too close for her to reply without being heard. "Hi."

"Hi," Danny said. "You look great." He held out the potted plant. "It's a peace lily. They're great for improving the air quality of your home."

"Thank you."

He put his hand on his dad's shoulder. "This is my father, Miguel."

"For you," Miguel said, holding out the bottle of wine. He had bright eyes that showed even behind his glasses.

She took the wine. Were her cheeks red from her sister's comment about Danny? She hoped not. "Thank you for the plant. Why don't you put it on the coffee table over there?"

"Sure," Danny said.

She smiled at his father. "Thank you for the wine. It's a pleasure to meet you, Miguel." She tipped the wine bottle toward Jules as Danny rejoined them. "This is my sister, Julia."

Jules shook both of their hands. "Nice to meet you guys. Call me Jules."

Miguel looked at his son. "You didn't tell me the house next door was filled with beautiful women."

Jules laughed. "You're sweet." She picked the tray off the table and hooked her thumb toward the elevator. "I need to run back up and get the rest of the crew and food."

"Thanks," Claire said to her sister before looking back at her company. Danny really was handsome. "I'm so glad you could come."

"Me, too." He took the cooler off his shoulder and held it out. "I brought some ginger beer."

"Oh, great!" She took it and put it on top of the cooler already downstairs. "Please, make yourself at home. I need to check on the chicken."

Kat came down the steps. She was carrying a

Bluetooth speaker and a plate of cornbread. She waved at the men. "I'm Kat, the daughter."

"Nice to meet you," Danny said. "I'm Danny and this is my dad, Miguel."

"Hi. You guys mind a little background music? I won't turn it up too loud."

Miguel shook his head. "We love music."

"Great." She set it up on the coffee table in the seating area where Danny had put the plant.

Danny came over to Claire. "I just want to say I thought you looked very nice before, but the new hair is...very sexy. And definitely not boring."

Claire smiled but couldn't look at him for fear she might embarrass herself with her reaction. She would never again hear that word and not think about kissing him. She kept her eyes on the chicken as if it might burst into flames without her watchful gaze. She swallowed and found her voice. "T-thank you."

Roxie came down with the beans, Trina behind her carrying a couple of Diet Cokes in can holders. Roxie met Claire's gaze, then looked at Danny. A big smile spread across her face. "Hello, there."

This was going to be a very interesting dinner.

Chapter Forty-three

J ules yelled down the steps to whoever was still down there on the first floor that it was time for dinner before going into the bedroom to let her mom know, then put the rest of the food on the tray to take it downstairs. Her mom came with her in the elevator, carrying a basket with salt and pepper grinders, butter for the cornbread, extra napkins, and serving utensils.

The elevator stopped at the first floor and Willie got on, a large plastic tumbler in one hand. It held clear, bubbly liquid over ice, along with a fat slice of lime.

"Roxie and Trina took the steps," the older woman explained. "But my hip's acting up." She shook her head. "All that time sitting on a hard stool while Trina was doing my hair. I guess what they say is true. Beauty is pain."

Margo nodded, a little half-smile curving her mouth. "I had to do the same, but thankfully it didn't seem to bother my knee. Getting old is not for the fainted-hearted."

"No, it is not," Willie agreed.

They got off the elevator and joined the party.

Kat glanced up and locked eyes with Jules, but then she quickly looked away again.

Jules stared after her, but Kat didn't make eye contact again. Jules didn't understand it. She felt like she'd done something to upset her niece, but she couldn't imagine what that might be. She'd gone through her last few interactions with Kat and come up blank. Maybe she'd just flat-out ask her after dinner. Jules took the tray to the table and starting setting the dishes of food out. Margo was doing the same with the things in her basket.

Roxie was at the grill with Claire and Danny. Looked like there were burgers on with the chicken now, all of which smelled amazing.

Miguel was sitting at the table already. Jules went over to him. "Miguel, have you meet my mom, Margo?"

They both smiled at each other before Jules continued. "Can I get you something to drink,

Miguel? Water? Wine? Your son brought ginger beer, as I'm sure you know."

He nodded. "Water would be fine, thank you."

She looked at her mother. "Mom? Do you want something? I'll get it."

"A glass of wine would be great."

She got Miguel a bottle out of the cooler, getting one for herself, too, and brought the white wine with her. She opened it and poured her mom a glass, then Jules sat next to Miguel, leaving the ends of the table for Claire and possibly Danny. Although maybe Claire would want to sit next to Danny. Jules was curious to see how that played out. Her mom had already picked a spot on the other side. "I understand your family owns the Mrs. Butter's Popcorn stores?"

Miguel nodded as he took the top off his water bottle. "That's right."

"That's quite a business you've got there. You can't hardly walk through town without seeing someone carrying a bag of it."

He smiled. "It's addictive."

Jules nodded. "You know what else is addictive? The smell that comes out of your shops. It's impossible to go near one without that buttery, sugary scent making your mouth water. It's irresistible. Gets me every time."

He laughed and leaned toward her. "You know, we have special fans that carry that smell out to the street. It's deliberate."

She let out a sound that was half gasp, half laugh. "Get out of here! That's marketing genius."

"Thank you." He bowed his head. "My best idea. But I'm retired now. Danny handles the business, along with his kids."

"That's nice."

Miguel looked at his son with pride in his eyes. "He's a good boy." He turned back to Jules. "What do you do?"

"I'm a singer and a songwriter and a musician."

His eyes lit up. "That's marvelous. Music is everything, don't you think?"

She could only nod and smile. "It certainly is for me. Do you play?"

"A little guitar, but not too much anymore." He lifted his hands. "The arthritis makes it hard. But I love listening and I appreciate the work that goes into making a living as a musician." He chuckled. "Assuming you make a living?"

She laughed. "I do." And now that she'd felt the first tendrils of inspiration growing inside her, she felt better about actually continuing to make money. The beginnings of a new song had come to her this afternoon in a way they hadn't in quite a while. All thanks to Willie's suggestion of writing a letter. For some reason, that had kicked off the idea in her and she'd started brainstorming on paper right away. She was eager to turn her musings into lyrics.

Jules waved at Willie to join them. She was sitting alone on the sofa. "Come on over, Willie."

The woman looked up, bright-eyed and clearly pleased at the invitation. She pushed to her feet and came over, tumbler in hand.

Jules did the introductions. "Willie, this is Miguel. He and his son Danny live next door."

Willie glanced at their house. "That's a nice place you've got there."

Miguel couldn't seem to take his eyes off her, although Jules thought it probably had a lot to do with her hair color. "Thank you." He wiggled his gnarled finger at her. "I like your hair. Hard not to be happy looking at that color."

A big grin spread over Willie's face. She sat down next to him. "Thanks. It's one of my favorite colors."

Miguel nodded. "Mine, too, now."

Jules stood up. "Willie? Can I get you anything else to drink?"

"I'm just fine, thank you."

Jules slipped away and let them talk. Her mother
was on her phone anyway, and Jules wanted to go
see what Roxie, Claire, and Danny were laughing
about by the grill, but her phone buzzed just then.
She pulled it out of her back pocket and took a look
at the screen.

It was Jesse. She smiled and answered, walking
toward the pool for a little privacy. "Hey, there."

"Hey. How are you?"

"Good. How are you?"

"I'm...well, I'm in a bit of a jam, to be honest."

"What's going on?"

"I hate to even make this call. It's a huge imposi-
tion and I fully expect you to say no but I'm out of
options and you're my only hope."

Her brow bent. "You might need to back up and
explain a little more."

He sighed. "Yes, absolutely. Sam Mayfield was
booked for the club's nine o'clock show but his son
was just taken to the ER with appendicitis and Sam's
on a flight back to Austin as we speak."

Jules understood. She'd once had to cancel a gig
because her youngest boy, Fender, had broken his
arm. Fen was twenty-six now. "And you're hoping I
know someone who could fill in?"

Jesse laughed, but there wasn't much humor in it. "I was actually hoping I could get *you* to fill in." He groaned. "I know, huge ask, last minute, awful idea. I'm sorry. Like I said, I was out of options, and you've been on my mind all day and I just thought—"

"I'll do it." She was smiling. How long had it been since she'd been on a man's mind all day? Besides that, she could use the boost. Performing always gave her a huge lift in mood and spirit. It might be just the thing to put her over the creative edge. "I'm about to sit down to dinner with family and friends, though, so I won't be able to be there too early."

"I can't believe you said yes."

She laughed. "Me, either. I'll be there as soon as I can but it probably won't be until eight or eight-thirty. I hope that's all right." She was already thinking about what she might wear. She hadn't really brought any stage wear with her.

"I owe you, big time. Which is not to say I'm not also paying you, because I am. But thank you."

"You're welcome. See you later." Jules hung up, smiling. It had been a little bit since she'd done a show, but she'd just do the set she'd done for the last one. She still didn't know what she was going to wear. At least she'd brought her guitar.

She wandered over toward the grill.

Claire was putting the chicken onto a big serving plate that Danny was holding. Roxie was adding cheese to the burgers.

Claire stopped, tongs midair. "You're all smiley."

"I have a gig tonight. As a favor for a friend."

Claire's brows lifted. "Is that the same friend you went to breakfast with?"

Jules nodded. "Yes. Jesse."

"Does that mean you're not going to be here for dinner?"

"No, I'll be here, but I'll have to leave right after."

"Ok, good." Claire went back to adding chicken to the platter.

Jules went to the table and found a seat. She hadn't anticipated seeing Jesse tonight, but she was happy about it. Something she didn't want to read too much into.

Chapter Forty-four

*R*oxie made up a plate of cheeseburgers on buns and brought them to the table. She wasn't sure anyone would actually eat them, so she was pleased when Trina helped herself to one right away.

"Thanks, Ma."

Roxie smiled. Trina passed the plate around. Danny took a burger, too, as did Willie, who was seated on the other side of Miguel. Roxie added one to her plate, then helped herself to a drumstick and a little bit of all the sides.

She listened to the conversations going on around her, but didn't chime in. She was too busy thinking about the conversation she'd had earlier, with Charles Kinnerman.

He hadn't been able to give her any reassurances. All he'd really said was that he wouldn't have anything to tell her for a few more days and that he was working on getting things finalized. Whatever that meant.

She watched Claire, wondering if she knew anything Roxie didn't.

Like who Bryan had left everything to. Roxie didn't care about *everything*, but she did need to know if she was going to have to find a full-time job or, worse, a cheaper place to live. She also cared that her daughter wasn't left out. In fact, she'd gladly be passed over if it meant Trina was taken care of.

If Bryan had made accommodations for Kat but not for Trina, Trina would be crushed. She loved her father. Even though he hadn't always been around, they'd developed a special bond. At least Roxie had always thought they had.

In a perfect world, Trina would get a portion of Bryan's estate and life insurance, enough that she could open her own salon.

That's all Roxie really wanted. For her daughter to be able to realize her dreams. Wasn't that what all mothers wanted? For their kids to have an advantage in life? For them to achieve the things their hearts desired?

Roxie's gaze shifted from Claire to Kat. Certainly Kat had been given an advantage, hadn't she? She'd gone to college. Gotten a degree. Mingled with the right kind of people who could give her even more advantages.

Trina had never had that opportunity. It wasn't fair. She was such a good girl with such a giving spirit and a generous attitude. All she wanted to do was help people.

Bryan had said there were a lot of ways to do that without going to college.

And that's what worried Roxie. If Bryan hadn't thought college important enough for Trina to provide those funds, would he also pass her over when it came to an inheritance? She was pretty sure she knew the answer to that, and it soured her stomach.

She sighed, wishing that life could just be easy for a while. If this place went to Claire and got sold, Roxie knew there was no way Claire would give them even the smallest share of the proceeds.

Why should she? Claire already felt like Bryan owed her for all the lies he'd told. That much was plain.

Claire caught Roxie looking at her. She stared back for a moment, then raised her fork. "These beans are very good. Thank you for making them."

Roxie smiled. It was always nice to be appreciated. "You're welcome. Thank you for including us."

Willie raised the enormous gin and tonic she'd
insisted on bringing. "I'll cheers to that."

Kat raised her bottle of water. "And thank you to
Trina for spending her entire day making us look
fabulous. Your skills with hair are unmatched."

Trina grinned, lifted her diet soda, and smiled.
"It was my pleasure."

Danny looked impressed. "You did everyone's
hair?"

Trina nodded. "I did my Mimi's yesterday, but
then I did Margo's, Kat's and Claire's today. It's what
I do."

"Do you have a salon around here?" Danny
asked. "My daughter is always saying it's hard to find
a good hairdresser."

"No, not around here. I work at a place called
Tangles back home in Port St. Rosa. It's a little over
two hours from here."

He nodded. "If you were closer, I'd send her to
you."

"Thanks." Trina's expression was mixed.

Roxie understood her daughter's look. Trina
wanted her own place more than anything, but she
didn't even live on her own right now, mostly to save

up money, but she helped out by contributing to the household bills and with Willie, when she needed it. Trina owning her own salon was a long ways off.

"So," Jules started. "Strange question, but do any of you ladies have some sparkly accessories I might be able to borrow?" She was mostly looking at Roxie and Trina. "I have a spur-of-the-moment gig at the Dolphin Club tonight and I didn't bring any of my stage wear."

Trina nodded. "We can hook you up."

Jules smiled. "I had a feeling you'd be able to. Thanks."

"Just come to my room with me after dinner and I'll show you what I've got."

"Perfect," Jules said.

Willie's hip bag buzzed. She pulled out her phone and looked at it. "Hmm. That's probably spam. I better not answer it." She put the phone down on the table and spooned up another helping of the potato salad. "Who made this? It's about the best potato salad I've ever had."

Jules lifted her hand. "Guilty. I'm kind of known for my potato salad."

"I can see why," Willie said. "What's your secret?"

Jules grinned a little harder. "If I tell you, I'll have to kill you."

"Well," Willie said. "You could try." She laughed loudly at her own joke, making everyone else laugh, too.

Roxie watched Miguel, who seemed to be watching Willie with something like fascination in his eyes. Earlier, he'd picked her napkin up for her when it had fallen off her lap. He'd pulled the bowl of potato salad closer when she'd gone for a second helping.

Willie had been chatting with him since she'd sat down, but as far as Roxie knew, Willie hadn't noticed his focus on her yet. Then again, Willie had been a man-magnet all her life. The chances she didn't know what she was doing to the man next to her were slim.

Roxie smiled, trying to keep her grin to herself. If she could bottle whatever Willie had, she'd be a millionaire.

Willie's phone buzzed with another incoming call. Willie picked up the phone to look at it, then set it back down, rolling her eyes. "Stupid telemarketers."

Roxie glanced at the screen. Her eyes narrowed. "Ma, isn't that a Las Vegas area code? Maybe you should answer it."

"Vegas?" Willie squinted at the phone. "Are you sure? I don't have my reading glasses on."

"Yes, I'm sure."

"I guess I'll get it." She picked up the phone and tapped the button to answer. "Hello?" She frowned. "Hang on, I can't hear you."

She got up and walked toward the conversation area. As soon as she sat down, she looked back at Roxie and waved her over.

"Excuse us for a second." Roxie got up and joined her, sitting next to her on the sofa.

"Who are you now?" Willie asked. She nodded. "I see." She listened, then her eyes narrowed. "Is this some kind of joke?"

She blinked a couple of times. "You're sure?" A pause. "No, I'm at my daughter's beach house. Okay, that would be all right. Hang on."

Willie dug into her hip bag again, pulled out a little pink notebook she kept important information in, opened it to a certain page and read off a string of numbers.

"Ma," Roxie said in a hushed voice. "What are you doing? Is that your bank account?" If her mother was being scammed into sharing that kind of information—

"Shh," Willie said, waving her hands to keep Roxie quiet.

Roxie frowned. Willie was the last person she'd expect to be taken advantage of. Her mother was sharper than that. But it happened to people far smarter than her all the time. She inched closer, trying to hear the other side of the conversation, but there were too many other sounds around her to pick any of it up.

Willie nodded some more. "Thank you. I don't know if I'll really believe it until I see it, but it's exciting all the same. He was a lovely man and..." She sniffed, her voice breaking. "I am so sorry he's gone. I wish I could have been there."

A few more seconds passed, then Willie said goodbye and hung up. A tear trickled down her cheek. She wiped it away and let out a long sigh.

Roxie was going out of her mind with not knowing what had just happened. "Ma. Are you going to tell me what that was all about or what? You gave your bank account number to someone. I think I deserve to know why. What's going on?"

Willie wiped at her eyes again, then looked at her daughter. "That was a nice young man from the law firm handling Zippy's estate. They'd been looking for me, apparently, and when I left that note of condolence on his Facebook page, they tracked me down that way."

Roxie leaned back. "Why were they looking for you? Did he leave you something in his will?"

Willie nodded, the blank expression on her face completely unreadable. "He did. Seven and a half million dollars."

Roxie sucked in air but had no words. She just let her mother's news wash over her.

Maybe life was about to get easy after all.

Claire's Lemon Bars

Ingredients

For The Crust:
1 cup (2 sticks) salted butter, melted
2 cups all-purpose flour
1 teaspoon fresh lemon zest
½ cup powdered sugar
Extra powdered sugar for dusting

For The Filling:
2 cups granulated sugar
¼ cup all-purpose flour
½ teaspoon baking powder
4 eggs (room temperature)
6 tablespoons fresh lemon juice
1 teaspoon fresh lemon zest

Instructions:

Preheat oven to 350° F. Grease and flour a 9 x 13-inch glass baking dish.

For The Crust:

In a large bowl, mix together the melted butter, flour, zest, and powdered sugar until combined. Press the crust mix into the greased & floured baking dish until it's even.

Bake for 15 minutes, or until golden brown, then remove dish from the oven and set aside.

For The Filling:

Do this while the crust is baking. In another large bowl, whisk together the sugar, flour, and baking powder. Add the eggs, lemon juice, and lemon zest. Keep whisking until thoroughly combined.

Pour the filling into the glass baking dish. Put it back in the oven for another 25 minutes.

Cool completely. (A wire rack works nicely for this.) Once cooled, dust with powdered sugar, slice into squares and serve.

Want to know when Maggie's next book comes out? Then don't forget to sign up for her newsletter at her website!

Also, if you enjoyed the book, please recommend it to a friend. Even better yet, leave a review and let others know.

About Maggie:

Maggie Miller thinks time off is time best spent at the beach, probably because the beach is her happy place. The sound of the waves is her favorite background music, and the sand between her toes is the best massage she can think of.

When she's not at the beach, she's writing or reading or cooking for her family. All of that stuff called life. She hopes her readers enjoy her books and welcomes them to drop her a line and let her know what they think!

Maggie Online:

www.maggiemillerauthor.com
www.facebook.com/MaggieMillerAuthor

Made in the USA
Middletown, DE
30 August 2023